"My lord, please be so kind as to release my hand immediately," said Helena with the utmost politeness.

In response, Lord Varington raised his gaze to hers and lifted her hand until it was just short of his mouth. Then slowly, carefully, never taking his eyes from hers, he touched his lips to the center of her palm. It was as if he had touched the very core of her being. A spontaneous gasp escaped her, and she found she could not take her eyes from his, could not move, could barely breathe.

"My lord, I must protest!" she said in a breathy whisper.

"You are beautiful," he said, and she sat as if mesmerized, watching his head bending toward hers until he was so close that she could examine every detail of his face. Helena knew that he was going to kiss her, and, despite the knowledge, she did nothing.

"Helena," he whispered, and her name rolled off his tongue as if it had been made to do so. There was a richness to his voice, a sensual ripeness.

She felt her eyelids flutter shut. Tilted her mouth to accept his.

The carriage suddenly swerved to the side, throwing Lord Varington off balance and bringing Helena to her senses in an instant.

* * *

Untouched Mistress
Harlequin® Historical #921—November 2008

Praise for
Margaret McPhee

"A fresh new voice in Regency romance.
Hugely enjoyable."
—Bestselling author Nicola Cornick

THE WICKED EARL
"McPhee skillfully weaves a tale of revenge,
betrayal and an awakening love in this emotional
and compelling romance about an innocent young
woman, a forbidding lord and an evil villain."
—*Romantic Times BOOKreviews*

MISTAKEN MISTRESS
"McPhee spins a lovely Cinderella story."
—*Romantic Times BOOKreviews*

THE CAPTAIN'S LADY
"Captivating high-seas adventure."

—*Romantic Times BOOKreviews*

MARGARET McPHEE

UNTOUCHED MISTRESS

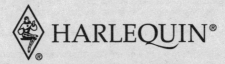

HARLEQUIN®

TORONTO • NEW YORK • LONDON
AMSTERDAM • PARIS • SYDNEY • HAMBURG
STOCKHOLM • ATHENS • TOKYO • MILAN • MADRID
PRAGUE • WARSAW • BUDAPEST • AUCKLAND

ISBN-13: 978-0-373-29521-0
ISBN-10:   0-373-29521-9

UNTOUCHED MISTRESS

First North American Publication 2008

Author Note

I've always enjoyed reading Harlequin's historical novels, and I still do. I love to lose myself in a good romantic story, preferably set in Regency times, with a dangerous dashing hero, a heroine I'm rooting for and a happy ending. With Harlequin I know that's what I will get. I'm so pleased and honored to be a part of this famous romantic tradition with my own few books.

Knowing how much Guy hated the countryside in his brother's story, *The Wicked Earl*, made me mischievously place him on the rugged coastline of western Scotland for his own story—*Untouched Mistress*. It was during a cycle along the shore on a cold gray day, with a stiff breeze blowing and a smir of rain in the air, that I thought of the idea of Guy stumbling upon a beautiful, half-drowned woman washed up with the seaweed on the sands. And so came about Guy and Helena's story. I hope you enjoy reading it.

DON'T MISS THESE OTHER NOVELS AVAILABLE NOW:

Chapter One

1 November 1815—Ayrshire, Scotland

A white froth of waves crashed against the rocks as the solitary figure picked its way along the shore. The morning sky was a cold grey and the fine drizzle of rain had penetrated the woollen cloth of his coat and was beginning to seep through his waistcoat to the cotton of his shirt below. Beneath his boots the sand was firm, each step cutting a clear impression of his progress. A gull cried its presence overhead, and the wind that had howled the whole night through stung a ruddy rawness to his cheeks and swept a ruffle through the darkness of his hair. Guy Tregellas, Viscount Varington, ignored the damp chill of the air and, not for the first time, thought longingly of London: London that had no gales to part a man's coat from his back. No incessant rain. No empty landscape that ran as far as the eye could see, with only the hardiest sheep and cattle for company. Guy suppressed a shudder and continued on, avoiding as best he could the mounds of seaweed and driftwood that the sea had cast upon the sand during the night's storm. The pain in his head was dulling and the nausea in his stomach had almost disappeared; the memory of just how much whisky he had drunk had not. And so he continued, walking off his hangover in this godforsaken place. He crossed the stream that ran down to meet the sea, taking care not to lose his balance on the stepping stones, and followed the curve of the shore round. It was then that he saw the body.

A dark shape amidst the seaweed. At first he thought it was a seal that had been unfortunate enough to suffer the worst of the storm in open water. But as the distance between him and the shape lessened, he knew that what lay washed upon the shore was no seal. The woman was curled on her side, as if in sleep. The dark sodden skirt of her dress was twisted around her body to expose the white of her lower legs. Her feet were bare and the one arm he could see was bloody and bruised beneath the torn sleeve of her dress. Guy rolled her over on to her back and cleared away the long strands of hair plastered across her face. She was not old, in her middle twenties perhaps, and even in her bedraggled state he could see that she was beautiful. He bent closer, touching his fingers to her neck, feeling the faint flutter of her pulse. Guy had seen too many dead bodies in his life. He breathed a sigh of relief that this was not one of them, and as he did so her eyelids flickered open and a pair of smoky green eyes stared up at him.

'An angel,' she whispered with something akin to awe. 'A glorious dark angel come to fetch me.' Her mouth curved to a small peaceful smile before her eyelids closed once more.

'Wait!' Guy gripped at the soft flesh of the woman's

upper arms. He shook her, fearing that she was giving up her fight for life. Her body seemed limp and lifeless beneath his hands. He shook her harder, spoke louder, more urgently, all trace of his hangover gone, leaving in its place a twist of dread. 'Come on, damn it! Do not dare die on me, girl.' And then, just when he thought that it was too late, she came to.

She lay still and silent for a few seconds, as if trying to remember where she was, what had happened. And then her eyes focused upon him.

'Agnes.' It was little more than a whisper, slipped from lips that scarcely moved. He could see the anxiety in her gaze.

'Thank God!' Guy sighed his relief before stripping off the coat from his body and draping it over her. 'I need to get you back to Weir's.'

'Agnes?' she said again, this time with a note of despair in her voice. 'My maid…with me in the boat…and Old Tam.'

He scanned the shoreline, knowing that there was nothing else there save sand and sea and rocks, seaweed and shells and driftwood; no more bodies, definitely no Agnes, and no Tam, old or otherwise.

'They are not here,' he said gently. 'Can you tell me your name?'

'Helena.' The reply was uttered so weakly as to almost be carried off completely by the wind. Nothing else. Just that one name. Her lungs laboured to pull in another breath of air; such a small noise against the howl of the wind and the distant roar of the sea. A few yards away the water rushed in a steady rhythm against the sand.

Guy could see that she was fighting the darkness that threatened to claim her. Her eyelids dipped and her eyeballs rolled up as she fought to remain conscious. Her lips moved again.

He bent his ear to her mouth to catch the faint words.

'Please…' What she would have said he would never know. The woman's eyes fluttered shut, and he sensed that she was slipping away from him.

'Helena.' Guy touched her cheek; the touch became a light slap.

No response.

'Helena,' he said more loudly, pressing his fingers to her neck.

There was only the faintest pulse of an ebbing life.

Guy muttered an expletive and in one motion gathered her up against him.

She was heavy with the weight of seawater soaked through her clothing, and cold; colder than any other living person he had felt, almost as cold as a corpse. Her body was limp and fluid, her head lolling against his shoulder. He wasted no more time. With the woman secure in his arms Guy headed back across the expanse of rocks and sand towards Seamill Hall.

Helena opened her eyes and blinked at the sight of what she thought was her own plasterwork ceiling above her. Mercifully she seemed to be alone. No dip in the other side of the mattress; no possessive hands pawing at her; nothing of his male stench. Just the thought of it caused her bile to rise and a shudder to ripple through her. Her fingers scrabbled to find the top of the blanket. And then she noticed that there was something different about the ceiling. She stilled her movement, and became aware that the daylight seemed much brighter than normal. Forcing herself up on to her elbows, she ignored the pounding in her head and stared at the room in which she found herself.

It was a small bedchamber, decorated predominantly in a cosy shade of yellow, shabby but genteel. The bed was smaller than her own and higher, too, with yellow-and-green striped curtains that had been fastened back. A fire roared on the hearth. Everything was clean and homely. Close by the fireplace was a comfortable-looking armchair. A large painting depicting a panoramic view of the Firth of Clyde and its islands was fixed to the wall above the mantelpiece. Near the door was an oak-coloured wardrobe, and over by the window, a matching tallboy set beside a small ornate dressing table in the French style. Next to the bed sat a table with a blue-and-white patterned pitcher and basin and various other small items. Helena recognised none of it.

Where am I? But even as she thought the question, a sinking sensation was dipping in her stomach. The mist began to clear from her mind. Helena swallowed hard. It was coming back to her now. All of it. Agnes had been with her. Old Tam, too, rowing the boat out into the darkness of the night. There had been no wind, no rain, when they had first started out, just a heavy stillness in the air. They would be there before the rain started, or so Old Tam had assured her. It was as if she heard his voice again within the quietness of the room. *Didnae be feart, Miss Helena. I'll ha'e the pair o' you across to the mainland afore the rain comes on.* But Old Tam had been wrong.

Helena remembered the sudden pelt of heavy raindrops, and the waves that rose higher in response to the strengthening wind. The sea had seemed to boil with fury, leaping and roaring until their small rowing boat had been swamped and the water had claimed the boat's occupants. She had not seen Agnes or Tam through the darkness, but she had heard the maid's screams and the old man's shouts amidst the furore of the storm.

The water had been cold at first, but after a while she had ceased to notice the icy temperature, pitched as she was in her battle to fight the heavy fatigue that coaxed her to close her eyes and yield to the comfort of black nothingness. She supposed that she must have done just that, for she could remember nothing else until she lay senseless and battered upon the shore with the angel staring down at her.

It was impossible, of course; even if angels existed, they did not come to save the likes of her. And yet the angel's face was so clear in her memory that she wondered how she could have imagined him. She struggled to recall what had happened on the beach, her head pounding with the effort. But she could remember nothing save the angel's face: dark sodden hair from which water dripped down on to his cheeks; pale skin and the most piercing eyes that she had ever seen—an ice blue filled with strength and concern. With him she had known she would be safe. Aside from that image, there was nothing.

She knew neither this place in which she now lay nor how she had come to be here. Knew only that she must leave before Stephen found her. Run as fast as she could. And keep on running. This was reality and there was no handsome angel to save her here. She had best get on with the task of saving herself. She pushed back the covers, swung her legs over the side of the bed, took a deep breath and, rather unsteadily, got to her feet.

The entirety of her body ached and she felt unreal and dizzy. But Helena moved across the room all the same. Determination and fear spurred her on. She washed in the cold water from the pitcher and hastily dressed herself in her own clothes that had been cleaned, dried and mended and placed within the bed-chamber. Unfortunately there was no sign of her shoes and stockings, nor of her hat or travelling bag.

The reflection in the looking-glass upon the dressing table showed a dark bruise on her temple. Her fingers trembled as she touched the tender spot, wondering as to how it had happened, for she had no recollection of having hit her head. Her face was paler than normal and there were shadows of fatigue beneath her eyes. She did not dally for long, but twisted her hair into a rope and tucked the ends back up on themselves, hoping that the make-do style would hold.

Quickly she smoothed the bedcovers over the bed to give some semblance of tidiness. Then she moved to the large wooden box positioned at the bottom of the bed and removed a single neatly folded blanket. Her eyes scanned the room, alighting on the silver brush-and-comb set sitting upon the chest of drawers, knowing they would fetch a good price. But, for all of her desperation, Helena could not do that to whoever in this house had helped her. It was bad enough that she was stealing the blanket. She hurried to the door, then turned and glanced once more around the room. The fire burned within the fireplace. The room was warm and cheery in its yellow hues. For a moment she was almost tempted to stay; almost. But then she turned and, still clutching the blanket to her chest, opened the door to pass silently through.

* * *

'It's a fine piece.' Lord Varington admired the rifle before him. 'Well balanced.' He weighed the weapon between his hands, set the butt of the handle against his shoulder and took aim.

John Weir laughed and looked pleased with his friend's admiration. 'It turns hunting into something else altogether. I can hit a rabbit at fifty paces and a grouse when the bird thinks it's got clean away. Thought you might like to try out the Bakers. I've two of them; this one here and the other kept oil-skinned in my boat.' He looked sheepish. 'Seagulls make for good target practice, you see.' Then his enthusiasm returned. 'I can have it fetched for you. We could go up onto the moor. You could give me some pointers on improving my shooting, if you've no objection, that is.' Then, remembering Guy's dislike of the outdoors, Weir added, 'Brown says the weather will clear tomorrow, that it might even be sunny.'

Guy's eyes narrowed in mock suspicion. 'You wouldn't be trying to tempt me, would you? I've been here a week and there's been no sight of the sun. Indeed, if memory serves me correctly, we've not yet had a day without rain.'

'Mark my words, tomorrow will be different.' Weir nodded his head sagely. 'And I wouldn't want to miss a few hours of rifle practice on a glorious sunny day. Besides, the views from the moor are magnificent. If the cloud clears, you'll see all of the surrounding islands.'

'I've not the least interest in "magnificent views", as well you know. But, fill my hip flask with whisky and I'll willingly accept your invitation.'

'Done.' Weir laughed. 'I do have a rather fine Islay

malt in the cellar, nice and peaty in flavour. I think you'll like it.'

'I'm sure I will,' said Guy.

'Does it take you back to your years in the Rifles?' Weir jerked his head in the direction of the rifle. 'The Baker, that is.'

Guy ran a finger along the barrel of the rifle. 'Naturally.'

'Do you miss it?'

Guy smiled in a devil-may-care fashion. 'Sometimes, but it's been years and there are…' he threw his friend a raffish look '…other interests that fill my time now, and if I've time to waste, then I'd rather waste it on them. Even if you are a married man, I'm sure you'll remember the fun that's to be had in that.'

'If you say so, Varington.'

Guy smiled a lazy arrogant smile. 'Oh, but I do.'

Weir reached down and lifted the Baker rifle. 'We'd best get back to preparing the guns.'

A comfortable silence ensued while the two men set about their task. Then Weir asked, 'What are we going to do about that woman upstairs? She still shows no sign of wakening, despite Dr Milligan's insistence that there's nothing wrong with her.'

'Save exhaustion and bruising.'

Weir nodded in agreement. 'Even so, it has been three days…'

'She'll waken when she's ready.'

'But we don't even know who she is yet.'

'A lady of mystery.' Guy crooked an eyebrow suggestively, making light of the matter. He did not want to think about what had happened on the shore, when the woman's life had literally expired before him, and his stomach had clenched with the dread of it. It reminded him too much of the darkness from a past that he wished to forget.

Weir rolled his eyes. 'You must admit that it is rather curious that a woman is washed up on a beach the morning after a storm and no one reports her missing?'

Guy shrugged. 'Maybe she has no family to notice her absence, or they, too, perished in the storm. What did the constable say?'

'That he would make his own enquiries into the matter.'

'Then you have nothing to worry about.'

'Save a strange woman lying upstairs in one of my bedchambers.'

Guy gave a roguish smile. 'If she was lying in one of my bedchambers, I wouldn't be complaining.'

Weir snorted. 'I doubt you would, but that's not the point. We know nothing about her. She could be anyone. Annabel says that the maidservant who laundered the woman's dress found a key sewn into a secret section in its hem.' Weir dug in his pocket. 'Here, take a look at it.' He extended a hand towards Varington, a silver key upon the outstretched palm.

The key was of a medium size and had been roughly fashioned. Beneath Guy's fingers the metal was cold and hard. 'Looks like the key to an internal door.'

Weir gave a shake of his head. 'Why on earth would she have a key in the hem of her dress? It doesn't make any sense.'

'Maybe she was hiding it from someone.' Guy shrugged his shoulders. 'How should I know?' Closing his fingers around the key, he placed it within his own pocket, patted the pocket and said, 'I'll see that it's returned to the lady at a more appropriate time.'

Weir said nothing, just gave a sigh.

'Has she spoken yet?'

'Nothing of sense. Apparently she cries out in her sleep as if in fear, but that is little wonder given that she seems to have survived some kind of boating accident.'

'To have survived the sea on a stormy November night, our mystery lady must have the luck of the devil.'

Weir gave a shudder. 'Don't say such things!'

Guy laughed.

'It's not funny,' said Weir with indignation. 'Not when the storm was on All Hallow's Eve. I cannot rid myself of the notion that she's a portend of bad things to come. Her very presence in the house leaves me with an uneasy feeling in the pit of my stomach. I wish you had not brought her here.'

'I think you may have been reading too many gothic novels, my friend,' teased Guy. 'Would you rather I'd left her out on the sand to die?'

'No, of course not!' retorted his friend. 'I could not, in truth, sentence anyone to such a death. And I would be failing in my Christian duty to do other than I've done. Yet even so…' An uncomfortable expression beset Weir's face. 'I do have Annabel and the girls' safety to think about.'

'What do you think she is? A thief? A murderess?' Guy's eyes narrowed and he floated his fingers in the air and said in a sinister voice, 'Or a witch, perhaps? She does have red hair.'

Weir frowned. 'This is not some jest, Varington. Maybe she's innocent enough, but I can't shake this feeling that something has been unleashed, something that was held safe in check before she arrived.'

'Weir, the woman is in no fit state to set about any mischief. Even were she conscious, I doubt she would have the strength to walk to the other side of the room, let alone anything else.'

'Are you not concerned, even a little?'

'No,' replied Guy truthfully.

'Well, you damn well should be. It was you who brought her here. If she turns out to be a criminal, the blame shall be on your head.'

'Guilty as charged,' said Guy cheerfully.

'What are we going to do if she doesn't wake up soon?'

'We?' questioned Guy in a teasing tone. And then, witnessing the rising irritation in his friend's face, he repented, sighing and saying in a maddeningly nonchalant voice, 'Well, as on first impression she seemed tolerable to look upon, I suppose I might be persuaded to take an interest in her.'

'Varington! The devil only knows why I was so insistent on your coming to stay at Seamill.'

'Something to do with my charming company I believe.'

Weir could not help but laugh.

A knock at the door preceded the manservant who moved silently to Weir's side to whisper discreetly in his ear.

'Can't he come back later?'

More whisperings from the manservant.

Weir's face pinched with annoyance. 'Then I had better come and see him.' The servant departed and Weir turned to Guy. 'Trouble with one of the tenants. It seems it cannot wait for my attention. Please excuse me; I shall be back as soon as possible.'

Guy watched his friend leave before turning his attention back to the rifle in his hands.

* * *

Helena froze as she heard a door downstairs open and close again. Panic gripped her, so that she stood there unable to move, to speak, to breathe. Men's voices—none that she recognised—footsteps and the opening and closing of more doors. Then only silence. Her heart was thudding fast and hard enough to leap clear of her chest. She forced herself to breathe, to calm her frenzied pulse, to listen through the hissing silence. She knew she had to move, to escape, before whoever was down there came back. Her bare feet made no noise as she trod towards the stairs.

Guy ceased what he was doing and listened. All was quiet except for the soft creaking coming from the main staircase. It was a normal everyday sound, yet for some reason his ears pricked and he became alert. He remembered that Annabel and the children had gone out for the day, and his sense of unease stirred stronger. Guy knew better than to ignore his instincts. Quietly he set the rifle down upon the table and turned towards the door.

Helena reached the bottom of the staircase and, with a nervous darting glance around, moved towards the heavy oak front door. The doorknob was round and made of brass. Her fingers closed around it, feeling the metal cold beneath her skin. She gripped harder, twisted, turning the handle as quietly as she could. The door began to open. She shivered as the wind rushed around her ankles and toes. She pulled the door a little wider, letting the wind drive the raindrops against her face. Up above, the sky was grey and dismal. Out in front, the gravel driveway was waterlogged with rain that still pelted with a ferocity. Helena made to step down on to the stone stair.

'Not planning on leaving us so soon, are you?'

The voice made her jump. She let out a squeak, half-turned and saw a man in the shadows behind the staircase.

Helena reacted instinctively. She spun, wrenched the door open, and fled down across the two wide stone steps and up the driveway. The blanket was thrown aside in her haste. Gravel and something sharp cut into her feet; she barely noticed, just kept on running, towards the tall metal gate at the end of the driveway, unmindful of the rain that splashed up from puddles and poured down from the heavens. Running and running, ignoring the rawness in her throat from her gasping breath, ignoring the stitch of pain in her side, and the pounding in her head and the heavy slowness of her legs. She could feel her heart pumping fit to burst. And still, she ran and just ahead lay the road; she could see it through the iron railings of the gate. So close. And then she felt the grasp upon her shoulder, his hand slipping down to her arm, pulling her back. She fought against him, struggling to break his hold, lashing out at him.

He caught her flailing wrists. 'Calm down, I mean you no harm.'

'No!' she cried, and struggled all the harder.

'Ma'am, I beg of you!' She found herself pulled hard against him, his arms restraining hers. 'Look at me.'

She tried to wriggle away, but he was too strong.

'Look at me,' he said again. His voice was calm and not unkind. The panic that had seized her died away. She raised her eyes to his and saw that he was the pale-eyed angel from her dream. No angel, just a man, with hair as dark as ebony, and skin as white as snow and piercing ice-blue eyes filled with compassion.

'What the—' He caught the words back. 'You are not yet recovered. Come back to the house.'

'I will not.' She began to struggle against him, but could do nothing to release his grip.

'You have no shoes, no cloak, no money. How far do you think you will get in this weather?' The rain ran in rivulets down his face. Even his coat was rapidly darkening beneath the downpour of rain. She was standing so close that she could see each individual ebony lash that framed the paleness of his eyes, so close that she could see the faint blue shadow of stubbled growth over his jaw…and the rain that dripped from his hair to run down the pallor of his cheeks. 'Come back inside,' he said, and his voice was gentle. 'There is nothing to fear.'

She closed her eyes at that, almost laughed at it. Nothing to fear, indeed. He had no idea; none at all. 'Release me, sir.'

He did not release her, nor did his eyes leave hers for a second, and she could see what his answer would be before he even said the words. 'I cannot. You would not survive.'

'I will take my chance.' Better that than sit and wait for Stephen to find her.

'We can discuss this inside.'

'No!'

'Then let us discuss it here, if it is your preference.'

A carriage rolled by on the road outside, its wheels splashing through the puddles. She glanced towards the gate, nervous that Stephen might arrive even as she stood here in this man's arms. 'You are getting wet, sir.'

'As are you,' came the reply.

She could see by the determined light in his eyes that he would not release her. He thought he was being a gentleman; he would be no gentleman if he knew the truth. She shivered.

'And cold,' he said. 'Come on.' And gently he began to steer her back up the driveway to where the front door lay open.

Chapter Two

G uy did not release the woman until they were standing before the roaring fire in Weir's gunroom. He poured two glasses of whisky, pressed one into her hand and took the other himself. The amber liquid burned a path down through his chest and into his stomach. The woman stood there, the glass untouched in her hand.

'Drink it,' he instructed. 'God knows, you need it after that soaking.'

She hesitated, then took a sip, coughing as the heat of the whisky hit the back of her throat.

He could feel the glow from the flames warming his legs and see the steam starting to rise from the dampness of the woman's skirts. 'Why don't you tell me what this is about?' They stood facing each other before the fireplace. He could see the rain droplets still glistening on her cheeks. His eye travelled down, following the thick snaking tendrils of hair that lay against her breast, their colour deep and dark with rain. The smell of wet wool surrounded them.

She was not looking at him; her focus was fixed on

the whisky glass still in her hand, and he thought from her manner that she would give him no answer. A lump of coal cracked and hissed upon the fire. The clock ticked. The wind whistled against the windowpanes, causing the curtains at either side to sway. And then she spoke, quietly with a cautious tone for all that her face had become expressionless. 'Who are you, sir, and where is this place?'

'I forget my manners, ma'am.' He gave the slightest of bows. 'I am Viscount Varington and we are in Seamill Hall, the home of my good friend Mr Weir.'

He thought that she paled at his words. 'Seamill Hall?' Her eyes closed momentarily as if that revelation was in some way unwelcome news, and when they opened again she had wiped all emotion from them. 'It was you that rescued me from the shore,' she said.

He gave a small inclination of his head. 'You were washed up near Portincross.'

'Alone?' She could not quite disguise the anxiety in her voice.

And then he remembered the companions that she had cried out for upon the shore, and understood what it was that she was asking. 'Quite alone,' he said gently.

She lowered her gaze and stood in silence.

He reached out his hand, intending to offer some small solace, but she stared up at him and there was something in her eyes that stopped him. 'I'm sorry for your loss,' he offered instead.

'My loss? What do you mean, sir?' He saw the flash of wariness before she hid it.

'The death of your companions. You alluded to them upon the shore.'

'I cannot recall our conversing.' She set the whisky

glass down. Her hands slid together in a seemingly demure posture but he could see from the whiteness of her knuckles how tightly they gripped. 'What did I tell you?'

Guy could feel the tension emanating from her and he wondered what it was that she feared so very much to have told. He gave a lazy shrug of his shoulders. 'Very little.'

There was the hint of relaxation in her stance, nothing else.

'The boat's other occupants are likely to have been lost. Had there been anyone else come ashore, we would have heard of it by now.'

She stilled. It seemed to Guy that she was holding her breath. And all of the tension was back in an instant, for all that she stood there with her expression so guarded. 'But it is only an hour or two since you found me.'

'On the contrary…' he gave a rueful smile '…you have lain upstairs for three days.'

'Three days!' There was no doubting her incredulity. The colour drained from her face, leaving her so pale that he was convinced that she would faint.

Guy set out a hand to steady her arm.

'It cannot be,' she whispered, as if to herself, and again there was the flicker of fear in her eyes, there, then gone. And then she seemed to remember just where she was, and that he was present, standing so close, supporting her arm. She backed away, increasing the distance, breaking the link between them. 'Forgive me,' she said. 'I did not realise.'

'You have suffered a shock, ma'am. Sit down.'

'No.' She began to shake her head, then seemed to change her mind and stumbled back into the nearest chair.

'To where were you running?'

She did not look at him, just said in a flat voice, 'You have no right to keep me here against my will.'

'Indeed I do not.'

Her eyes widened. He saw surprise and hope flash in them and wondered why she was so hell-bent on escape.

'Then you will let me go?'

'Of course.'

'Then why…' she hesitated and bit at her bottom lip '…why did you stop me?'

'I didn't save your life to have you throw it away again. You are not dressed for this weather.' And what the hell kind of woman woke from her sickbed in a strange place and hightailed it down the driveway in a torrent of rain without so much as a by your leave to those who had cared for her? He looked at the woman sitting before him.

'I must leave here as soon as possible.'

'Why such haste?'

She shook her head. 'I cannot tell you.'

'Then I cannot help you.'

Her mouth twisted to an ironic smile, and he thought for a moment that she would either laugh or weep, but she did neither. 'No one can help me, Lord Varington. I am well aware of that. Besides, I am not asking for your help.' And there was such honesty in her answer that Guy felt a shiver touch to his spine.

'You have no money, no *adequate* clothing—' his eyes flicked down over the creamy swell of her bosom '—and you are unwell from your ordeal. How far do you think you will get without some measure of assistance?'

'That should not concern you, my lord.'

'It should concern any gentleman, ma'am.'

There was the quiet sound of a sigh and she looked away. 'If you have any real concern for my welfare, you will take me to the door and wave me on my way.'

'Why are you in such a hurry to leave? You have been in this house for three days—what difference will one more make?'

'More than you can know,' she said quietly.

'Come, ma'am, tell me what can be so very bad?'

She gave a small shake of her head and looked down.

Guy knew he needed something more to push her to speak. 'Or should I address that question to the constable? Shall we have him back to speak with you now that you have wakened?'

She stared up with widening eyes, her fear palpable. He saw the way that her hands wrung together and he felt wretched for her plight. Yet even so, he let the silence stretch between them.

'Please…please do not,' she said at last, as if she could bear the silence no more.

He stepped towards her, drew her up from the chair to stand before him and said very gently, 'Why not?'

There was just the tiniest shake of her head.

She was exhausted, not yet recovered from battling a stormy winter sea. She had been half-drowned, frozen, battered and cast up to die upon a shoreline. Her companions had died that night in the Firth of Clyde. That she had escaped death was a miracle. He eyed the bruise still livid against the pale skin of her forehead and stepped closer, so that barely a foot separated them. 'Tell me.' He stared into her eyes—a beautiful grey green, as soft-looking as velvet. The desperation there seemed to touch his soul. 'I promise I will help you.'

Her eyes searched his, as if she were trying to gauge the truth of his words. He could sense her wavering.

'I…' She inhaled deeply.

He held his breath in anticipation.

'I—'

The door of the gunroom swung open and Weir strode in.

The moment was lost. Guy's breath released in a rush.

'The strangest thing, Varington. Brown has just retrieved a blanket from the…' Weir's words trailed off at the sight before his eyes.

Guy watched the woman step away from him, and inwardly cursed his friend's timing. All of the emotion wiped from her face and she became remote and impassive and untouchable. The transformation was remarkable, like watching her change into a different woman, or more like watching a mask pulled into place to hide the woman behind, he thought.

'What the blazes…?' Weir's eyes swung from Guy to the woman and back again. 'You're soaked through to the skin.'

'The lady and I stepped outside for a spot of fresh air,' said Guy. 'It felt a trifle stuffy in here.'

Weir seemed to have lost the power of words. His mouth gaped. He stared.

'I was just about to escort your guest up to her bedchamber. She needs a change of clothing.' He began to guide her towards the door.

'Varington.' It seemed that Weir had found his voice.

Guy glanced back at his friend.

Weir gestured down towards the woman's feet.

Only then did Guy notice the trail of bloody foot-prints that she left in her wake and the crimson staining that crept around the edges of the skin on her feet.

But the woman continued walking steadily on towards the door.

'Your feet... I will carry you.' He caught her arm.

'There is no need, my lord, I assure you.' She appeared so calm that he wondered if it were he that was going mad. Hadn't she just tried to run away, leaving the warmth and protection of Weir's house, and for what? He was quite sure that she had nowhere else to go, why else had she taken the blanket? And when he had tried to stop her, she had fled from him, fought with him, pleaded with him to let her go. He had seen the terror in her eyes, the utter anguish. And now she stood there as if there was nothing wrong in the slightest. Guy stared all the harder.

Her face was white, the shadows beneath her eyes more pronounced. The bruise on her head told him that it undoubtedly throbbed, and the blood on her feet only hinted at the damage beneath. Yet she looked at him like she felt nothing of the pain; indeed, like she felt nothing at all. He wondered again who this woman was and what it was that she was hiding and why she so feared the constable. And he remembered Weir's allusions to her criminality.

He glanced at his friend.

Weir gave a nod, his face taut, unsmiling, worried.

Guy turned and accompanied the woman from the room.

It was all Helena could do to put one foot in front of the other. The soles of her feet were stinging red raw and her legs seemed unwieldy and heavy. Her head was throbbing so badly that she could barely think straight, and it seemed that her eyes could not keep up with the speed of the things moving around her. She swallowed down the nausea that threatened to rise. Yet through the pain and the discomfort she kept on going. One step and then another. Each one taking her closer to the bed-chamber. Keep going, she willed herself. Think of another way out. She wouldn't give up; she couldn't, not now, not while there was still breath in her lungs and blood in her veins. So she walked and focused her mind away from the pain. She thought of her plan; she always thought of her plan at such times.

The gunroom door closed behind them.

'Allow me…' Lord Varington held out his arm for her to take.

Her immediate reaction was to reject his offer, but in truth she felt so unwell that she was not confident that she could make the journey without stumbling. Better to take his arm than to fall. So she tucked her hand against his sleeve and slowly, without a further word between them, they made their way along the passage-way towards the stairs.

Helena was both resentful and glad of the support of Lord Varington. His arm was strong and steady, his presence simultaneously reassuring and disturbing. His sleeve was warm beneath her fingers and she could feel the hard strength in the muscle beneath. He smelled of cologne and soap, and nothing of that which she asso-ciated with Stephen. Everything of him suggested expense: his looks, his manner, his tailoring. Even his accent betrayed his upper-class roots. But Helena knew a rake when she saw one.

With his oh-so-charming manner and his handsome looks, she supposed Lord Varington was a man used to getting what he wanted when it came to women—and she felt a fool for so nearly trusting him and blurting out the truth. She wondered how much she would have revealed had the other man, Weir, not returned to the gunroom exactly when he did. The thought seemed to sap the last of her energy. She focused her attention on reaching her bedchamber.

Every step up the staircase drained her flagging strength. Her head was swimming with dizziness and her legs felt so weak that she scarcely could lift them to find the next stair. She leaned heavily, one hand on the worn wooden banister that ran parallel to the staircase, the other on Lord Varington. At the end of the first flight she paused, trying to hide the fact that her breathing was as heavy as if she had been running rather than tottering up the stairs.

'I think it might be easier if I were to carry you up the remainder of the distance,' he suggested in that deep melodic voice of his.

'No, thank you.' Even those few words seemed an effort. She did not look round at him, just concentrated all her effort on remaining upright, and tried to ignore the perspiration beading upon her brow and the slight blurring of her vision. She forced herself to focus upon the banister beneath her right hand. The wood was worn smooth and dark from years of use, and warm beneath the grip of her fingers.

The smile in his voice rendered it friendly and sensual and slightly teasing. 'That's a pity,' he said, 'after the last time, I was rather looking forward to it.'

She stayed as she was, unmoving, her gaze fixed upon the banister. 'I don't know what you mean, my lord.'

'Surely you cannot have forgotten your journey from Portincross to Seamill Hall—I carried you in my arms.'

The banister began to distort before her eyes. She squeezed them shut and gripped at it even harder.

'Ma'am?' The teasing tone had gone, replaced now with concern.

'I require only to catch my breath,' she managed to murmur.

'I see,' he said, and before she realised his intent, he had scooped her up into his arms and was walking up the staircase.

She struggled to show some sense of indignation. 'Sir!'

'You may catch your breath a mite easier this way.' He crooked a smile.

'Lord Varington…' she started to protest, but her head was giddy and her words trailed off and she let him carry her the rest of the way.

He laid her upon the bed.

She knew that she was wasting precious time, tried to push herself to sit up.

'Rest a while,' he said, and eased her back down. Only then did she notice the maid in the background setting down a pitcher and some linen. Lord Varington saw the girl, too, and beckoned her over. He took off his coat, casting it aside on one of the chairs by the fireplace. Helena watched him move to stand at the bottom of the bed and she knew she should get up and run. His intent was clear. Why else did a man take off his coat? But Helena did not move. She couldn't. It was as if she was made of lead. Her arms, her legs, her body were so heavy, all of them weighing her down. She stared as he rolled up his sleeves and she heard the sound of water being poured. And then, unbelievably, Lord Varington began to wash her feet. 'Sir!' she gasped, 'You must not!' The pale eyes flickered up to meet hers, and she saw in them a determination that mirrored her own.

'They must be cleansed if the cuts are not to suppurate,' he said.

She could see the maid's face staring in disbelief. But Lord Varington's hands were on her feet, wiping away the dirt and the blood and picking out the embedded gravel. His touch was gentle, caressing almost. One hand held her foot firmly, the other stroked the pad of linen against the sole. No man had ever touched Helena with such gentleness. His fingers were warm and strong and sensitive. Carefully working around each cut, each tear of skin, as if tending wounded feet was something that he did every day. The movement of his hands soothed her. And it seemed to Helena that something of her pain eased, and her head did not throb quite so angrily, nor her body ache so badly. So she just lay there and allowed him to tend her, and it seemed too intimate, as if something that would happen between lovers. She raised her eyes to his and looked at him and he looked right back, and in that moment she knew that she was as aware of him as a man as he was of her as a woman. And the realisation was shocking. She tore her gaze away, feeling the sudden skitter of her heart, and traitorous heat stain her cheeks. Lord Varington's hands did not falter. When he had finished with the cleansing he dabbed her soles with something that stung.

Helena bit her lip to smother her gasp.

'Whisky,' he said. 'To prevent infection.' Then he dried her feet and bound them up in linen strips.

He spoke to the maid. 'Bring some dry clothing for

the lady and help her change. And put some extra blankets upon the bed and more coal upon the fire.' Then he took up his coat and moved to stand by the side of the bed.

Helena pushed herself up to a sitting position, leaning back heavily against the pillows. 'Thank you.'

The expression on Lord Varington's face was unfathomable and yet strangely intense. 'Rest now, we will speak tomorrow.' And the door closed quietly behind him.

She looked over to where the maid was placing several large lumps of coal from the scuttle on to the fire. The room was quiet save for the wind that rattled at the window and the drip of water from the guttering. He would want to know everything tomorrow— who she was, how she had come to be washed up on the shore. Her heart sank at the prospect and she knew that she had to find a way out of this mess in which she now found herself.

'Well? What the hell just happened?' demanded Weir.

'Our mystery lady decided to leave in rather a hurry,' said Guy.

'What the blazes…? You mean, she tried to run away?'

'Unbelievable that it may be for any woman to flee from me, I know, yet…' he smiled mischievously '…in this case, true.'

'But what on earth can have possessed her?' Weir looked pointedly at his friend's damp clothing. 'I mean, she must have only just come to, and it isn't exactly walking weather, is it?'

'Hardly,' replied Guy.

'Then why?'

Guy shrugged. 'The lady is reticent to reveal her reasons. She does, however, appear unwilling to prolong her stay. Most probably she does not wish to inconvenience you further,' he lied. More likely she was fleeing the constable, but there was no need to make mention of that if he did not want Weir to eject her immediately.

'Damn and blast it! Can't be turfing her out when the woman is so clearly ill recovered. But…'

'But?' prompted Guy.

'You know that I do not like having her here.'

'Oh, come on, Weir, you cannot tell me that she is not a beauty.'

'She looks like a doxy.'

Guy smiled. 'Aye, but a damnably attractive doxy.' Indeed, she was quite the most beautiful woman Guy had seen, and Guy, Lord Varington, had seen a great many beautiful women.

'All that hair, and that dress, and bare feet and those ankles.'

Guy put his fingers to his lips and blew a kiss. 'Divine.' He smiled. 'But it is the sea we have to thank for her appearance. You judge her too soon, my friend. Perhaps she is the height of respectability.'

Weir snorted. 'That is profoundly unlikely.'

Guy laughed. 'I fear that her beauty has prejudiced you.'

'Nonsense! Did any of the neighbours see her outside?' He rubbed at his forehead with undisguised agitation. 'Hell, they're bound to draw only one conclusion.'

'Which is?' Guy raised an eyebrow.

Weir cleared his throat. 'I don't need to spell it out

to you, of all people, Varington. She'll have to be found some more suitable clothing.'

'More is the pity.'

'Will you not take this seriously?' Weir poured himself a glass of whisky and topped up the one that Guy had previously emptied. 'You must see my dilemma. I cannot have that sort of woman in this house, not with Annabel and the girls, nor can I ignore my Christian duty to help those in need. I cannot cast an unwell woman out into the street.' He broke off to take a gulp of whisky and said, 'Who is she anyway? Has she told you her name?'

Guy's hesitation was small and unnoticeable. 'We did not get to that.' He had no real way of knowing, other than his gut instinct, of whether the words she had spoken upon the shore were the truth or just the ramblings of a confused and barely conscious mind.

'One minute she's out for the count in my guest bed-chamber and the next she's running down my blasted driveway dressed like a doxy!' Weir's mouth drew to a tight straight line. 'Lord help us, Varington, what am I to do?'

'Given her determination to leave Seamill Hall I do not think that you will have to do anything.'

'I don't like this one little bit. I think I should have the constable over to speak to her.'

Guy thought of the woman's fear at the mention of the constable. 'No need for that just yet.' This was one mystery that Guy intended on solving by himself.

Weir took another sip of whisky. 'And what the hell happened to her feet?'

'She ran barefoot across the driveway, must be some glass still out there from the broken lantern. Never had a woman running away from me—well, not one outwith a bedchamber and that didn't want chasing.'

Weir winced, but smiled all the same. 'Dear God, Varington.'

'Quite shocking,' agreed Guy good-humouredly. 'But there's a first for everything.'

Weir's eyes rolled. 'I was referring to the woman's feet.'

Guy laughed. 'The cuts are not deep. She'll recover quick enough.'

'Good,' said Weir. 'The sooner that she's gone, the better. It's as I said before. There's something about her that makes me uneasy and what with her trying to run off and our not even knowing who she is…' Weir stopped and looked at Guy. 'And she *was* trying to steal that blanket, was she not?'

'She was indeed,' said Guy, with a twinkle in his eye. 'Fortunately I managed to apprehend her before she could make off with the item.'

'You see…' Weir nodded sagely '…did I not say she could be a criminal?' And then caught a glimpse of Guy's face. 'Will you not be serious? Would you see Annabel and the girls suffer over this woman?'

Guy knew his friend's predisposition to worry and so he let something of the playful teasing drop away. 'I shall make it my duty to ensure that neither Annabel nor the girls suffer in the slightest. As you said, the woman is here because of me and she is therefore my responsibility.' His responsibility indeed, and for once Guy was being entirely serious.

Weir gave a nod. 'Amen to that.'

'Amen indeed,' said Guy, and drained the whisky from his glass in a single gulp.

* * *

Sunlight lit the sky as Helena sat by the window, looking out at the stretch of sea that was calm and clear and so pale a blue as to be almost white, water that mirrored the colour of Lord Varington's eyes. Seagulls called, circling in the sky and from the shore beyond came the rhythmic wash of waves against sand. She was dressed, as she had been since six o'clock that morning when she had given up watching the slow crawl of the hours on the clock.

She adjusted her legs, making herself more comfortable, and felt the press of the linen around her feet, bindings that Lord Varington had put in place. A wash of guilt swept over her, and yet she knew she could not allow guilt to stop her. Lord Varington would not understand. He did not know what it was to be so desperate that it was worth risking anything, even death, to escape. She thought of the words he had spoken yesterday, of his offer of help, of the kindness of his voice and the gentleness of his hands and the smile in his eyes, and Lord only knew how she wanted to believe him. Once upon a time she would have. Not now. Five years of Stephen had taught her better. And yet there was nothing of Stephen in Lord Varington.

She thought again of the tall dark-haired man, just as she had thought about him throughout the night. There was an attractiveness about him, both in his looks and his character. He was handsome and charming and flirtatious…and were it not for his interference she would not still be sitting here in Seamill Hall. Indeed, she reflected, she would never have been here in the first place; most likely she would have perished out upon the shore. It was a sobering thought.

She wondered why he was so concerned with her. The man Weir wasn't. Mr Weir would not have chased her the length of the driveway in the pouring rain; judging from the look upon his face he would have let her go and been glad of it. But then Mr Weir hadn't looked at her like he wanted her in his bed. Heaven help her, but she had troubles enough in her life without Lord Varington.

Helena sighed and let her gaze wander to the islands that lay beyond. St Vey was so clear that she could see the different shades of green and brown and purple grey, could see the glint of the sun picking out a brook that flowed over the rocks to the south, and in the north the dark outline of Dunleish Castle. It looked so close, close enough to swim the short stretch of sea that separated it from the mainland, as if she could reach across the water and touch it. St Vey lay only four miles off the coast, and that four miles had cost Agnes and Old Tam their lives. She felt the terrible stab of guilt and of grief. Helena stared for a long time at the island and the water and the sand, and mentally rehearsed her story.

She could go nowhere without owning an identity; that much was obvious. If she told the truth, her fate was sealed: a rapid return to Stephen and Dunleish Castle. She had thought long and hard about her problem, until, at last, in the wee small hours of the morning, came the seed of an idea. As a widow not from these parts, Helena could borrow some money, enough to finish what she had started, and leave Seamill Hall quite properly, without affecting anyone's gentlemanly sensibilities. Just enough money to finish what she had started: escape to a place where Stephen would not find her.

Helena would speak to Mr Weir's wife today, and

make the necessary arrangements. She would have to lie to them all—to Mr Weir and his wife and to Lord Varington. She ran a hand down her skirt, smoothing out the creases as she stood to go down to breakfast, and remembered a time when she had thought dishonesty to be the most reprehensible of sins. Such naïvety; Stephen had changed that. And yet she found the prospect of lying so blatantly, particularly to Lord Varington, did not sit comfortably with her. Part of her wanted to laugh at the absurdity of the situation. A few lies to a stranger were the least of her problems. But she heard the whisper of a little voice that this stranger had saved her life, and she remembered the touch of his hands upon her feet and the intensity in those pale eyes. She thrust the thoughts away, forced herself on. Survival was everything.

Chapter Three

The woman—Helena, as he suspected she was called—was already seated next to Weir's wife, Annabel, at the breakfast table when Guy entered the sunlit dining room. She was wearing a drab black dress, clearly something borrowed from one of the servants as Annabel was so much shorter. Pity, when her own sea-shrunken attire was so very much more becoming. Still, even in the servant's guise, there could be no mistaking that she bore herself with dignity. She was of average height and build. But Helena had a face that marked her out from other women, a face that any man would not easily forget: almond-shaped eyes, a small straight nose and lips that were ripe for kissing. Guy's eyes lingered over the deep flame of her hair, the cream velvet of her skin and the smoky green of her eyes.

She was exuding an air of calm watchfulness, as if all her actions, every answer, was considered most carefully before given, as if she desired to reveal nothing of the real woman. Yet beneath her composure he thought that he could detect an undercurrent of tension.

'Good morning, ladies.'

'Guy!' Annabel, all pretty and pink and blonde, gushed. 'We thought you had quite slept in, didn't we, Mary?' She glanced at Helena.

Mary? He allowed only the mildest surprise to register upon his face as he turned to look at her. The harsh black of the woollen dress served only to heighten the pale perfection of her skin and the vivid colour of her hair, which had been caught up neatly in a chignon. She did not meet his eyes.

'It seems that I have missed the introductions.' He sat down at the table, poured himself some coffee and looked expectantly at the woman who it now seemed was calling herself Mary.

'Oh, Guy,' said Annabel. 'Poor dear Mary has suffered so much—'

'Perhaps,' interrupted Weir, 'Mrs McLelland would be kind enough to recount her story again for Lord Varington? If it is not too much trouble, that is.'

Guy noticed how there was nothing of emotion upon her face, that she wore the same mask-like expression he had watched her don on Weir's entry to the gunroom yesterday.

'It would be no trouble at all,' she said.

Guy sat back, sipped his coffee and waited.

Helena took a deep breath and ignored the way her stomach was beginning to churn. It had not seemed so bad telling her lies to Mr and Mrs Weir alone. It was not something that she would have chosen to do, but needs must, and Helena's situation was desperate. But now that Lord Varington was sitting across the table, watching her with those pale eyes of his, her determination felt shaken. She forced herself to begin the story that she had spent the hours of the night rehearsing.

'My name is Mary McLelland and I am from Islay.' By choosing an island of the Inner Hebrides she was effectively ensuring that any trace that they might set upon her would be slow, so slow that by the time the results of any investigation arrived Mary McLelland would have long fled Scotland. She could see that Lord Varington was still watching her. She forced herself to stay focused, shifted her gaze to where the sunlight reflected upon the silver jug of cream set just beyond her plate. 'I am the widow of James McLelland, and I am travelling to London to stay with my aunt.'

'How came you to be washed upon the shore?' asked Lord Varington.

'A local boatman from the island agreed to take me on the first leg of my journey, for a fee, of course. When first we started out, the weather was cold and damp, but with little wind. Indeed, the sea was remarkably calm, but that soon changed during the sailing.' That bit at least was true, and so was the rest of what she had not yet told the Weirs. 'First the wind fetched up and then the rain began. I have never seen rain of its like. All around us the sea grew wilder and higher, tossing us from wave to wave as if we were a child's plaything, until the lanterns were lost, and we were clinging to the boat for dear life.'

Helena could no longer see the jug of cream, nor was she aware of the dining room or its inhabitants. Her nose was overwhelmed with the stench of the sea; her skin felt again the rawness of the battering waves. She heard nothing save the roar of the water. It seemed that she could see only the darkness, feel only the terrible fear that had overtaken her as she realised that they were going to die. Agnes was clinging to her, sobbing, wailing. Old Tam's shouts: *Hold fast, lassies. Hold as you've never held afore. And pray. Pray that the Lord will have mercy on our souls*. Struggling to stay within the boat as it bucked upon the water's surface. Soaked by the merciless lash of the waves. Gasping for breath. She sucked in the air, fast, urgent. The cry muffled in her throat by the invading sea. Felt the waves lift the boat, so high as to be clear of it, time was suspended. Agnes's hand in hers, clinging hard. And then they were falling. It was so dark. So cold. And silent…just for a while. The water filled her eyes, her ears, her nose, choked into her lungs, as the sea pulled her down. She could not fight it, just was there, aware of what was happening and strangely accepting of it. Just when she closed her eyes and began to give in to the bursting sensation in her lungs, the sea granted her one last chance, thrusting her back up to its surface, letting her hear Agnes's screams, Old Tam's shouts. Her skirts bound themselves around her legs and she could kick no more. And then there was only darkness.

'Ma'am.'

She opened her eyes to find Lord Varington by her side. She was alive. Agnes and Old Tam were dead… and it was her fault. The sob escaped her before she could bite it back.

His hand was on her arm, dragging her back from the nightmare.

She blinked her eyes, smoothed the raggedness of her breath.

'Drink this.' A glass was being pressed into her fingers.

'There is no need,' a voice said, and she was surprised to find that it was her own.

'There's every need,' he growled, and guided the glass to her mouth.

The drink was so strong as to burn a track down her throat. Whisky. She coughed and pushed the glass away.

'Take another sip.'

She shook her head, feeling revived by the whisky's fiery aromatic tang.

'She must go and lie down at once!' Helena became aware of Mrs Weir by her other side. 'The trauma of re-counting the accident has quite overwhelmed her.'

The dreadful memory was receding. And Helena found herself back sitting at the breakfast table in the dining room of Seamill Hall. Only the rhythmic rush of sea upon sand sounded in the distance. She took a deep breath. 'Thank you, Mrs Weir, Lord Varington...' she turned to each in turn '...but I am recovered now. I did not expect to be so affected. Forgive my foolishness.'

'Dear Mary, you are not in the slightest bit foolish. Such a remembrance would overset the strongest of men,' said Mrs Weir stoutly.

Helena gave a stiff little smile.

'There is no need for you to continue with your story.' Mrs Weir looked up imploringly at her husband. 'Tell her it is so, John.'

Mr Weir looked from his wife to Helena. There was the slightest pause. 'You need not speak further of your shipwreck, Mrs McLelland.'

'There is not much more to tell,' she said, anchoring down all emotion. 'I do not know what happened other than I landed in the water. From there I remember nothing until I awakened to find myself here.'

'Mary, you are the bravest of women,' said Mrs Weir, and patted her arm.

Guilt turned tight in her stomach. 'No, ma'am.' She shook her head. 'I am not that. Not now, not ever.' There was a harsh misery in her voice that she could not disguise. Lord Varington had heard it, she could see it in the way that he looked at her.

'You should rest,' he said.

She turned to him with a slight shake of the head. 'I am fine, really, I am; besides, I must make myself ready to leave.'

'To leave, Mrs McLelland?' He raised an eyebrow.

'Mary means to catch the coach to Glasgow,' said Mrs Weir by way of explanation. 'She is intent on continuing her journey to London…by stage'

'Mr and Mrs Weir have been kind enough to agree to lend me what I need. I will, of course, return everything that I have borrowed as soon as I have found my aunt.'

'You must not worry, Mary. You need return nothing. The maid will be delighted to have a new dress, and John sees that I have more than enough money,' said Mrs Weir.

Weir said nothing, just sat with a look of undisguised relief upon his face.

Varington resumed his seat opposite Helena. 'Leaving so soon, Mrs McLelland?' She remembered that he had spoken similar words within the hallway when she had tried to flee, and that memory brought others that she did not wish to think about—Lord Varington carrying her up the staircase, Lord Varington tending her feet.

'I am quite recovered and can therefore no longer impose upon Mr and Mrs Weir's hospitality, and besides…' Helena folded one hand over the other, keeping a firm grip on her emotions '…my aunt is expecting me and shall be worried over my continued absence. I do not wish to add to her concern.'

Varington stretched out his legs and made himself comfortable within the chair. 'Write her a letter explaining all.'

'What a good idea,' said Mrs Weir.

Weir turned away, but not before Helena had seen the roll of his eyes.

'I would rather see her in person.'

'Have you no other relatives?'

'No,' said Helena, worrying just how far Lord Varington's questioning and her lies would lead them.

'And that is why you left Islay—to visit your aunt in London?'

'Yes.' Experience with Stephen had taught her it was better not to elaborate.

'I know London very well. It is my usual abode, apart from when I am coaxed away under extreme duress.' Varington smiled and glanced meaningfully towards Weir.

Helena swallowed, knowing instinctively that he was leading up to something.

'Where exactly does your aunt live?' he asked.

Helena had never visited London in the entirety of her life. She had not an inkling of its streets. *Be sure your lies will find you out*. The words whispered through her mind. 'It is not precisely in London,' she said, racking her brains for a village, any village in the vicinity of the capital.

All eyes were upon her, waiting expectantly.

Hendon was near London, wasn't it? For once Helena wished she had taken more interest in geography. Her mind went blank. 'Hendon,' she said, and hoped that she had not got it wrong.

'Your aunt lives in Hendon?' There was a definite interest in Guy's tone.

'Yes.'

'Do you know the place, Guy?' asked Annabel.

'Indeed,' he said with more confidence than Helena wanted to hear. 'I have a friend that lives there. What a coincidence.'

Helena's heart sank. He would ask her now her aunt's precise direction in Hendon, and what answer could she give? She dropped her gaze, staring down at her hands and waited for his question.

'And what travel arrangements have you made, Mrs McLelland?'

She glanced up at him, surprise widening her eyes, relief flooding her veins. 'I leave this afternoon on the one o'clock mail to Glasgow. From there I will take the stage and travel down the rest of the way.'

'May I be so bold as to suggest an alternative?'

Helena felt a stab of foreboding. 'Please do.'

'I will be returning to London myself at the end of the week. You are most welcome to travel with me.'

It seemed that her heart had ceased to beat. 'Thank you, my lord, you are generous to think of me, but I cannot wait so long to leave. I must find my aunt as soon as possible.'

Mrs Weir patted Helena's arm. 'But it shall be so much safer to travel with Guy than by stage, won't it, John?'

Lord Varington crooked a sensual smile in Helena's direction.

There was nothing remotely safe about Lord Varington, Helena thought.

Weir's eyes slid to meet his friend's.

'The stage is inconveniently slow,' said Lord Varington. 'You do know that it will take you practically four days to make the journey, don't you?'

In truth, Helena had no idea how long the journey would take. She had planned to travel by stage rather than mail for the majority of the journey because it was significantly cheaper and she had no wish to indebt herself to Mr and Mrs Weir for any more than was necessary. 'Of course,' she lied.

'I can do it in two,' he said.

'And so he can,' added Mrs Weir, 'it took him even less to reach us. But I imagine he would have some consideration for a lady passenger and drive a little more sedately than normal.'

Varington laughed. 'Indeed, I would.'

Helena could feel the noose tightening around her. 'There is no need to inconvenience yourself, Lord Varington. Besides, I really must reach my aunt before the end of the week. I will take the stage as I planned, and you—' she gave a kind of breathless forced laugh '—may travel every bit as fast as you wish without the encumbrance of a passenger slowing you down.'

'Mary!' Mrs Weir scolded.

'Then you really believe it a matter of urgency to arrive in London before Friday?' Varington turned the full force of his gaze upon her.

She could feel the guilty warmth in her cheeks. 'Yes, my lord. I thank for your offer, but you can see why it is impossible for me to accept.'

'Very well.' He nodded.

Helena almost sighed her relief aloud…too soon.

'We will leave on Monday morning and I will have

you in London by Tuesday evening…a full day earlier than the stage's arrival. I cannot offer better than that.' A handsome smile spread across his mouth.

Mrs Weir clapped her hands together. 'Oh, Guy, you are too good!'

Helena froze.

'Isn't he, Mary?' Mrs Weir demanded of Helena.

'Indeed,' said Helena weakly, and cast wildly around for some excuse that might extricate her from the mess that her lies had just created. 'But I could not impose on you to change your plans in such a way. It would be most unfair.'

'It is no imposition, Mrs McLelland. I look forward to your company,' he replied, never taking his eyes from hers. 'Besides, I couldn't possibly allow a lady to travel alone and by stage.'

'Thank you,' said Helena, and forced a smile to her face, knowing that there really was no way out this time. Lord Varington had neatly outmanoeuvred her and there was not a thing that she could do about it.

Lord Varington rose and helped himself to some ham and eggs from the heated serving dishes on the sideboard.

'Please excuse me,' Helena said wanly, and escaped to the solitude of the yellow bedchamber, knowing full well that she must wait the rest of this day and all of tomorrow before travelling with Lord Varington to London. She could only hope that he would not insist on taking her directly to the home of her make-believe aunt.

Guy did not see the woman calling herself Mary McLelland again until the next afternoon. She descended the staircase at exactly two o'clock, just as he had known that she would. There was a hint of colour in her cheeks that contrasted prettily with her clear creamy complexion. Several strands of her hair had escaped her pins and she swept them back with nervous fingers. Guy cast an appreciative eye over the image she presented.

'Lord Varington,' she said rather breathlessly, 'I came as your note requested.' He noticed that she surreptitiously kept her hands folded neatly behind her back… out of sight…and out of reach.

'Mrs McLelland.' He moved from where he had been lounging against the heavy stone mantel in the hallway, and walked to meet her. 'I see you have had the foresight to have worn a cloak. You seem to be eminently practical; not a trait often observed in beautiful women.'

She ignored his comment completely. 'You said that a boat had been found, that it might be…' Her words trailed off. 'Where is it now?'

'The remains have been carried to Weir's boat shed, a mere five minutes' walk from here.' He waited for her protest at having to walk. None was forthcoming. She just gave a curt nod of her head and started to walk towards the back door. She had almost reached the door when he called softly, 'Helena.'

Her response was instinctive. She stopped and glanced back over her shoulder.

He smiled, and watched as the realisation of what she had just betrayed registered.

The blush bloomed in her cheeks, and something of fear and anger passed transiently across her features. 'My name is Mary McLelland,' she said quietly, but she did not meet his eye.

'If you say so…Mary McLelland,' he said, moving in a leisurely manner towards her.

He offered his arm. She took it because she could not

politely do otherwise. Together they walked down the back garden until they reached the start of the over-grown lane that led down to the shore and the boat-house.

Guy looked down at her thin leather shoes. 'Perhaps I should carry you,' he suggested. 'The grass is still wet from last night's rain and I would not want you to spoil your shoes or dress. And, of course—' he looked directly into her eyes '—there is the matter of your wounded feet.'

She threw him an outraged look. 'My feet are per-fectly recovered, thank you.' And she blushed again.

And Guy knew very well that she was remembering, just as he was, the intimacy of that moment in her bed-chamber. He smiled. 'Or if you prefer, we can turn back.' He waited with all the appearance of politeness, knowing full well what her answer would be.

'I am perfectly capable of negotiating the pathway, Lord Varington.'

'As you will, Mrs McLelland, but I must warn you that the surface is rather uneven.' Having successfully goaded her, he smiled again and waited for her to set off.

Wild bramble bushes seemed to have taken over on either side, their long thorny branches encroaching far into the path. Not only that, but the grass underfoot was wet, and peppered with jagged nettles, small rocks and shells and copious mounds of sheep droppings. Long riding boots protected Guy's feet and legs. He sauntered nonchalantly over every obstacle. The same could not be said for Helena. Despite picking her way with the greatest of care, it was not long before her shoes and bandaged feet were soaking. And to make matters worse, water was wicking from the grass up and over the edge of her skirt. Three times a bramble branch managed to snag her skirt most viciously, and twice upon the cloak borrowed from Annabel, the last of which to her chagrin necessitated Guy's assistance in freeing it. All around them was the smell of damp undergrowth, of earth and sea and fresh air.

The path eventually led them out to the shore and a rather dilapidated-looking large hut. The wood was a faded ash colour, bleached and beaten into submission by years of hostile weather. Guy slipped the key from his pocket. It turned stiffly in the lock. The door creaked open under the weight of his hand. And they were in.

It was a boathouse without a boat. The floor consisted of creaking wooden planks that were covered in a damp sugaring of sand. Over in one corner a pile of crates and lobster pots had been neatly stacked. In another was a sprawl of ropes and nets and in yet another a few barrels and casks. In the middle of the floor lay a small mound covered with a rumpled canvas sheet.

'But where is the rowing boat?' Helena peered around the hut.

Guy saw her pull the cloak more tightly around her body. He had made no mention of the type of boat in his note to her. And having viewed a map of the exact location of the island of Islay, Guy was quite willing to bet that no boatman worth his salt would have attempted to row the distance single handed in so small a boat as the remains of which lay in this boat shed. 'Here.' He indicated the canvas.

'But…' Her words trailed off as he moved forward and pulled the sheet back to reveal the pile of broken timbers.

He watched her face closely for any sign of reaction. 'I thought…'

'I should have warned you that it was badly shattered.' He crouched and began to separate the remnants of the boat, laying them out across the floor with care. 'Part of the bow is still intact.' He placed it close to her feet.

She dropped to her knees beside him, unmindful of the hardness of the wooden floor or the sand that now clung to the damp wool of her dress. She reached out a hand, caressed fingers against what had once been the bow of a small boat.

'I do not know. I cannot tell if it is the same boat.' She shook her head, a look of frustration crossing her brow.

'And there is this,' he said, uncovering a ripped piece of timber on which a string of bright letters had been painted.

He sensed the sudden stillness in the figure by his side. It seemed that she did not so much as breathe, just leaned forward, taking the torn planking from his hand to trace the remnants of the name.

'*Bonnie Lass*.' Her voice was just a whisper. She swallowed hard; without moving, without even laying down the wood, she closed her eyes. She looked as if she might be praying, kneeling as she was upon the floor with her eyes so tightly shut. Her face appeared bloodless and even her lips had paled.

'Mrs McLelland,' he said, and gently removed the wood from between her fingers to place it on the ground. 'Do you recognise what remains of this boat?'

She made no sign of having heard him.

He heard the shallowness of her breathing, saw how tightly she pressed her lips together in an effort to control the strength of the emotion assailing her. 'Helena,' he said quietly, and touched a hand to her arm.

Even then she did not open her eyes, just stayed as she was, rigid and unwavering.

He pulled her kneeling form against him, his hands stroking what comfort he could offer against her back, his breath touching against her hair. Yet still, she did not yield.

His fingers moved to caress her hair, not caring that several of her hairpins scattered upon the floor in the process.

He heard the pain in her whispered words, 'They should not have died. It was my fault. They were only there to help me. And now they're dead.' For all her agony she did not weep.

Guy held her, awkward and stiff though she was, and looked down into her face. 'How can it be your fault?' he said. 'It was an accident, nothing more than a terrible accident. A small boat out in a big storm.'

'You don't understand.'

'Then explain it to me,' he said gently.

Her eyes slowly opened and looked up into his. And for a moment he thought she would do just that. Every vestige of defence had vanished from her face. Stripped of all pretence she looked young and vulnerable…and desperately afraid. 'I…'

He waited for what she would say.

'I…'

And then he saw the change in her eyes, the defensive shutters shift back into place.

'I must be getting back. Mrs Weir will be wondering where I am.' She began to gather up her hairpins.

'Annabel knows very well where you are,' he said with exasperation.

Helena carefully picked each pin from the sandy floor before rising and turning to leave.

'Wait,' he said, catching her back by her wrist. 'You are certain that this is the boat in which you travelled?'

A nod of the head sent a shimmer down the coils of hair dangling against her breast. 'Yes.'

'With whom did you sail?'

He saw the pain in her eyes, the slight wince before she recovered herself. 'The boatman who agreed to take me.'

'Who else?'

'No one,' she said, and averted her eyes.

'Not even your maid?'

Her gaze darted to his and then away. He heard her small fast intake of breath and released her. She folded her hands together, but they gripped so tightly that her knuckles shone white. 'I have told you my story.'

He reached one finger to tilt her chin, forcing her to look at him. 'And that is exactly what you've told me, isn't it, Helena? A story.'

He saw the involuntary swallow before she pulled her head away.

'When I found you upon the shore you told me that your maid, Agnes, had been with you in the boat. In your distress just now you spoke of *them*, rather than *he*. Why will you not tell me what happened?'

She shook her head, stumbling back to get away from him.

He snaked an arm around her waist, pulling her to him, until he could feel the wool of her dress pressing against his thighs, feel the softness of her breast against his chest. He lowered his face to hers, so close that their lips almost touched. He could see each fleck within her eyes, every long dark red lash that bordered them, the delicate red arc of her eyebrow. His lips tingled with the proximity of her mouth, so close that they shared the same breath. 'The truth has a strange way of making itself known sooner or later, sweetheart. Are you sure that you do not want to tell me yourself?' Much more of this and he would give in to every instinct and kiss her as thoroughly and as hard as he wanted to.

The tension stretched between them.

His eyes slid longingly to her mouth, to the soft ripeness of her lips. He was so close as to almost taste her.

'Please, Lord Varington,' she gasped.

It was enough to bring him to his senses. Slowly he released her. Watched while she began to coil her hair back into place.

He replaced the boat wreckage in an orderly pile and re-covered it with the canvas, and when he looked again she had tidied her hair.

'We should return to the house.' She spoke calmly, smoothing down the creases in her skirt, fixing the cloak around her body, as if she hadn't just discovered the boat that had claimed the life of her servants and very nearly her own, as if she was not grieving and afraid. There wasn't even the slightest hint that he had just pressed her the length of his body and almost ravaged her lips with his own. Yet he had felt the tremor ripple through her, the strength of her suppressed emotion. There was no doubting that the woman before him was a consummate actress when it came to hiding her feelings. But Guy had glimpsed behind her façade, and what he saw was temptation itself. What else was she

hiding and why? Guy was growing steadfastly more determined to discover the mystery of the beautiful redheaded woman.

Chapter Four

Later that afternoon Guy was sharing a bottle of whisky with Weir in the comfort of Weir's gunroom.

'Do you think that she was lying about the boat?' Weir poured yet another tot of whisky into Guy's glass and added a splash of water. 'Could be she'd never set eyes on the blasted thing before. I'm beginning to wonder whether this whole thing of her being apparently washed up on the shore that morning isn't just some kind of farce.'

'Her reaction to the boat seemed genuine enough. She'd have to be a damned good actress to have feigned that.' Guy accepted the whisky with thanks.

'Well, maybe that's exactly what she is.'

'Maybe,' he conceded. 'Certainly her name is not Mary McLelland, nor did she travel alone with a boatman from Islay. But whoever she is, and whatever she's up to, I think she recognised the wreckage of the *Bonnie Lass.*'

Weir stood warming himself at the massive fire that roared in the chimney place. 'Doesn't mean she was in it when it went down.'

'Maybe not,' said Guy.

'Don't you think it rather incredible that anyone, let alone a woman, could have survived being shipwrecked in such conditions?'

'Incredible, yes, but not impossible.'

'She might have arranged herself on the shore like that for some passing soul to find.'

'Come on, Weir. You saw the state she was in when I brought her here. Had I not chanced upon her when I did she would have died. And no one could have known I'd decided to walk along the beach when I did. It's not exactly my usual habit.'

'That's true. But even had you not gone out walking that morning, someone would have found her. Storms wash up all manner of things. The villagers would have been down looking for firewood and Spanish treasure.'

'There was firewood aplenty, but nothing of treasure,' said Guy with a grin, 'unless one counts a half-drowned woman in that league.'

Weir rolled his eyes.

'Besides,' said Guy, 'if she contrived the whole thing to land herself a bed here, why has she been so determined to leave since regaining consciousness? It doesn't add up.'

'Whether she was shipwrecked or not, that woman is bad news.'

'Don't worry, old man. I'll have her off your hands and out of your house tomorrow morning.'

'You seem rather determined to have her travel down to London with you. I must confess that although I'll be relieved to see the back of her, I beg that you will exercise some level of caution where "Mrs McLelland" is concerned.'

Guy gave a laugh. 'What exactly do you think that she's going to do to me?'

'God only knows.' Weir sighed. 'Just have a care, that's all I'm asking. I don't want anything happening to you. Tregellas would kill me.'

'And there was me thinking you had some measure of friendship for me, when in truth your concern is because you're afraid of my brother.'

'Everyone's afraid of your brother!' Weir took a gulp of whisky.

Guy smiled and refilled the two glasses. 'Still got your feeling of impending doom?' he teased

'Don't laugh at me. The blasted thing's lodged in my gullet and showing no signs of shifting. I'm serious, Varington, take care where that woman's concerned.'

'No need to be so worried, Weir. I mean to pay very close attention to Mrs McLelland for the entirety of our journey together.'

Weir's eyes became small and beady with suspicion. 'I don't like the sound of that. Just what are you up to?'

One corner of Guy's mouth tugged upwards. 'We wish to know the truth of the woman who is at present your guest, and by the time we reach London I tell you I will have it.'

Weir leaned back in his chair and gave a weary sigh. 'And just how do you intend to do that? She'll just feed you more lies as she's done so far. I wish you'd let me send for the constable.'

'Not at all, my dear Weir. You see, it's really quite simple.' Guy smiled. 'I mean to seduce the truth from her.'

A groan sounded from Weir. 'I beg you will reconsider. You can have women aplenty once you're back in London. And if musts, then even in the coaching inns on your way down, though the Lord knows I must counsel you against it.'

'Alas, my friend, you know that I have a penchant for widows with red hair.' Guy was smiling as if not quite in earnest. 'And it will be an easy enough and rather pleasant distraction from the tedium of the journey. By the time I'm home I shall know the truth of her, just in time to kiss her goodbye and set her on her way.' He loosened his neckcloth and made himself more comfortable in the chair.

'I have a bad feeling over this.'

'Relax, Weir. I've had plenty of practice in the art of seduction. I'll have Mrs McLelland spilling her secrets before we're anywhere near the capital.'

'I only hope you know what you're doing, Varington.'

Guy raised his whisky glass and made a toast. 'To Mary McLelland.'

'Mary McLelland,' repeated Weir. 'And an end to the whole unsettling episode.'

At half past seven the next morning a murky grey light was dawning across the skyline. The noise of horses and wheels crunched upon gravel and gulls sounded overhead. Helena inhaled deeply, dragging in the scent of the place, trying to impress it upon her memory. Salt and seaweed and damp sand. It was a clean smell and one that she had known all her life. After today she did not know when, or indeed if, she would ever smell it again. Mercifully the weather seemed to have gentled. Only a breath of a sea breeze ruffled the ribbons of her borrowed bonnet and whispered its freshness against her cheeks. Despite the early hour Mrs Weir was up, wrapped in the largest, thickest shawl that Helena had seen.

'I simply could not let you go without saying goodbye, my dear Mary.' Mrs Weir linked an impulsive hand through Helena's arm. 'You will write to me, won't you?'

'Of course I will.' Helena smiled, hiding the sadness that tugged at her heart. Once Mrs Weir knew the truth she would not want letters. In short she would not want anything to do with 'Mary McLelland'.

Mrs Weir pulled her aside and lowered her voice in a conspiratorial fashion. 'Mary, there is something I must say to you before you leave.' She patted her hand. 'There is no need to look so worried. It is just that...' She bit at her lip. 'Promise me that you will not heed any rumours that you may come to hear concerning Lord Varington or his brother while you are in London.'

'Rumours?' Helena stared at her, puzzled.

'Promise me,' said Mrs Weir determinedly. 'Guy is a good man.' Mrs Weir smiled and let her voice return to its normal volume.

'I do not let gossip influence my opinion of people,' said Helena.

'You must come back and visit me soon. London is such a long way and John is most reticent to leave his lands, else I would visit you myself.'

John Weir could not quite manage to force a smile to his face. 'Come now, Annabel, we must let Lord Varington and Mrs McLelland be on their way. They have a considerable distance to travel today.' So saying, he moved forward and drew his wife's hand into his own. The message was very clear.

Helena made her curtsy, thanked Mr and Mrs Weir

again for all their kindness and finally allowed herself
to look round at Lord Varington.

He was watching her while fondling the muzzle of
one of the four grey horses that stood ready to pull the
carriage. 'Mrs McLelland, allow me to assist you,
ma'am.' He moved towards her, took her hand in his and
helped her up the steps into the carriage.

Helena gave a polite little inclination of the head,
ignored the awareness that his proximity brought and
quelled quite admirably the fear of being enclosed
within a carriage for two days with the man by her side.
'Thank you, my lord,' she said stiffly.

Only once she was comfortably seated with a travelling rug wrapped most firmly around her knees and a
hot brick beneath her feet, all fussed over personally by
Lord Varington himself, did the carriage make ready to
depart. The door slammed shut. Lord Varington flashed
her a most handsome smile.

Helena experienced a moment of panic and struggled
out from beneath the blanket, which in her haste seemed
to be practically binding her to the carriage seat. But
Lord Varington had already thumped the roof with his
cane.

She heard Mrs Weir's voice through the open
window. 'Goodbye, Mary. Take care.'

The carriage moved off with a lurch, the horses'
hooves crunching against the gravel.

'No, wait!' she gasped.

Varington smiled again. 'Have you changed your
mind about visiting your aunt, Mrs McLelland?
Perhaps you wish to remain here at Seamill Hall. Shall
I stop the carriage?'

She looked into those ice blue eyes, and wondered

if he would do it. Leave her here, to wait for the next mail, to travel half the country by stage, all the while looking over her shoulder for Stephen. She was being foolish, letting her fears get the better of her. Lord Varington might well know that she was not being honest, but he could know nothing of the truth. Quite simply, she would not be sitting here now with him if he did. He might be flirtatious. He might be a little too curious for comfort, asking too many questions, tricking her into revealing things that she did not want to reveal, but Helena McGregor was no innocent when it came to the devices that men used for their own ends. At seven-and-twenty she had seen more of the dark side of life than most women could bear. But Helena had survived, because Helena was strong.

Lord Varington might well ask the questions. It did not mean that he would receive the answers that he wanted. Quite deliberately she closed herself off to her emotions, resuming the mantle of calm poise that she knew from years of experience would protect her…and deflect any attempt to come close to the real Helena. Her only aim in life was to escape Stephen. Nothing else mattered. She would do whatever she had to, just as she had always done. She hardened her heart and her resolve. She could weather whatever Lord Varington would throw at her.

'Mrs McLelland?' he prompted, recalling her from her thoughts.

'Thank you, my lord,' she said calmly, 'but that will not be necessary.' She turned her face away to the open window and raised her hand in response to Mrs Weir's waving. She waved until the carriage reached the bottom of the driveway and turned out on to the road, and the couple standing before the front door of the big house were no longer visible. Then the horses got into their rhythm, their hooves clipping against the stones and mud of the road surface.

Helena was sitting bolt upright, facing the direction of travel, her hands neatly folded together upon her lap. Across from her, Lord Varington seemed to be taking up the whole seat. His head was against the squabs, his legs stretched out so that the ankles of his long riding boots were crossed rather too close to Helena's skirts. She made an infinitesimal motion to shift her feet away from him.

Varington saw it and smiled. 'You might as well make yourself comfortable, Mrs McLelland. It's going to be a very long day. Long enough for us to dispense with formalities.'

In Dunleish Castle on the island of St Vey, Sir Stephen Tayburn was standing at the top of the north-east tower, leaning on the crenellations looking out at the sea. The sky was a pale muted grey streaked with brush marks of deep charcoal and a wash of delicate pink. The sea was calm—for now. The calm would not last. Sir Stephen knew that. What more could be expected? They were already into November and slipping closer towards winter, to the time when days grew shorter and nights grew longer and darkness prevailed—just the way he liked it. The wind caught at his cape, swirling it up and out as if it were the wings of some great dark bird. Everything of Sir Stephen was black—his clothing, his eyes, his heart, everything excepting his hair, which was a stark white. He sipped from the goblet in his hand, relishing the slightly sour taste of the wine. The door behind him creaked open. A figure emerged, hesitated, cap in hand.

'Sir.'

Stephen Tayburn did not look round, just continued surveying the scene before him.

There was the quiet shuffling of feet and a nervous cough.

'You have news for me, Crauford?' It was an imperious tone, a tone that barely concealed an underlying contempt. Still, he kept his face seaward, not deigning to look at the man.

'Aye, sir. I made the enquires, discreet like you instructed. Nosed around in the taverns and howfs o' the villages on the mainland.'

'And?' He moved at last, turning his dark terrifying gaze to the hook-nosed man standing so patiently by.

'There was talk o' a woman found washed up on the shore near Portincross. They tain her to Mr Weir's house and had the doctor look at her.'

Nothing of emotion showed upon Tayburn's face. 'So she was still alive?'

'Aye, sir, she was alive, all right. They've kept her there in the big house, on account of her bein' in a swoon.'

'How very convenient,' he mused. 'Has the woman a description? Was she seen by any of your…sources?'

'Oh, aye, sir.' Rab Crauford crept a little closer towards his master. 'Ma source has a pal whose lassie works at Seamill Hall.' His grin spread wider. 'The woman frae the shore has red hair.'

Tayburn's eyes narrowed and the set around his mouth hardened. 'Has she indeed.' His gaze raked the tall thin man before him. 'Have McKenzie ready the boat. I've a mind to visit the mainland this morning, Kilbride, perhaps…'

'Very good, sir,' said Crauford. 'I'll see to it right away.'

Sir Stephen Tayburn did not wait for his servant to leave before presenting his back and turning once more to look out across the rolling waves below. He drained the rest of his wine and belched loudly. The door closed behind him, and he heard the sound of Crauford's footsteps running down the winding stone stairs. Only then did he say beneath his breath, as if the words were a thought murmured aloud, 'I have found you at last, my darling Helena. What a homecoming you shall have, my dear.' A cruel smile spread across his mouth and over the sound of the waves and the wind was the dull crack of crystal as the grip of his fingers shattered the fine goblet within.

Helena's back was beginning to ache and her right hand was growing numb from clinging so hard and so long to the securing strap. The bouncing and rocking of the carriage was threatening nausea and she had long since closed her eyes to block out the view of the countryside racing by in a blur of green and brown. And still, they had not made their first stop, aside from the rapid change of the horses. She was just gritting her teeth and wondering how much longer she could endure it when she heard a thump upon the roof and the carriage began to slow. Her eyes opened and as the carriage ground mercifully to a halt she could do nothing to contain the sigh of relief that escaped her. The door was open and Lord Varington was leaning out, shouting something up to his driver. He withdrew back inside, shutting first the door, then the window and sat back in his seat.

'Is something wrong, my lord?' she managed to say

with what she hoped was a tone of polite enquiry, whilst disentangling her hand from the strap.

'Wrong, Mrs McLelland?' he replied.

'The carriage seems to have stopped. Have we reached the coaching inn?' she said, trying not to sound too wishful. Just as the words had left her mouth the coach began to move off, albeit at a much more sedate pace. Her fingers grabbed for the strap.

'Not yet.' One corner of his mouth turned up, as if he knew very well the measure of her desperation to reach their stop. 'I thought perhaps you might prefer that we travelled at a more comfortable pace for a while.' His eyes slid from her face to her fingers that wound themselves so tightly around the strap, and back again to her face.

Helena felt a flush of self-consciousness and released the strap in an instant. 'There is no need to alter your plans on my account. If you wish to travel faster, please do so. In fact, I would prefer that you did.'

He just looked at her in that knowing way. 'I am content to travel slower, for now.'

'Very well, my lord.' Surreptitiously she massaged her fingers, coaxing the blood to flow to the tips she could not feel, grateful for the break, but anxious also not to lose any time.

Lord Varington stripped off his gloves and then without pausing in the slightest, reaching smoothly across to take her right hand into both of his. 'My name is Guy,' he said in a slow delicious drawl.

'Lord Varington!' exclaimed Helena in as frosty a tone as she could summon, and tried to withdraw her hand.

Lord Varington's hands were firm but gentle in their imprisonment of her fingers. He showed not the slightest inclination to release them. Instead, he carefully peeled the borrowed glove away from her until her hand was bare. 'I fear that the strap has left its mark upon you,' he said, and traced a finger over the impression on her skin.

Helena shivered and gave another tug of her hand.

Lord Varington's fingers tightened by the slightest degree. 'Such a dainty little hand,' he said, and slid his thumbs across the back of her hand. 'Such slender little fingers.' His thumb caressed the length of her index finger, from knuckle to the tip of her nail.

'My lord, please be so kind as to release my hand immediately,' said Helena with the utmost of politeness.

In response, Lord Varington turned her hand over and began to stroke a sensuous massage across her palm, his thumb pressing first lightly, then leaning a little more strongly, sweeping small slow circles over her skin. His hands were warm, their movement against hers blatantly erotic. She shuddered beneath the pleasure that it ignited, tried to quell the inappropriate response that it engendered.

'Lord Varington,' she said again, with just the slightest of emotion in her voice. 'Release my hand.'

The Viscount did not oblige. Instead he ran both thumbs slowly down the full length of either side of her forefinger, moving then to do the same to each adjacent finger in turn. Skin slid against skin in a slow sensual slide until Helena's hand burned beneath his touch. A flame sparked low and deep in her belly and the breath shook in her throat.

'My lord, I must protest!' she said in a breathy whisper.

Lord Varington raised his gaze to hers, and in his eyes seemed to burn a pale blue fire of passion. Helena had never seen such a look in any man's eyes. He raised her hand until it was just short of his mouth, and then slowly, carefully, never taking his eyes from hers, he touched his lips to the centre of her palm. It was as if he had touched the very core of her being. A spontaneous gasp escaped her, and she found she could not take her eyes from his, could not move, could barely breathe.

'You are beautiful,' he said, and she could feel the tickle of his lips against her skin with his every word. 'Beautiful,' he said again, and lowered her hand back down to cradle it within his own.

She sat as if mesmerised, watching his head bending towards hers until he was so close that she could see the dark eyelashes that framed his magnificent eyes, could examine every detail of his face: the pallor of his skin, the way that his eyebrows were smooth and dark, the strong line of his jaw that led down to the cleft in the square of his chin. A lock of hair dangled dangerously close to his eye so that she longed to just reach across and smooth it away. But she could not, for Helena knew that he was going to kiss her and, despite the knowledge, she did nothing. Everything seemed to be in slow motion. He filled her vision. His cologne filled her nostrils. Her lips parted as if of their own will. She seemed drugged, powerless to stop the move of his mouth towards hers.

'Helena,' he whispered, and her name rolled off his tongue as if it had been made to do so. There was a richness to his voice, a sensual ripeness.

She felt her eyelids flutter shut. Tilted her mouth to accept his.

The carriage suddenly swerved to the side, throwing Lord Varington off balance and bringing Helena to her senses in an instant.

'What the he—?' He caught the curse back before it left his mouth and resumed his seat just as the coach came to a halt. A thud of feet sounded and the door swung open to reveal a rather red-faced coachman.

'Beggin' your pardon, m'lord,' he said. 'But a sheep ran out before us and it was all I could do not to hit the animal. It was a good thing that we weren't goin' at no speed else we would have like come off the road.' He clutched his hat between his hands. 'I hope that you and the lady were not harmed by the abruptness of my change of direction.'

'No harm at all, Smith,' said Lord Varington with an ironic twist of one corner of his mouth.

An exceedingly apologetic coachman retreated, and soon the coach set off at what seemed an even slower pace.

'Forgive my man's driving, ma'am. He is usually most proficient at handling the ribbons. Indeed, this is the first incident of its kind in all the years he has worked for me. But then I do not usually expect him to drive through the wilds of the country. I trust you are not too overcome by the shock?' Lord Varington's voice was filled with concern.

Helena gripped firmly on to the leather of the seat on either side of her. Lord Varington had unknowingly hit the nail on the head with his question. Helena was completely shocked and aghast, but not at anything the unfortunate coachman had done. Rather she was in a state of horrified disbelief at her actions immediately preceeding the swerving of the carriage. She had been on the verge of allowing Lord Varington to kiss her! And would have done so had not a sheep happened to stroll out into the path of his carriage. Lord, oh, lord!

He leaned forward towards her. 'Mrs McLelland? You seem to have gone rather pale. Are you feeling unwell?'

'I am quite well, thank you, my lord.' Helena flattened herself against the leather seat back, trying to make the space between her and Lord Varington as large as possible. Her emotions were in turmoil. She felt thoroughly undone. In all of five years with Stephen, Helena had not experienced anything that prepared her for the effect that Lord Varington seemed to exact upon her person. It was utterly ridiculous!

'It would seem that something has rendered you a trifle overwrought, ma'am.' There was that knowing half-smile playing about his lips. 'You appear to be a little breathless. It becomes you very well.'

Helena had never felt so vulnerable and the knowledge made her angry, not only with herself but also with Lord Varington. 'I assure you that you are mistaken, my lord,' she said curtly.

'Am I, Helena?'

'My name is Mary McLelland,' she snapped, 'and I would trust you, sir, to remember that you are a gentleman, and to behave accordingly.'

Lord Varington's head bowed in mock humility. 'Forgive me, dear lady, if I have done anything to…' those stark eyes lingered over her face '…offend you.'

There was nothing of sincerity in his attitude, Helena noted with more than a touch of asperity.

'Allow me to make reparation for my blunder.' He extended a hand in her direction.

Helena shrank back further, if that were at all possible given that she was practically plastered against the back of the carriage seat. 'That will not be necessary, my lord,' she said rather more quickly than was polite.

'But I insist.'

'No!'

Lord Varington leaned back against his seat with a bemused expression.

'What I mean to say, my lord, is that it would be better if we just put the incident from our minds, and forget that it occurred. We do, after all, have some considerable distance to travel together, and…and…' She ran out of words and glanced up at him, her cheeks stained a peachy pink.

His eyes held more than a hint of amusement. 'And it is better that there are no misunderstandings between us,' he finished.

She nodded.

'Very well, Mrs McLelland.' He smiled and extended his hand once more towards her.

She stared at it in dismay.

'Let us shake hands on our now newly defined friendship.'

Much as she had no wish to touch him, she could not very well refuse his suggestion. With a great deal of reticence she reached her fingers to touch his. It was a mistake. In her flustered state Helena had not yet fitted her glove back on, and neither, it became apparent, had Lord Varington fitted his. Bare skin met and touched. On the surface it was nothing more than a handshake. But Helena's skin tingled beneath the touch of his warm strong hand, and she felt the sudden stampede of her pulse. He did nothing improper, neither holding her hand for too long nor overly personal. He did not have to, not when he looked at her with that smoulder in his eyes.

'To new friendships,' he said, and smiled a most charming smile.

She said nothing, but Helena had the feeling that the journey with Lord Varington was going to be a great deal more challenging than she had anticipated.

Chapter Five

Lord Varington's carriage finally rumbled into the yard of the Graham Arms in Longtown, situated between Gretna and Carlisle. It was not where he had planned to stay, but Helena did not argue when Lord Varington said that they would go no further that night. The sky was now shrouded in black and dark grey clouds conspired to hide the light of the moon. Rain had been pattering against the carriage roof for the past two hours and the howl of the wind could be heard even over the racket of the wheels and the clatter of the horses' hooves upon the road. The coach stopped and the door swung open to reveal a sodden coachman struggling to fetch the steps into position.

'Leave those. See to the horses. The sooner we're all out of this weather, the better.'

The coachman did not argue, just hurried away to do his lordship's bidding.

Lord Varington jumped down, mud splashing up from where the soles of his leather boots impacted on the rain-soaked ground. Rain pelted against his coat, sitting upon the dark blue wool as sparkling droplets against the burst of lights from the building in the background. He turned to Helena, holding out his hand towards her. 'Come quickly, Mrs McLelland, if you do not wish to receive a thorough soaking.'

Helena pulled the hood of her cloak over her head and hesitated for just the slightest moment before placing her hand in his. The journey had been the longest of her life. She was exhausted, cold, and sore, and the thought of entering into yet another disagreement with Lord Varington was just too much to bear. A strong arm curled around her waist, and before she knew it, Lord Varington had lifted her out of the carriage and placed her feet upon the ground. At least her feet were well recovered, she thought ruefully. A loud bang as the door swung shut, and then his arm was around her shoulder, shielding her from the worst of the weather as they ran together across the yard.

Helena blinked at the sudden blaze of light. Heat rushed up to meet them as they entered through the heavy wooden door. The taproom was crowded with bodies. There was laughter and the buzz of chatter, the deep burr of male voices interspersed with the occasional high-pitched laughter of a female. Men in thick coats that were still steaming and damp, and two women, both of whom wore dresses cut indecently low to reveal their ample cleavage. Over on the opposite wall was a massive fire set in an old-fashioned stone hearth. Men were crowded round its heat, sitting where they could, some even upon the pile of logs that had been neatly stacked ready for the burning. All around was the smell of wet wool, beer and tobacco.

Several curious male stares were focused upon her

person. Helena drew her cloak more tightly around herself, and for the first time since setting off that morning was profoundly glad that she was with Lord Varington. Had she been travelling by stage, she would be in the position of having to negotiate her own room at the overnight stops. Entering places like this on her own, conscious of how precious little money she had in her purse.

The landlord was a small man with a large girth. He wiped his hands upon the apron stretched across his waist when he saw Lord Varington and made his way across to the bar, knowing an aristocrat when he saw one. 'My lord.' He nodded. ''Fraid all our rooms have been taken for the night.'

Varington pulled a purse from his pocket and sat it upon the bar. 'Are you quite sure about that?'

The landlord's small eye dropped to the purse, which Varington obligingly unlaced until the glint of gold could be seen within.

Helena had no idea how many gold coins the purse held, but there seemed to be a great many.

'Let me see what can be done,' said the landlord.

'We require two rooms,' said Lord Varington.

The landlord hurried off, leaving Helena standing at Varington's side. Five minutes elapsed before he returned with an oily smile. 'It's your lucky night, m'lord. Two rooms have just become available.'

'How fortuitous.' Lord Varington smiled.

The landlord grinned and in a single swipe the purse had gone, stuffed beneath his apron.

Helena saw the landlord's gaze switch to her, saw too the presumption in it.

'Directly across the landing from each other the rooms are, m'lord.'

'It just gets better and better,' said Varington, and smiled at Helena.

She did not need to see the crudity that crept into the landlord's expression at Lord Varington's words to know what conclusion the man had drawn. She felt the warmth rise in her cheeks, and all of her gratitude to Lord Varington vanished in an instant.

'And a private parlour?' Lord Varington looked expectantly at the landlord.

The landlord sucked in his breath and grimaced. 'Packed to the gunnels we are, m'lord, packed to the gunnels.'

Varington raised an eyebrow.

'It'll be ready in twenty minutes.'

'Most obliged.' Lord Varington flicked another coin into the landlord's hand. Then, turning to Helena, he positioned his arm for her to take. 'Shall we?'

The landlord bellowed for his daughter to show the lord and lady to their rooms. A pretty plump girl appeared, made her curtsy, glanced first at Varington, and then at Helena, gave a very knowing smile for one so young, and then led off towards a low wooden door.

Helena drew Lord Varington a look of pure ice, held her head erect, and touched only the barest tips of her fingers to his sleeve. Even with such minimal contact she could feel that the wool was damp. Causing a scene within the crowded taproom would only draw more attention to herself and, although there was a most definite irony in her taking umbrage at being thought Lord Varington's mistress, she found herself unwilling to be the focus of such attention.

As if knowing her every thought, Lord Varington threw her his most charming smile and then guided her in the serving wench's wake out of the taproom and up the narrow staircase, only pausing once he reached the door to her chamber.

There was a jangle of coins and the girl disappeared with an even bigger smile upon her face.

Helena disengaged her fingers immediately.

'Shall twenty minutes suffice?' he asked.

'Twenty minutes?' she parroted without the least idea to what he was referring.

'To dine. In our private parlour. Regardless of the quality of this place, we need to eat.'

Exhaustion was buzzing in Helena's head, and she was still damnably angry that Lord Varington had done nothing to repudiate the conclusion reached by the landlord, and indeed had seemed positively to foster the impression. 'I am tired, my lord. I think I would rather just go to bed.'

'You have scarcely eaten a bite all day, Mrs McLelland. Can I not tempt you to my table?'

'No,' she said, too weary to be polite.

'You wound me, madam,' he said, and touched a hand to his heart.

'For that I am sorry, my lord.'

There was a cynical flicker of his mouth. 'Much as I fear to incur your displeasure, I feel, speaking purely in the capacity of a concerned gentleman and friend, you understand,' he said as if in an aside to her, 'that I cannot enjoy the pleasure of a meal if I allow you to retire on an empty stomach.' The pale eyes twinkled.

Helena gave a sigh. She had the feeling that Lord Varington would not give up his persuasions anytime soon. The ache in her back intensified. She longed for nothing other than to shut the bedchamber door against the world and curl up safely and alone in the bed. 'Very well, my lord. I shall partake of a little food.'

'Excellent decision, Mrs McLelland,' he said, and before she knew what he was going to do, he raised her hand to his mouth, brushed his lips against her knuckles and released her. 'Twenty minutes,' he said with a bow, and stood back against the door frame that led into his own room, watching her.

Helena did not linger. She entered the room designated as her bedchamber, aware that, even as she closed the door, Lord Varington's eyes were still upon her.

Exactly twenty minutes later Guy knocked on the door leading to the room in which Helena was housed. He had washed and changed into fresh clothing. Now he waited to see Helena again—to work a little harder at learning the secrets that she was so desperate to keep hidden. The task was not onerous. If truth be told, he was enjoying flirting with the woman who called herself Mary McLelland immensely. She was beautiful; he had not lied to her of his opinion. All creamy velvet skin, flowing red hair and a figure that most men would appreciate. Nor had he lied in his words to Weir of his liking for fast widows and redheads. Helena most definitely came into the second category, and perhaps even the first. Dinner with a green-eyed vixen. He smiled at the thought. It had proved easier to persuade her to join him than he had anticipated, but then again she was clearly tired and Guy had been prepared to stand there all night if need be. He flicked a speck of invisible dust from the lapel of his coat and smiled as the door opened.

Helena was still wearing the same dark travelling

dress that she had been wearing all day. She had tidied her hair and, judging from the smell of her, had applied some lavender water.

'Mrs McLelland,' he said, and presented his arm.

She said nothing, just took his arm and together they made their way down to the private parlour.

The light from the candelabra in the centre of the dinner table showed the fatigue around her eyes. Her cheeks seemed to have taken on a slight ashen hue and there was a tightness around her mouth. Something of the rigidity had gone from her deportment and she was leaning every so slightly into the support of the chair at her back. She looked exhausted and extremely vulnerable. Guy felt a twinge of conscience.

The maid had left a newly opened bottle of claret and two clean glasses on the table beside the place settings of china and cutlery. He filled her glass and then his own, and still, she said nothing.

'It seems that the journey has exhausted you, ma'am.'

'I am a little tired, my lord.'

'Then that must be remedied. We shall travel more slowly tomorrow. I would not want you arriving at your aunt's in a state of fatigue.'

'I shall be refreshed after a night's sleep, sir. You have already reduced your pace on my account. I beg you will slow it no further.'

'You are too thoughtful of me, Mrs McLelland,' he said silkily.

'Not at all, my lord, I am but impatient to reach my aunt,' came the retort.

Guy smiled. Helena was trying hard to appear unperturbed, but he had not missed the nervous flutter of her fingers against the stem of her glass. 'Then have I no hope of winning your favour, ma'am?'

He saw the movement of her breast, the rise and fall of her shoulders as if she had taken in a deep breath of air and then released it. 'My lord, I thought that I had made my position clear earlier today.' There was no censure in her tone, only the unmistakable sound of bone weariness.

'You are a very attractive woman, and a man can but hope.' He stared across the table at her, willing her to meet his gaze, but she determinedly kept her eyes averted.

A knock at the door and the landlord and a small posse of servants hurried in, bearing numerous serving plates and dishes. Only when they had exited did he speak again. 'Shall I serve you?' he asked with deliberate *double entendre*.

She glanced momentarily up at that, and he could see from her expression that she had understood his meaning only too well. 'No, thank you, my lord.'

'As you wish,' he said, and inclined his head.

He sampled a little of every dish.

She sipped at her wine and took nothing.

'Can I not tempt you even a little?' he said, and looked meaningfully at her lips. 'The chicken is more than edible.'

Her face remained impassive. 'Thank you, my lord, but I am not hungry.' She took another taste from her glass before setting it carefully down upon the tablecloth.

Guy continued to eat his dinner. 'The cabbage is not soggy, Mrs McLelland, and the pork is nicely crisped.'

A faint tummy rumbling sounded across the table. A hint of colour touched Helena's cheeks. 'Please do excuse me,' she mumbled.

The corners of Guy's mouth curved. 'I think you

have not been honest with me, ma'am.' And reaching across, he took up her plate and placed a little from every dish upon it.

The colour in Helena's cheeks intensified at his words, but she began to eat the food he had set before her.

'Honesty is such an important attribute. What is your opinion on the matter, Mrs McLelland?'

'I have little opinion, my lord.'

'Come now, you do not seem to me to be a simpleton. You must have your own thoughts on the matter,' he said, refilling her glass.

'Very well, I am sure that you are right, sir.'

'So you agree that dishonesty is a sin?' he asked with an exaggerated expression of surprise.

She set down her knife and fork upon her plate, and looked up at him. 'I believe there are some cases where the sin may be excusable.'

'Such as?'

She took a gulp of wine and glanced away to the left, to where the flickering flames of the fire danced against the wall. 'Such as when a person is in fear for their life,' she said in a voice so quiet he had to strain to catch her words.

Something kicked in Guy's gut. And he had the sudden thought that he might have grossly misjudged the woman sitting opposite him.

There was silence between them.

'If that were to be the case, then that person need only appeal for help, and help would be forthcoming. That is something I could guarantee, ma'am.'

'In some situations there is nothing that can be done to help.'

'Perhaps it might appear that way to the individual within that circumstance, but there is always something that may be done to assist them.'

She looked at him then, and in that moment he knew that he was seeing the real woman behind the façade, the real Helena. And Guy thought he had never seen a more hauntingly beautiful woman.

'There are some cases that are beyond all hope.'

'Helena.' He reached across and took her hand in his, and this time there was nothing of his sensual teasing. 'Nothing is beyond hope.' He paused, then said, 'Let me help you.'

He saw the longing in her eyes, the need to unburden the terrible truth that she carried with her. Her fingers lay still and quiet against his, trusting, open. She parted her lips to speak…

A knock at the door.

The serving wench breezed in. 'Anything else I can get for you, m'lord?'

Helena quickly withdrew her fingers from his.

'There is nothing, thank you,' he said in a cooler tone than normal, and dismissed the girl.

But it was too late. The moment had gone, and so, too, had Helena's trust, for when he looked at her, there was that familiar wary caution in her eyes and her mouth was closed firm. He raked a hand through his hair with ill-disguised frustration. 'Helena—' he began.

But she cut him off. 'My name is Mrs McLelland. Forgive me, my lord. I am tired and would like to retire to bed now. We have an early start in the morning.'

Helena had gone, and in her place sat Mary McLelland.

'Of course,' he said, rising from his chair.

They did not speak again until he watched her slip

through the door to her chamber. 'Good night, Mrs McLelland,' he said softly.

'Good night, Lord Varington,' came the quiet reply.

He lingered a moment longer in the passageway, staring at the door through which she had vanished. Then slowly he turned around and walked alone into his room.

The evening had not gone quite according to Guy's plan.

It was a long time before Helena finally found sleep, despite her body aching with fatigue, despite her mind being so tired that she could not think straight. She wriggled out of her borrowed dress, and into her borrowed nightgown. She removed the borrowed hairpins and combed through her long tresses with the borrowed comb. And all the while she could think of nothing save that she had nearly revealed all to Lord Varington. Quite how it had happened she did not know. One minute she was deflecting his flirtatious behaviour quite well, the next, she was on the verge of pouring out her heart to him. Something about him had changed. It had happened while they had been talking in double meanings about the subject of dishonesty. The rake had vanished, replaced instead with a man whose eyes were filled with compassion and concern, whose hand was strong and reassuring, a man who said he would help her…and she had believed him. A moment's weakness. And had not the serving maid come into the parlour when she did, Helena would have told him all of it. She shuddered at the thought, lying there in the bed in the darkness of the inn room.

Through the wall came the muffled sound of snoring. Outside an owl hooted in the darkness. The tips of naked branches tapped a rhythm lightly against the glass panes of the window. How easy it would have been to have told, and how dangerous. If he knew who she was, what she was, his kindness would have vanished. In this one thing she had spoken the truth to him: there was nothing and no one who could help her. And Stephen would ensure that anyone who tried would regret it most bitterly.

Helena rolled over on to her other side, trying to find comfort, trying to find sleep. Both proved equally elusive. Stephen would be playing his own game for certain. She did not allow herself the luxury of imagining that he believed her drowned in the sinking of the *Bonnie Lass*. She could only be thankful that she had lied about her identity at Seamill Hall, especially given that Mr Weir might well speak to the constable again and Stephen was not unknown to that official. She prayed for the protection of Mrs Weir and her husband. She hoped that Stephen would not find them—for all their sakes.

She thought of Lord Varington's handsome face; thought, too, of the sincerity in his offer of help. But he did not know who she was. And she would warrant that his offer would change to something else altogether were he to discover that truth. The thought did not shock her. For the first time she considered exactly what being under the protection of Lord Varington might be like. It did not seem such a bad prospect. Her face grew hot at the idea. She thrust it away, ashamed of where her thoughts had led, mortified by what Stephen had made her. Even if by some slim chance she managed to escape him, she could never escape that... Stephen had ruined her for ever. And he had said that he would keep her for ever. She knew what he would do to anyone who tried to help her.

For the first time she realised that by accepting Lord Varington's offer of transport to London she might have actually endangered him. It was one thing to risk herself, quite another to involve the lives of others. The wrecking of the *Bonnie Lass* had taught her well. Agnes and Old Tam were dead. It was Helena's fault. And that was something she would have to live with for the rest of her life. She would not risk having another's life on her conscience. The sooner they reached London, the better. London: a big place, a busy place, somewhere into which she could disappear unnoticed. Helena's eyes stung raw in the darkness, but she did not allow herself the indulgence of tears. Such weakness would not help her, not when safety was still so far away. She closed her eyes and willed sleep to come. Sleep refused her call. Thoughts of Guy, Lord Varington came in its stead.

The journey the next day began slowly. Guy had instructed his coachman well. Instead of flying at breakneck speed, the coach was moving at an almost leisurely pace.

'My lord, we seem to be travelling a great deal more slowly than yesterday.' There was just the faintest hint of worry about her eyes. Yes, indeed. Helena hid her feelings well…but not quite well enough.

A smile played about his lips. 'A more considerate pace for a lady, I think you will agree.'

'You did not think so yesterday,' she pointed out.

'Yesterday I was attempting to reach Catterick.'

'But we did not make it.'

'No, we did not,' he agreed. One corner of his mouth curled up in a most suggestive manner.

'And where must we reach tonight, my lord?'

He turned the full weight of his gaze upon her and allowed a small pause before saying softly. 'That remains to be seen, Mrs McLelland.' He saw her comprehension before she abruptly turned her face to stare out of the window.

There was nothing save the rhythmic thud of hooves and the noisy rumble of the carriage wheels.

'I would prefer that we travel faster, my lord.' The words were spoken quietly and she did not take her eyes from the passing scene to look at him.

'You enjoy being shaken around a speeding carriage?' He gave a little laugh of disbelief.

'No.' She was no longer looking at the passing countryside. Rather her eyes moved round to find his. 'But I am eager to reach London.'

'To minimise the time you must spend in my company?'

'No.' Surprise washed over her face, then was gone as quickly as it had come. 'I wish to see my aunt, that is all.'

'In Hendon?'

'Yes, in Hendon,' she agreed, and dropped her gaze to examine the carriage floor.

Guy smiled. 'Tell me about this aunt of yours. Hendon is a small place and perhaps your aunt is not unknown to my friend.'

There was nothing in Helena's expression that gave her away. She made no telling movement, no sign that his request was not perfectly reasonable. Indeed, it was by her very stillness that Guy knew that he had caught her on the back foot. Like a swan, Helena was all tranquil and serene; underneath the surface told quite a different tale. Quite deliberately he sat back and waited, interested to hear what story she would tell. One lie would beget another, and each of those would spawn another two. Before she knew it, the lies would overtake her…unless she was a very accomplished liar. And for all his cynicism there was a part of Guy that hoped it was not so.

Eventually, after too long a silence, she found her voice. 'My aunt is an elderly spinster, quiet and unassuming, with little financial wealth. It is most unlikely that she would have come to your friend's attention. You are very polite, my lord, but I'm sure that my relatives are of no real interest to you.' She gave a small stiff smile that did not touch her eyes. 'Shall we not speak of London instead? I have never been there. Indeed, I have never left Scotland before yesterday.' Another forced smile before she continued with her chatter. 'Mrs Weir told me that you live in London all year round. You must know it very well, sir. Perhaps you could tell me something of the place. I would be delighted to hear it.'

'As I would be delighted to tell it. But you do me a disservice by doubting my sincerity. I assure you that I am almost as interested in your aunt as I am in you.' His eyes never left her for a minute. 'Pray tell me of your aunt.'

The green eyes met his. He could sense the tension in her.

'There is very little to tell,' she said.

'You could start with her name.'

Another pause.

'Miss Morgan…Miss Jane Morgan.' The knuckle of her forefinger touched against her lips.

'Miss Jane Morgan—an elderly spinster, quiet and unassuming, with little financial wealth,' he said in a parody of what she had already told him.

'Yes.' Her hand dropped from her mouth and she no longer looked at him.

'Then I look forward to meeting her.'

Her startled gaze swung round to his. 'What do you mean, my lord?'

'The next time I am in Hendon I will visit both you and your aunt.' He adopted an expression of bland innocence. 'What else did you think that I meant, Mrs McLelland?' he asked in feigned puzzlement.

'Why, nothing at all, sir.' But her cheeks were tinted peach, and he could see the uneasy air that hung about her.

'I must remember to take a note of your aunt's precise direction once we reach London.' Then he looked at her. 'You would not forbid my visit, ma'am?'

'No,' she uttered weakly, 'I would not forbid your visit.'

'Glad to hear it, Mrs McLelland.' He settled back against the squabs, stretched out his legs and smiled. 'Don't mind if I catch up on a bit of shut-eye, do you?'

She gave a faint shake of her head. 'Please go ahead, my lord.'

Another smile before he closed his eyes, confident that he had just launched a successful assault on the façade that was Mary McLelland.

'Will you take some refreshments, Sir Stephen?' enquired Annabel of the man sitting within their drawing room as if he owned the place.

Sir Stephen Tayburn turned to look at her, and it was all Annabel could do not to quail. 'No, thank you, Mrs Weir. I have not the time for such frivolities.' He spoke slowly, enunciating each word with meticulous care. His gaze lingered on her a moment longer before he turned his attentions to her husband, who was sitting closest to him. 'I understand you have a lady staying here at Seamill Hall.'

The look upon John Weir's face was not one of friendship. He knew of Tayburn and did not care for him. 'May I enquire of your interest in our house guests, sir?'

Tayburn's dark gaze met the younger man's. 'I believe that the lady may be a friend of mine.'

'Your friend?' Annabel's face flushed crimson. 'Oh, no, sir, I fear you are mistaken. The lady we found upon the shore was a poor widow by the name of Mary McLelland.'

'Indeed?' queried Tayburn and arched a black eyebrow. 'Pray be so kind, Mrs Weir, as to furnish me with a description of this poor widow.'

'Oh, she is of average height, with long red hair, and…green eyes, yes, I do believe that Mary's eyes are green.'

'Annabel, let me deal with this,' said her husband with a frown.

Annabel's mouth trembled into a moue.

Tayburn smiled and it was a terrible sight to behold. 'And you said that you found this *poor widow* washed upon the shore?' He stressed the words *poor widow* with particular malice.

'Well, not *us* precisely,' said Annabel in defiance of her husband. 'It was Guy.'

'Annabel!' said Weir with irritation.

'Guy?' The name sounded sinister upon Tayburn's lips.

'I contacted the constable directly that the woman was found and there have been no reports of a missing female in the past days,' said Mr Weir.

'My friend left to visit her cousin last week, on the night of the storm. I had no reason to think that she had not arrived safely until a letter arrived from her cousin this morning enquiring as to her whereabouts.' Tayburn held Weir's gaze directly. 'Upon hearing the news I acted immediately and made the appropriate investigations. They, sir, have led me here. I need not tell you that the description of the woman that you found matches that of my friend.'

'Except that the lady goes by the name of Mrs McLelland, and is a respectable widow,' said Weir.

Tayburn's upper lip curled with undisguised contempt. 'Perhaps. But then again my poor friend may have been rendered unconscious by her accident; such a state in women may result in subsequent confusion of the mind. Was this "Mrs McLelland" perhaps unconscious when she was found?' he asked nonchalantly.

Weir could say nothing other than the truth, even though it was dragged quite grudgingly from his lips. 'She was, sir.'

'Ah,' said Tayburn with a degree of satisfaction. 'Then you will not object to my meeting the "lady" in question.' It was a statement rather than an enquiry.

'I'm afraid that is not possible, my lord.' Weir took his place before the fireplace, standing with legs astride, hands behind his back, every inch the master of Seamill Hall.

Tayburn got slowly to his feet and walked over to stand directly before Weir, closing the distance between them until he was too close. 'And why might that be, Mr Weir?' he said in a deathly quiet voice.

Tension crackled between the two men.

Weir swallowed convulsively, but stood his ground. 'Because, sir, Mrs McLelland is no longer here.'

Tayburn's eyes narrowed until they were nothing more than black slits in the sallowness of his face.

'She has gone to stay with her aunt.'

'Indeed? And where is Mrs McLelland's aunt to be found, sir?' The *sir* was a hiss at the end of his sentence.

'I do not know.'

Tayburn stepped closer, forcing Weir to step back towards the fire. 'Come now, Mr Weir, put your mind to the task.'

'I think you should leave my house, Sir Stephen.'

'And I think you should damn well tell me the truth. I'm going nowhere until I know where the hell she's gone.' Another step closer to John Weir.

Weir was looking straight into the empty blackness of Tayburn's eyes and he knew that the stories he had heard concerning this man had all been true. And yet if he told the truth then he knew that Tayburn would go after Guy. 'I believe she said that her aunt lives in Northumberland,' he said.

Tayburn laughed and Weir paled at the sound of it. 'Try again, Mr Weir. The truth this time, if you please.' One more step and Weir was backed against the mantel, and there was the smell of scorched wool. Weir formed a fist and made to punch Tayburn, but not fast enough. Tayburn had the muzzle of a pistol pressed to the coat lapel that covered Weir's heart.

'No!' cried Annabel from the other side of the room. 'Leave him alone!'

'Tell me what I wish to know if you do not want your wife to become a widow by the end of this day,' said Tayburn. 'I'm very good at comforting widows and orphaned children…' he cocked the trigger '…especially pretty little blond ones.'

'Mary McLelland left here yesterday, travelling to Hendon near London,' said Weir from between gritted teeth.

'Better.' Tayburn smiled. 'Now, tell me the rest.'

'There's nothing more to tell.'

Tayburn gave a sigh and tightened his finger on the trigger.

Annabel shouted, 'He's telling the truth. Mary left for London with Guy. We can tell you nothing else.'

Tayburn relaxed the gun and moved back.

Weir heaved a sigh of relief.

It did not last long, for Tayburn moved swiftly towards Annabel. 'And who exactly is this "Guy"?'

Annabel's blue eyes opened wide with fear. 'L-Lord Varington,' she said, shrinking away from him.

'Varington offered to take Mrs McLelland in his carriage as he was travelling back down to London.' Weir manoeuvred himself to stand between his wife and Tayburn.

Tayburn's lips pressed narrow and hard. 'Varington... Varington...' he whispered softly, as if to himself, then suddenly snapped the question, 'Tregellas's brother?'

'Tregellas's brother,' confirmed Weir, hoping that association would be enough to deter Tayburn.

One side of Tayburn's lips snarled back, revealing rather discoloured teeth. 'So she's with Varington, is she, eh? Then I had best fetch my dear Helena back.'

Tayburn threw Annabel a chilling smile. 'Goodbye, Mrs Weir,' then swiveled his gaze to her husband. 'Mr Weir. If I find you have withheld anything of the truth, I shall be sure to call upon you both again.' His eyes bored into those of John Weir. 'Such a charming little creature, your wife. Evil days are upon us, Mr Weir. Have a care that nothing of misfortune befalls her.' And with that he was gone, as quickly as he had arrived, leaving Annabel and Weir alone in the drawing room of Seamill Hall.

Chapter Six

Lord Varington was sleeping peacefully.

Helena was sitting rigidly staring out of the window.

His face was relaxed in repose, with nothing of the usual rakish sophistication and everything of a boyish innocence.

Her eyes were focused on the passing countryside, the huge rolling hills and deep carved valleys of northern England, majestic, awe inspiring, but Helena saw none of it.

The Viscount moved in his sleep, instinctively adjusting his weight on the seat, shifting his legs closer to Helena. His movement distracted her from the dismal route down which her thoughts were racing. She unwound her hands that were clinging so firmly together, placed them on the seat on either side of her, and looked at him, really looked at him. She examined every plane, every angle of his face, the fall of the dark hair across the pale forehead, the straight dark brows that swept low across his eyes, the strength of his nose, the sensual lips that, even in sleep, had just the faintest suggestion of a smile about them. It was a most appealing face, Helena decided, a face upon which the character of the man that bore it was indelibly stamped. Strong and sensual, but with a vulnerability that was hidden in his waking.

She found that she was staring at his lips. His was a mouth made for kissing, and Helena did not doubt that it would not want for practice. Just his touch upon her fingers had been enough to stroke a quiver of desire within her. She wondered what it would be like to feel his mouth on her own. Despite the coldness of the carriage, she felt a heat rise in her cheeks and jerked her gaze away. She was fleeing Stephen, for goodness' sake, not looking for some other man who would call himself her protector and give her nothing of protection! Taking a deep breath, she resolved to push such thoughts from her mind.

She was just concentrating on not looking at Lord Varington when it happened.

There was a noise like the splitting of wood, followed fast by an almighty thud forceful enough to shake Helena to the bone. The carriage collapsed violently on one side, but did not stop. She grabbed for the securing strap, held tight, felt the scrape of the carriage's body against the road. It happened so fast there was no time to scream, no time to cry out, or protest; so fast and yet in that moment time seemed to slow. The carriage was still moving, not forwards but somewhere to the side. Horses whinnied, the coachman bellowed and Helena could hear the terror in both the cries of man and beast. And then there was a scream and the world turned upside down and she had the sensation that the whole carriage was falling, dropping weightlessly through the air. *Lord Varington*! She tried to speak, to shout, to cry, but she could not find her voice. And amidst all of the chaos her mind was calm and quiet, thinking in such an everyday way, *We're going to die*. She knew it in that small flash of time that encompassed her lifetime, knew it with an absolute certainty. It was as if she was standing outside all of the frenzy, watching dispassionately, uninvolved, accepting. And she wanted to laugh at the absurdity of it.

Her arm felt as if it was being wrenched from its socket and she knew that she could not hold on much longer, and even as she thought it she felt the leather of the securing strap begin to slip through her fingers. She hung there, like a haunch of meat suspended from its hook, the securing strap and her failing arm above her head, the other arm useless by her side. Her back was against what had been the roof of the carriage. She could see the fine needlework on the leather of the carriage seat, the intricate even little stitches, the pile of the dark brown cushions. She tried to grab the strap with her other hand, but it was no use. Time stretched and elongated: the man's shouts, the horse's screams, the carriage falling, the slide of the leather within her fingers…and then all noise ceased and she was holding her breath, waiting. The almighty thud when it came sounded as if a whole woodland had been shattered into tiny twigs. It was a roar, an explosion. The carriage hit solid ground and came to a halt. Helena's body flicked like a whip from the force of it and she was flung downwards. A silent scream. An involuntary closing of her eyes. Arms flailing wide.

'Mrs McLelland!' Helena heard someone shout a name before she landed hard, her legs buckling beneath her, her body collapsing. She lay there stunned and still at last amidst the quietness of the wind and creaking timber. A tiny window of peace, in which there was no movement, no sound, just the silence of the moment. And then the horses were shrieking again, and the man was yelling again, and she felt the slight shift of the carriage body beneath her.

'Mrs McLelland,' he said more loudly, and this time she realised that it was Lord Varington, and that she was the Mrs McLelland to whom he was speaking.

She opened her eyes to find most of her view obscured by the remnants of the grey bonnet that had bent and twisted around her face during her fall. For all that she could not see, she could feel that she was lying curled on her side, her legs drawn up, her weight lying on top of her left arm. Beneath the fingers of her right hand she could feel the jagged timber carcass of the carriage, the dampness of soil and the coarse spring of grass. There was a pressure on her left shoulder and her head was resting on top of something solid and warm and alive. Lord Varington. She struggled to move, to sit up.

Lord Varington's voice sounded close by. 'Do not move, Mrs McLelland. Stay exactly as you are. Any sudden movement may risk tipping the carriage more.' His fingers touched firm against hers. 'Are you hurt?'

In truth Helena did not know. 'I do not think so.' Nothing throbbed in pain. In fact, she felt numb all over, numb and shocked and relieved all at the same time.

'Thank God,' he said, and there was a definite relief in his voice.

'We're alive,' she said, scarcely believing it. 'What happened?'

'Sounded like we lost a wheel and have come off the road.'

The horses began to shriek and the carriage creaked and began to move again.

'Lord help us,' she whispered, and she felt Lord Varington's hand close around hers. The shrieks turned to screams, terrifying, gut-wrenching screams that made the hairs on her head stand on end, and then the screams faded into the distance and there was only silence. There was no more movement of the carriage.

'M'lord, m'lord! Are you alive in there?' the coachman shouted from outside.

'I believe that we are, Smith.'

'Don't move, m'lord. Please, dear God, don't you or the lady move.'

Helena could hear the fear in the coachman's voice.

'Where are we, Smith?'

'Gone over the edge of the road, down a sheer drop towards a valley, m'lord, couldn't stop the team, I could see it was going to happen and I still couldn't stop them. Horses just went mad with fear. Panicked. I thought we were gonners.'

'Where has the carriage come to rest?'

The coachman's voice was hoarse. 'On a ledge, a ruddy great ledge, about ten feet down from the road. Horses damn near pulled us off it again. Had to cut them free, m'lord, all of them are lost.'

'You did what you had to, Smith, and for that I'm grateful. Can you open the uppermost door?'

There was a pause before the coachman replied. 'M'lord, the carriage is balanced right on the edge. I fear my weight upon her will send her over.'

Helena felt the sinking in her stomach. There was

no way out. They were trapped on the edge of a precipice and the only direction that the carriage would
be taking was down.

She felt the slight squeeze of Lord Varington's
fingers around hers, and still, she could see nothing
because of the crush of her bonnet over her eyes.

'Is there anything around us that could be used as
an anchor, Smith?' Lord Varington spoke loudly, but
did not shout.

A silence that seemed too long, while the coachman
looked around.

'Aye, m'lord, there's a tree growing where the ledge
meets the hillside. Only a small tree, mind, not strong
enough to take the weight of the carriage.'

'It doesn't need to,' replied Lord Varington. 'Fetch a
rope, Smith, and secure one end around the tree. Tell me
when you've done that.'

'Aye, m'lord.'

There was the sound of Smith moving about outside.

'Lord Varington.' She could feel the strong steady
beat of his heart against her cheek and knew that her
head must be lying against his chest. And then his
fingers were beneath her chin, unfastening the ribbons
of her bonnet, one hand carefully prising the remainder of the bonnet from her head, until at last Helena
could see the true nature of their predicament. The
carriage was on its side with Helena lying curled
across the remnants of the door. Her head was on
Lord Varington's chest, his left arm was pinned in
place by her left shoulder. Lord Varington lay where
he had landed, his head positioned close to the edge
of the carriage's shattered window. But Helena was
not looking at Lord Varington. Instead she stared at

the view through the hole that had housed the glass of the window.

'Mrs McLelland,' he said, drawing her focus to himself.

She turned her gaze up to his.

His face was so pale as to be powder white, which seemed only to exaggerate the darkness of his hair and the deep crimson of the blood splattered and smeared upon his forehead, cheek and chin, and the stark pale clarity of his eyes.

'You're hurt,' she whispered, feeling the fear grip tight in her stomach.

'A scratch,' he said. 'Do not let the blood fool you.'

But Helena knew that what marked Lord Varington's face came from no scratch. 'What are we going to do?'

'Hire another carriage. This one seems to have seen better days.' He smiled a mischievous sort of smile.

How could he joke at a time like this? Perhaps he didn't realise. She let her gaze drift once more to what lay beyond Lord Varington's head, to the view from the gap where the window had been. The bottom section of it, the section closest to where Helena and Lord Varington lay, was filled with the firm solidity of ground, scrubby grass on damp brown soil. But halfway up the ground stopped, and beyond was only the sheer drop into the valley below. The grass way down there looked very green, lush almost for the time of year. And she could see the small white dabs of sheep and the rich chestnut of the broken horses mixed with the red of their blood. She knew then what the screaming had been, she knew too why it was now so silent. And she felt sick.

'Do not look at it.'

At the edges of her vision the cold draught of the wind fluttered Lord Varington's hair. 'We're going to die, aren't we?'

'Look at me,' he said.

But it seemed that she could not draw her eyes away from the view below.

'Helena.'

She looked at him then.

'I will get us out of here. Trust me.'

Trust, the one thing Helena could not give.

'Trust me,' he said again.

Their eyes locked together and it seemed that she could look into his very soul and see his honesty. Her ears were filled with the steady reassuring beat of his heart. And Helena trusted him.

She gave the smallest of nods, feeling the brush of the superfine of his coat against her cheek.

'My lord, it is done,' Smith shouted.

'Very well.' Lord Varington did not take his gaze from Helena's face. Then spoke for Helena's ears only. 'We can escape this.'

Escape—everything came back down to that. 'Or die in the trying,' she said, and heard the huskiness in her own voice.

'My lord?' shouted Smith again.

'Stay back, Smith, until the door opens, then throw the rope as quick as you can. Mrs McLelland shall climb out first. See to her safety.'

'Yes, m'lord,' said the coachman.

His hand released hers, moved to touch gently against her cheek. 'Stand up as slowly and as easily as you can, keeping your weight back towards the side furthest from the drop. No sudden movements. Just slow and easy.'

'If I climb out first, will not that cause the carriage to tip?'

'Not necessarily.'

'But it is a possibility, is it not?'

'Yes…' he smiled '…it is a possibility.'

Helena was not fooled by the lightness of his manner. She knew that Lord Varington was offering her her life at the expense of his own. Her flight from Stephen had already cost two innocent lives. Helena could not let there be another. 'I think it would be better if you were to climb out first, my lord.'

He smiled again. 'I have escaped from worse situations than this. Much as I am touched by your concern,' he said in a teasing tone, 'you need not worry about me.' His thumb touched gently to her cheek. 'Climb out of the carriage and I will follow you.'

A small silence.

'I will not leave you to die,' she said with determination in her words. 'You must climb out first.'

'Really?' he drawled, and she saw the sudden smoulder in his eyes and the sensual tilt of his mouth. 'I did not know you had such a care for my welfare, ma'am.'

She just looked at him.

His smile deepened. 'I understand perfectly, dear lady. You are too shy to admit the truth of your feelings towards me. Come, now, there is none to witness our speech or our actions, Mrs McLelland, or may I call you Helena?'

She stared at him in disbelief. 'No, you may not,' she snapped. 'Have you forgotten our circumstance? That we are within a carriage in imminent danger of tipping over a precipice?'

'Why let a little thing like that stop us, Helena?' And his voice was mellow and teasing with sensuality.

'My name is not Helena,' she said.

'Is it not?' came the reply. 'That's a pity, for it's a name that suits you well.' His thumb slowly traced the contours of her face—'It's from the Greek, *helenos* meaning bright'—so lightly as to scarce be a touch—'and you would brighten any of my days'—and then was gone.

'Have you run mad, Lord Varington?' Her heart was thumping in her chest. 'You cannot seriously be seeking to take advantage of our situation?'

She heard the smile in his voice. 'As if I would do such a thing.' He winked, and blew her a kiss.

It was the final straw. 'You wish me to climb out first. Very well, I shall do so, sir.' And before she could change her mind, she looked away from him and got slowly to her feet.

Varington said nothing.

She turned and reached up to the door handle, twisting it with infinitesimal care. The handle did not budge. She tried again, applying a little more pressure, but the handle remained unyielding. 'The door is stuck,' she said. 'The handle cannot be moved.' She glanced back down at him then. 'My lord…'

'Try the handle again.'

She gave a nod and turned away to work at the handle until her fingers grew red and sore, and still, the handle did not shift. A noise sounded behind her, the creaking of wood, and then Lord Varington was at her back with his hand upon the carriage handle. His exertion brought a grunt to his lips and a fresh drip of blood down his face. Helena heard the click of the lock move and the door began to open. Lord Varington stood behind her, leaning over her. He took the full weight of the door on to his hands, pushing it up first, then edging it back gently to rest upon the carriage body. He was so close she could feel his warmth, his strength, smell the now familiar scent of him. The carriage creaked again as the door rested back against it.

'The rope, Smith!'

And in response a length of rope partially still coiled appeared at the open doorway, raining down towards them. Varington caught it in his hands and fastened part of it around Helena's waist.

She felt his breath by her ear. 'I shall lift you up through the doorway. Climb down the carriage body and jump clear of it as soon as you are able. Smith will help you.' Not one trace remained of his teasing flirtation. His voice was steady and serious. Realisation slipped into place. 'Lord Varington.' She turned her face to the side so that she might at least see him as he stood behind her. 'You were not intent on seducing me at all, only on making me leave the carriage first.' She saw his smile.

'Are you disappointed?'

Helena gave a half smile, half laugh, knowing full well the brink on which they stood. She twisted her head further round that she might look the better at him. 'Thank you for all that you have done for me…for all you are doing. Thank you,' she said again softly.

Only the soft hush of their breath sounded. Blue eyes held green. He lowered his face towards hers, and laid his lips against the edge of her eyebrow. It was a chaste kiss, a gentle kiss, a kiss that acknowledged her gratitude and more. And then his lips were gone, and she knew it was time. She felt the press of his hands just above her hips and then he was lifting her up and through the doorway. She half-fell on to the carriage body, hearing it grunt and creak beneath her weight, slid down it, jumped away from the wheels. Then the coachman was there, grabbing her arms, pulling her to safety, untying the rope and throwing it back down to the carriage. And behind her sounded the scrape of wood, the rip of leather and the crunch of glass.

'No!' The cry tore from her throat and she struggled to her feet, pushing away the coachman's arms, turning back towards the wreckage of the carriage. But where the carriage had stood there was nothing save for the crushed, torn grass and the rope that stretched across it.

'No!' she shouted, and stared at where the carriage had been. From far below came the crash and splintering of wood, the carriage being torn apart on impact. She had seen the horses. She did not want to see the carriage…or what remained of Lord Varington. She stood there, frozen in her disbelief. The horror was too enormous to comprehend. 'Varington!' and her whisper was stolen by the wind and carried away.

'Mrs McLelland.' She barely heard the coachman's words. 'Look, ma'am, look!' Smith was running towards the scarred edge from where the coach had slipped. And she did not know why… until she saw a hand appear, a bloody hand gripping at the rope, and she saw what she had not seen before—that the rope was taut and moving in tiny jerks, as if it supported a man's weight, as if someone were climbing up it. And then Smith was pulling him up, grabbing hold of him to heave him back up on to the ledge.

Lord Varington sat for a minute catching his breath in the grey drizzle of rain. Mud caked his riding boots and smeared the front of his clothing. The pale buff of his pantaloons was unrecognisable beneath the blood and filth, and his coat was torn and stained. His head was bent low and his dark hair fluttered in the wind.

She walked towards him, hardly knowing that she moved. 'Lord Varington.' She heard the relief in her own voice. 'I thought…' Her eyes flickered to the edge of the ledge, then back to his face. She dropped to her knees, unmindful of the mud and broken glass. She did not know how she came to be in his arms, his hands warm around her, pulling her into him, holding her close.

'We're safe now, Helena.'

And she clung to him.

The tremble started in her ankles and spread up through her legs, into her stomach, her chest and even her throat, until everything was quivering. Helena strove to hide the signs of weakness, yet the tremble grew. She made to pull away so that he would not know that she was shaking, but the strong arms just held her tighter. Her mouth opened to forge an excuse. The excuse did not come. There were no calm words of politeness, no ladylike poise. The façade that Helena had carefully sculpted during the years with Stephen crumbled. A sob sounded. Just a single sob. But that one sob led to another, and another, until, to her extreme mortification, Helena realised that she was crying. Crying for how close Lord Varington had come to death. Crying for Agnes and for Old Tam. Crying for everything she had lost through the years. And all the while the rain drizzled down around them.

'Hush,' he soothed. 'I have you. You're safe.' He cradled her against him and there was nothing of the rakish sensuality in the softness of his voice or the gentleness of his hands. 'You're safe,' he whispered again and again, until at last the tears and the trembling had stopped, and all that was left was the shudder in her throat.

She laid her cheek against his chest and let herself feel what it was like to be held by a good man. For the first time in many years Helena was truly safe. She relaxed against him, feeling the hardness of his body, smelling the clean scent of his cologne, absorbing his warmth. Something in her heart blossomed. For all of his flirtatious behaviour, this was a man who had saved her life upon the shore, a man who had changed his plans to take her to London rather than see her travel alone by stage, a man who had almost died to free her from the wreckage of a carriage. And what had she given him in return? Dishonesty. Distrust. Suspicion. She crooked her neck, looked up into his face, seeing again the bloody gash down the side of his face. 'You're hurt. We must seek help.'

'It is a scratch. But you are right, we must seek help. We have the climb back up to the road to negotiate.' He glanced up. The rain was falling in earnest now and, although it was still early in the day, the skies were dark and foreboding.

Lord Varington coiled the rope around his waist and made the climb up to the road. The grass was slippery from being wet and there was little purchase for his feet. Helena watched, the breath catching in her throat with every slip of his foot, until he disappeared over the top and on to the road. From there he secured the rope and threw the end down to Smith. The coachman fastened a length around Helena's waist and she half clambered, was half hoisted up to the road, where she untied the rope and cast it back down to Smith. The coachman was just scrabbling clear of the valley when the distant rumble of a coach sounded. It rounded the corner, its pace somewhat cautious in view of the weather, and slowed even before Lord Varington flagged it down.

Helena and Lord Varington stood side by side waiting for the carriage to halt.

'There is something I need to tell you, my lord,' she said. Her heart was beating too fast. *Truthfulness comes at a price*, the little voice inside her head was whispering. It was madness to tell him, and yet she knew that she had to. It was the least that he deserved.

'I know,' he said.

'I do not think that you do,' she said quietly, knowing full well that once he knew the truth everything would be changed. 'I've lied to you from the start.'

One corner of his mouth curved up in a wry smile. 'Not quite from the start,' he said. The coach came to a stop and the window dropped open, and Lord Varington stepped forward to speak to the man whose face appeared there. Then the door was opening and the steps being put into place.

Helena sat beside Lord Varington opposite the gentleman traveller. Outside, Smith climbed up to sit beside the coachman. And the coach trundled off down the road towards Appleby, through the mud and the heavy teeming rain. The truth would have to wait…for now.

Chapter Seven

Helena stood in the small bedchamber of the inn, naked save for the sheet wrapped around her. Her shift and stays were draped over both the chair and the fire-guard that she had positioned a little way from the fire that burned in the grate. The flames leapt high and golden, throwing out a heat that was too hot against the linen wrapped around her, yet still she made no move to shift away. She was sitting too close to the hearth, trying to dry the wetness of her hair. It hung heavy and damp over her bare shoulders, drying slowly into wild curls and waves. The fire scalded her skin pink, yet it did nothing to chase the chill that she had felt since the carriage crash. She closed her eyes, leaned her head back the better to dry the top of her hair and tried not to think at all.

A soft knock sounded at the door. 'Mrs McLelland.'

She jumped at the sound of Lord Varington's voice, scrambling to her feet, heart suddenly pounding.

'I am not dressed, sir,' she said with what she hoped sounded to be a reasonable and calm voice.

'You tempt me to abandon what I am here for.' She could hear his smile. 'The landlady has sent some spare clothing for you to wear while she dries that which you have given her. I have it here for you.'

She had not thought that he would bring her the clothing in person. She walked over to stand by the door, speaking through the thick wooden panels. 'Thank you, my lord. If you would be so kind as to leave the clothing there, I will collect it.'

'Very well,' he said. 'When you are ready, come downstairs. There is a private parlour for our use and I have requested some hot food.'

And once they were alone in the parlour, there would be no more hiding. She would have to tell him the truth. Dread squirmed in her stomach and it seemed she could not face a confrontation with Lord Varington, not tonight. She would be stronger in the morning. Then she could tell him, not now. 'I am not hungry, just tired. I would rather retire early, my lord, if you do not mind.'

Nothing sounded through the wood. She moved closer, straining to listen. Still nothing. 'My lord?'

Finally he spoke. 'As you wish, Mrs McLelland.' His voice sounded tired. There was none of the persuasions he had used the previous night. Indeed, he did not even wait for a reply before she heard the tread of his footsteps recede along the corridor.

Part of her was relieved, part disappointed. She sighed, ensured that the sheet was tucked securely around her bosom and turned the key in the door. The door opened a few inches. The bag of clothing lay where Lord Varington had left it immediately outside the door. Her line of vision showed the corridor to be empty. Stooping, she extended an arm cautiously through the aperture. Her fingers closed tight around the handle of the bag and she pulled it towards her. Just as she opened the door wider to admit the bag, a booted foot appeared between the door and the door frame. Helena gave a gasp, released her grip on the bag and tried to slam the door.

'Allow me,' said Lord Varington, and carried the bag into the room.

'Lord Varington!' Helena exclaimed. 'What on earth do you think you're doing?'

'Carrying a lady's baggage,' came the smooth reply.

Her mouth gaped and her eyes flashed wide with shock. One hand clutched defensively across her breast, ensuring the sheeting was tucked securely, the other moved to grip the door edge. 'Please leave at once.'

He walked across the room and set the bag down on the floor by the window, giving no sign that he had heard her.

'Lord Varington.' There was anger and indignation in her voice.

'Close the door, Helena. The draught from the passageway will give you a chill.'

She stared at him as if she could not believe what he was saying.

'We have much to discuss tonight, and if you do not intend coming down to the parlour, then we had best speak of it here and now.'

'I am not dressed, my lord!'

He let his eyes rove from the perfection of her face to the glorious curtain of hair that hung heavy and still damp over the creamy white of her bare shoulders. Above the winding of the sheet he could see the rise of her breasts, and could imagine exactly what lay beneath.

The imagining caused certain obvious reactions within his body, even though it was cold and fatigued. He clamped his jaw tight and let his gaze sweep lower. The sheet ended just past her knees. Her legs were pale and shapely; her feet bare and free from linen bindings. 'I had noticed,' he murmured, and forced himself to look away. He made a show of walking over to the fireplace, stirring at the coals with the poker.

Voices sounded from the direction of the staircase: women's laughter, the thud of feet.

Helena quickly closed the door and hurried over to where he was crouched. Her voice dropped low. 'What can you be thinking of, my lord? This behaviour goes beyond the pale.'

His head ached like Hades and there was a distinct pain in his leg. Fatigue sat like lead in his muscles. Hunger gnawed at his belly. He straightened and turned to look at her. 'Now will you come down to the parlour?' he said softly. 'It has been a long day and I did not wish to waste time hovering in the passageway coaxing you to do so.'

She blinked and stared up at him with those bewitching green eyes. She looked very much as if he had just snatched the wind from her sails. 'Can we not wait until morning?'

'No.' He twitched his eyebrows and gave a rueful smile. 'You'll have changed your mind come morning, and I would like to know the real identity of the woman that I'm accompanying to London.' He moved past her, heading towards the door.

'But the carriage… We are still for London?' It was Mrs McLelland that spoke, not Helena, yet Guy could hear the subtle undertones of hope and of desperation.

He stopped and looked round at her. 'We must wait

for a hire carriage to become available, which may take a day or two. Our arrival in the city will be delayed, but, yes, we are still for London.'

It seemed that her skin paled. 'Is there nowhere else from which we can hire a carriage more immediately?'

'Unfortunately not. I tried all of the surrounding villages. There are none to be had.'

Something akin to panic passed over her face, and then it was gone. 'There must be something?'

He gave a subtle shake of his head.

Helena looked away, thought furrowing her brow. 'Then I must catch the stage…or the mail.' As if remembering he was still there, she glanced back at him. 'Are we on the mail route? If so, I could be on the next coach coming through. The landlord would know. I must ask him at once.' He could see the sudden tension that racked her body, hear the higher pitch of her voice. She knelt down by the bag of clothes, and was struggling with small frenzied actions to unfasten it with one hand, while the other still clutched the sheet to her breast.

He did not move. He did not need to. 'Would you abandon me so readily, Helena?' he asked quietly.

The question seemed to pull her up short. Her hand ceased its motion. The green eyes shot up to his. And to his surprise he could see the pain in them. 'I must,' she whispered. 'I have no choice.'

'We both know that is not true,' he said.

Her teeth caught at her lower lip, and as she bowed her head, her hand resumed its work upon the bag. 'You know nothing of my situation.' He heard the struggle within her voice. 'I thank you for everything that you've done for me, my lord, but I cannot stay here. I have to get away.'

'From whom are you running?'

A sudden sharp intake of air, and when she looked at him there was a look of terror upon her face. 'No one!' The denial was too swift, too easy.

'You said that you would tell me the truth.'

She looked away in anguish. 'Please do not ask me, not now…'

'I offered you my help, Helena, and I meant it.' He moved to stand beside her.

She stilled.

'Let me help you,' he whispered.

Slowly she rose so that they stood facing one another, with barely two feet separating them. 'You would not offer your help, sir, if you knew the truth.'

He searched her eyes, trying to fathom something of her, finding only hurt and fear and betrayed innocence. Whatever this woman had done, Guy could not imagine that it would change his offer. 'Let me be the judge of that.'

The tiniest flicker of hope. 'To help me would be to place yourself in grave danger. I cannot allow you to do that.'

'It's too late,' he said. 'I've already helped you.' He paused just long enough to let the implication sink in.

There was a hiss from the fireplace. The noise from the crowded taproom below was a faint buzz in the background. She gave a nod. 'You are right.' Her eyes closed as if gathering strength, and when they opened again he knew that she would tell him what he wanted to know.

Her voice was quiet but clear as she began. 'I beg your forgiveness, my lord, for my dishonesty. I never meant for anyone else to become involved in any of this.'

He did not speak, just let her continue in her soft lilt.

'My name is Helena McGregor. I am the eldest daughter of James McGregor of Ayr, and…' she hesitated, took in a deep breath and could not meet his eyes '…and I am the mistress of Sir Stephen Tayburn.'

Tayburn! God in heaven! A shiver rippled down Guy's spine.

'I tried to escape him. Fled with the help of my maid and my father's old servant that came with me to Dunleish. I did not dare to leave them behind for Stephen to punish for my crime. The story I told you of the boat and the storm was true, except that we sailed from the island of St Vey, not Islay.'

'That would explain why you were washed up near Portincross.'

She gave a small nod.

'Have you heard of Sir Stephen? Do you know what manner of man he is?' She looked at him then, not a shred of the mask left in place to cover her emotions. There, in place of the calm polished poise, was naked vulnerability.

'I doubt there is anyone who does not,' he said, and then wished that he had not, at the look that crossed her face. 'He keeps you at his castle? What of his wife? I thought he was married to Harris's daughter.'

'He is.' Her voice was very small. 'She lives at Dunleish too.' And again she would not meet his gaze.

'You all live together?' Guy felt his eyebrow rise of its own accord. Something turned in his stomach.

Another small nod. 'I did not want it to be that way. I did not understand the arrangement when I agreed to…'

'When you agreed to be his mistress,' he finished for

her, and could not keep the distaste from his voice. How in Hades could any woman, particularly the woman standing so defencelessly before him, agree to such a thing? Hell, the man was evil incarnate.

No reply.

'My God, what must he have offered you to tempt you to his bed? I cannot imagine that Tayburn would be a considerate lover.'

She winced at that.

And still, he could not stop himself. Knowing that she had willingly given herself to such a beast. Knowing what he knew about Tayburn. 'How long have you been with him?'

'Five years.'

'You've stayed with him for five years! Hell's teeth, Helena, are you out of your mind? Is your need for money so very great that you must sell yourself to the likes of him?'

She edged back, her face frozen and pale.

'Why?' he snapped. 'Do *you* not know the manner of the man? Do you not know of what he is capable? Or don't you care, is that it?'

She shook her head, continuing to expand the distance between them.

His hand shot out, closed around the soft flesh of her upper arm and pulled her back to him. Her skin was cool and smooth beneath his fingers. The smoky green of her eyes had darkened. The top of her head reached only to his chin. Her bare feet stood toe to toe with his riding boots. He was gripping her tightly, too tightly. It was the shock of hearing Tayburn's name. He loosened his fingers.

She made to pull away.

'No.' His voice was firm even if his grip was not. 'I'll hear the rest of it first, if you please.'

Helena gave up her resistance. He felt the resignation in the arm beneath his fingers. The scent of her tickled beneath his nose. She was so close he could have lowered his mouth to hers and taken it. She was looking at him as if he had just struck her, a look so wounded that he had to remind himself of what she had just told him. She was Tayburn's whore, for heaven's sake!

'You know the rest. You saw the wreckage of the boat. I can only assume that Agnes and Old Tam drowned.' She blinked several times and looked down to hide the moisture in her eyes. 'When I awoke to find myself in a place I did not recognise, my first thought was to run before I could be found. But then you fetched me back and…' her words faltered '…and I realised that you were not going to let me slip away unnoticed. I could not tell anyone who I really was; Mr Weir would have had me shipped back to Stephen in the blink of an eye, as would the constable. And so I became the widowed Mary McLelland. Under her guise I thought there was still a chance I could escape him.' She cast him a look that begged for understanding. 'I had to get away from Seamill Hall. If he knew where I was, then Mr and Mrs Weir would have been in danger.'

'They *are* in danger, thanks to you.' And him. It was Guy that had brought her into their home, and Guy that had laughed at Weir's feelings regarding Helena.

'I never meant for that to happen. What else could I do? I couldn't tell Mr and Mrs Weir the truth!'

'But you could let them clothe you and take their money.'

'I intend to pay them back, every penny of it.'

He shook his head, his mouth adopting a sneer. 'With what? Money from your non-existent aunt in Hendon?'

She was so pale he thought she would faint, but she didn't, she just looked up at him with those beautiful eyes. No wonder she had snared Tayburn, looking like she did. She could have snared any man in the country. Guy doubted that he had ever looked upon a more physically attractive woman. Superficial perfection. But beneath it Helena McGregor could have no heart to be mistress to such a man. That she could have given herself to that monster. Something crawled in his stomach and his blood ran cold as memories of a man not so very different from Tayburn resurfaced. The horror of those memories served only to heighten his outrage.

'No, I—'

He cut her off. 'Or maybe you were planning on selling yourself to raise the money. What is your price, Helena?'

'It wasn't like that! You don't understand!'

Guy Tregellas was a man not often moved to anger, but when the devil was unleashed in him the anger splurged hot and hard. 'You haven't answered my question. How much? Come, don't be coy. If the price is right, I may well be your next customer.'

Anger flashed in her eyes. The hand that had been clutched to her chest raised and moved to slap his face.

He caught the wrist, before her palm made contact, dragged it back down, imprisoned it with the other behind her back.

'Or maybe you find me not to your taste. After all, how can I compare to Tayburn?'

Her breath came in short sharp pants, her breasts rising and falling in fast rhythm.

'I know of men like him, Helena, of what they like to do.'

'No!' she cried out, and struggled against him.

Their bodies collided as she sought to escape.

He held her with a firm determination, ignoring the feel of her softness bumping against him, ignoring the sweet womanly smell of her.

And then the sheet moved. She must have felt the end of it loosen from where she had safely tucked it beneath her arm, for she suddenly ceased her struggle and froze. The sheet slipped lower, revealing the swell of her breasts, bathed golden in the glow from the fire.

He stared down at the tops of the pale mounds. The only thing holding the sheet in place was the fact that she was pressed so hard against him. He felt a familiar tightening in his groin, felt the burning of desire. Fatigue and hunger were forgotten. He licked his lips and let his gaze meander back up to her face.

She was staring up at him like a rabbit caught in a trap, all stunned fear and panic. 'Please, my lord…' The sob caught in her throat.

How many times had she uttered that word to Tayburn? Hell, he'd be damned if he'd take her against her will. Slowly he loosened his grip over her wrists and stepped back from her. She clutched at the sheet but not before a fleeting glimpse of the body that lay beneath it had been revealed.

There was no hiding his blatant arousal. He turned and walked from the room while he still had the self-control to do so, cursing the woman left standing within for being Tayburn's whore. Cursing himself all the worse because even that knowledge did not stop him wanting her.

The door closed with a firm click and still Helena did not move. She stood staring at the oaken panels through which Lord Varington had stridden. What other reaction had she expected? Understanding? Kindness? Compassion? She was a fool a thousand times over. She disgusted him. He loathed her. He would not help her, not now that he knew the truth. Just as she knew that no one would help her.

Silence rang in her ears. The imprint of Lord Varington's fingers burned around her wrists. At least there would be no more lies. The sheet clutched between her fingers was warm where it had been pressed against him. She remembered again the revulsion that had crossed his face on learning the truth. Her eyes shuttered as if that could dispel the image. No more pretending to be what she was not. For all the awfulness of the situation Helena found comfort in that. She was a fallen woman, a soiled woman. Nothing could change that. But she had survived all that Stephen had done to her. And she would survive the future.

When Helena's eyes opened again she knew that she would keep going, because she had to. Her travelling bag had been lost with the carriage, but at least she still had the purse that Mrs Weir had given her. The inn was on the main road to London. All she need do was wait for the next mail-coach to arrive, then take a seat to London. It was her only hope of safety. Slowly, Helena moved towards the bag of clothes sent by the landlady. Piece by piece she began to reassemble her defences around her. She had told the truth and the truth had cost dearly. The bag opened. With fumbling fingers she pulled out the clothing that she needed.

She was fully dressed and her almost-dry hair combed and pinned up into a neat chignon when the knock at the door sounded. Helena jumped and eyed the door with suspicion. 'Who is it?' She was half-expecting the deep tones of Lord Varington's voice, but a girl answered.

'It's Rose, ma'am. I work here, and I've brought your dinner.'

The smell of food wafted under the door. 'I didn't order any food.' She couldn't afford to. Helena thought of the precious money within Mrs Weir's purse and how long it would have to last.

'His lordship said as to bring you up a tray.'

There was a slight pause before Helena asked, 'Is Lord Varington there?'

'No, ma'am,' the voice said. She sounded young, little more than a girl. 'He's down in one of the parlours. It's just me.'

The key turned silently beneath Helena's fingers. Her hand hovered ready to engage the lock in an instant. Slowly she opened the door by the smallest crack and peered out.

A girl stood there, wearing a brown dress and an apron that had once been white. Her hair matched the wool of her dress and had been bundled up into the huge cap that was pinned upon her head. She looked fifteen at the most. Helena breathed a sigh of relief and opened the door wider to receive the tray.

The girl looked at her strangely, as if she wasn't sure of what to make of her. 'Shall I just set it down on the table for you, ma'am?'

Helena gave a nod. 'Thank you.'

The tray was placed on the small table close by the bed. 'Mind your fingers, ma'am. Plates are just out of the oven. Right hot they are.'

'Thank you,' Helena said again. The girl was almost through the door before she added, 'Did his lordship say anything else?'

The girl stared round at her. 'No, ma'am. Nothin.' Do you want me to take him a message?'

'No, thank you,' Helena said quickly. 'But there is something that you could find out for me, if you would be so kind. I need to know if the mail-coach stops here.'

The girl's feet padded back down the passageway. The key turned easily in the lock. The tray of food and wine beckoned. Her stomach growled. She moved the tray to her lap and sat down upon the bed.

It was only two hours later, when Helena lay down, still clothed in the landlady's dress, beneath the covers of the bed. The fire had burned low, leaving just a pile of glowing coals. The discarded emptied tray sat where she had left it, on the same small table on which it had arrived fully laden. Downstairs the carousing had diminished, but not died. Outside the night was miserable. Rain smattered against the windowpanes and wind howled. She nestled below the blankets and was glad of the shelter. Tomorrow night would see her in London. But she did not want to think about that. Not now. Not until she had to. She needed to rest, for the mail-coach passed early and it waited for no one. She sought the black comfort of sleep, but did not find it. The image of his face would give her no peace. Even with her eyes closed she could see it as if it was etched for ever upon her mind. But it was not the face of the man who had forced her into becoming his mistress that haunted her. It was another man altogether. A man that looked at her with both desire and distaste. A man whose smile had vanished with her revelation. Varington.

A slight noise sounded from her door. Helena stilled her restless turning and listened. There was a clatter as the key that she had left sitting within the lock fell suddenly to the floor. Something scraped in the lock. Helena sat bolt upright, staring at the door, alarm ringing in her head. Her throat was suddenly dry, her heart hammering in her chest. Dear God! She glanced about, eyes strained through the gloom to find something she might use as a weapon. There was nothing save the candlestick and the stub of her candle. Her fingers closed around the coldness of the metal, and she lifted it quietly to her. A creak. Then a chink of light showed as the door slowly, steadily began to open.

Stephen! The word stuck in her throat so that it seemed she could not breathe. Her hand tightened around the candlestick. Waited to see the dark promise she knew that his face would hold. The door widened. She readied herself. Tried to suppress the sudden churn of her stomach. A figure shielding a lit candle walked silently forward into her room. She shrank back, opened her mouth to scream, but none came. Stephen! The word formed upon her lips. 'Stephen!' This time his name escaped as a whisper. And it seemed that in that single word was all of her terror, all of her dread.

'Helena.' He uncovered the candle and moved towards her.

She stared all the harder, her pulse throbbing all the more. For the light of the candle had shown that his hair was not white like snow. The man who had just broken into her bedchamber was dark like a raven, and even through the sombre light of the single candle she could see that his eyes were pale.

'I'm not Tayburn. You needn't be afraid.'

'Lord Varington?' The candlestick slackened as relief coursed through her veins. 'I thought…I thought that he had found me.'

He stopped where he was, just short of the bottom of the bed. 'I didn't mean for you to think such a thing.' There was no smile on his face, but neither did it hold the distaste she had earlier witnessed. 'I would have knocked, but after what I said to you this evening I did not think that you would admit me. I apologise both for my uninvited entry now and for my earlier behaviour. I was a trifle…surprised…to hear mention of Tayburn's name.'

Her relief was rapidly evaporating. 'How did you get in? I locked the door.'

He pulled a key from his pocket and held it up to the candlelight. 'For the right price the landlord was willing to part with his spare key.'

She shivered. 'What do you want, my lord?' As if she needed to ask. What did any man want that came to a woman's bedchamber at night?

Just the slightest hesitation before he answered, 'To talk to you.'

'I would have thought you had heard enough of me to last you a lifetime.'

He ignored that. 'I hear you are planning to be away on the six o'clock mail.'

She looked at him, comprehension dawning. 'The serving girl told you.'

No reply.

'You need not concern yourself with me any more, my lord.' She spoke with quiet dignity.

'You cannot outrun him, Helena.' There was a weariness in his voice.

'I can try.' She swung her legs over the side of the bed and set the candlestick back down in its place.

'He will find Weir and Annabel eventually. It's just a matter of time before he discovers where you went and with whom.'

'Oh, God!' Her teeth found her bottom lip and bit down. 'I'm so sorry. I never meant for them or you to be involved.'

He gave a nod of his head. 'I know.'

She looked round at him at that. 'If he finds you, tell him the truth about the carriage accident and that I travelled on to London alone. Maybe then he'll just come after me.'

'You don't really believe that, do you?' He walked to the bottom of the bed and sat down on its edge. The candlelight cast shadows on his face. Beneath his eyes were smudges of fatigue.

'I pray that he will find neither of us.'

A little grunt of disbelief sounded in the room and he gave a cynical smile.

'You need not go back to London. Perhaps you could go abroad for a short while, just until things blow over.'

'I have no intention of hiding from Tayburn,' he said.

'Please,' she whispered. 'You asked me if I knew what he was capable of…' She tasted the blood from her lip. 'And I tell you I *know* him. So please, Lord Varington, if you value your life, do not let him find you. My conscience is already laden. Don't seek to weigh it any heavier.'

'Do not worry, Helena. Tayburn does not frighten me.'

'Then you're a fool or you do not know him!'

Something in his expression shifted and a cold distant look came into his eyes. 'I'm no fool, and I do not under-estimate him, for I once knew a man very like him.' He spoke softly but she could hear the deadly intent in his voice. 'I'll change nothing of my life for Tayburn.'

There was no point in pursuing the matter. She could see that he would not change his mind.

As suddenly as it had come, the darkness of his mood seemed to disappear. He glanced at her. 'What were you going to do when we reached London? I take it there is no aunt in Hendon.'

She gave a little shake of her head, and felt the long plait into which she had woven her hair sway against her back. 'It would be safer if you did not know, my lord.'

He gave a noise that was half disbelief and half laugh. 'For whom?'

'Both of us.'

'You're mistaken, Helena. If you run, Tayburn will pursue until he catches you.'

'I have to at least try,' she said. 'I've come this far.'

'Have you in the least idea what it will be like for you as a woman alone and penniless in London?'

'I will find myself employment. I'm not afraid of hard work.'

'Employment?' The word dripped with cynicism. 'And the nature of this employment will be…?'

'A governess, a seamstress, a maid…I do not know precisely. Whatever position I am able to secure.'

'Even the lowliest maid of all requires a reference from her previous employers.'

She was aware of the sinking feeling in her chest. He was right, of course. She realised that she had been naïve in her expectations; that her thinking had been too concerned with escaping Stephen and not enough with what she would do if she ever found that freedom. Lord Varington's words rendered her dreams of renting a clean and pretty sunlit room, of finding genteel employment, of saving her money to buy a small dressmaking shop, seem ridiculous. She raised her chin defiantly. 'I will find a way.'

'Except that the way might not be quite what you are expecting. You wouldn't last five minutes before some scoundrel had you in his grasp, forcing his attentions upon you. London is not a nice place for an unprotected woman, Helena. There are other men like Tayburn out there, some even worse than him.' And he could not keep the bitterness from his voice at the dark memories those words triggered.

She shivered at his words, but she could not let him dissuade her. She had to keep going if she wanted to survive. 'What do you suggest that I do? Go back to him? I'd rather take my chances in London.'

'There is another way,' he said quietly.

Another way? Could there be? She looked at him.

'A way that I believe would be beneficial to us both.'

She saw the look in his eyes, knew what he was going to say even before he said it.

'A certain proposition…'

She felt the blood drain from her face, felt the tightening twist within her stomach. 'No.' The denial was so faint that she was not sure that she had uttered it aloud.

But he did not stop. 'You're a beautiful woman, Helena. You cannot be unaware of the fact that I'm attracted to you. And I do not think that you're entirely indifferent to me.'

She knew what he thought her, what the whole world thought her. She just did not want to hear it confirmed from his own lips. 'Please, do not, Lord Varington.'

'A mistress may choose her protector. If you were to come under my protection...' He raised a suggestive brow. 'I assure you it would be preferable to what awaits you in London.'

'No. I cannot. It's—'

He held up his hand. 'Just hear what I've got to say before you give me your answer. As my woman, Tayburn could not touch you. You would be safe.'

'I could never be safe. He will not just let me go, especially to another man.'

'He would have no choice in the matter. You would have whatever you wanted, *carte blanche*.'

She turned her face away, stared down at the floor. He was offering to buy her, just as Tayburn had done, only then she'd had no choice, and now...

'I will set you up in your own establishment in London and give you money to do as you wish.'

Her eyes squeezed tightly shut. He was bidding for her services.

'I would protect you from him, Helena.'

Emotion cracked raw in her breast. Her hand balled in a fist and touched firm against her mouth. She did not speak.

'You need not decide right now. Think over what I have said. At best you'll end up in a hell-hole in London under some cove. At worst, you'll run for a little while longer, giving Tayburn the thrill of the chase, before he catches you. If that's what you want, Helena, then get on that mail-coach tomorrow morning. If you decide otherwise, then we will make our arrangements accordingly.' She could feel the force of his focus even though she was not looking at him. It seemed that there was something wrapped tight around her chest that was making it difficult to breathe. Slowly, almost against her will, she turned to meet his gaze.

Her eyes traced the line of the cut that ran down the side of his face. The paleness of his eyes seemed darker within the shadows of the room, his face menacingly handsome. Their gaze held for what seemed an eternity and then he rose, causing the small flame above his hand to flicker wildly. 'Sleep well, Helena.' And with that the tall dark figure walked towards the door and was gone. The key turned in the lock and then there was silence.

Chapter Eight

The morning was as dark and cold as the night. Helena shivered as she trod quietly down the inn staircase at a quarter to six the next morning. She had not slept at all. Lord Varington's words had made sure of that. She knew that he had only spoken the truth. Knew too that Varington was everything a woman could want in a lover; that there had always been some measure of attraction between them since he had found her upon the shore near Portincross. A small voice within told her she should grab his offer with grateful hands. Was it not the solution to all her problems? But her heart balked at what that would mean: that Stephen was right—that she was nothing better than a whore. Accepting his offer would confirm it to Lord Varington, and that thought hurt more than it should have.

She asked the landlord for a cup of coffee. Counted a few of her precious coins on to the table. Sat alone in the little parlour sipping on the hot bitter brew while she contemplated what he had offered her. She did not need to weigh the pros and cons. There had only ever been one answer to his offer and she could have given him that last night. Lord Varington's view of her and her thoughts of him did not influence the matter at all. Another sip of coffee and she roused herself.

'How much do I owe you for the bedchamber and the food last night?'

The small gruff man looked at her with confusion in his eyes. 'Lord Varington will settle the account.'

'I will settle my own, sir,' she said in a quiet determined voice. 'If you would be so kind as to tell me the sum owing.'

He named a price that seemed rather exorbitant to Helena. She showed nothing of her thoughts and pressed a pile of her rapidly diminishing coins into the landlord's hand. They disappeared from sight with surprising speed, as did the landlord himself when he spotted who had just come into the room.

The cup shook between Helena's fingers.

Lord Varington did not so much as look in the landlord's direction. He moved silently towards her, gave a small bow and sat down. 'Good morning, Helena.' And not once did his eyes leave her face. He was dressed in yesterday's clothes that had been cleaned and dried and repaired.

'My lord.' She quickly placed the cup down on the table so that he would not see the tremble of her fingers.

His eyes swivelled to the landlady's bag sitting on the floor by her side, then swung back to her face.

'You've made your decision, then.'

She said nothing, knowing that there had never been any decision to make.

The silence stretched between them.

'Before you go, will you tell me what it was that Tayburn offered for you to become his mistress?'

She looked him directly in the eye. 'My father's life,' she said.

The rumble of the approaching mail-coach sounded outside.

Shock registered across his face.

A knocking at the door and the landlord's face appeared. 'Mail will be in the yard in two minutes, ma'am.'

'Thank you.' She nodded her dismissal to the man and stood, gathering the bag into her hand.

'You should have told me,' he ground out from between gritted teeth.

'You didn't ask,' she replied softly, and walked towards the door.

'Wait!' There was an urgency in his voice.

She halted in her tracks.

'Is that not all the more reason to come to me?'

She turned and looked at him. 'And confirm what Stephen has made me?' She shook her head. 'I do not think so. I am not fleeing him to run to another man.' Then her chin raised a notch. 'I will make my way in life through honest and respectable means.'

'And you believe Tayburn will sit back and let you go? Your impatience to reach London is not so that you may see the sights! You know what manner of man he is, Helena.'

'Then I must ensure that he does not find me,' she said with a great deal more confidence than she felt.

'We both know that is an impossibility.' He stood up and walked slowly towards her. 'Men like Tayburn never give up. If it takes him one week or ten years, he will find you.'

She swallowed hard and looked away.

'And what of your family? Can you be so sure that Tayburn shall not mete his revenge at your flight upon them?'

Her breath shook. She clasped fiercely at the bag. 'That is why I go to London and not Ayr. I have made no visit to them, sent no note, no message while I was at Seamill Hall. Do you not think that I long to see them? I tell you it is infinitely so, but I would not risk bringing Stephen's attention to them. My family knows nothing of my escape; indeed, there has been no contact between us since he took me away. They kept their agreement with Stephen. It is I, not they, who have angered him.'

'Do you think that matters to a man like Tayburn?'

'All of Stephen's attention will be focused upon finding me. He will not think of my family.'

'If that's what you want to think, I shall not dissuade you from the comfort that you find in that delusion.'

A whisper of dread rippled down her spine. 'There's nothing I can do to help them…save go back to him.'

'It's too late for that, Helena.'

Her eyes rose to his. 'Should I then have stayed with him for ever? Am I wrong to have sought my freedom?' The bag hung awkwardly in her hand.

His gaze was intense. 'No.'

A clatter of horses' hooves sounded coming into the yard. Men's voices shouted.

'I must go,' she said, but it seemed that she could not tear her eyes from his. She wrenched her gaze away and, before her courage deserted her, walked briskly through the inn door. His voice sounded behind her.

'Helena, I can help your family. They can be protected. I give you my word that I will not let him harm them.'

The words echoed in her head as she ran across the inn's yard towards the waiting coach. And she thought—what if Lord Varington was right, what if Stephen took his revenge on her family? There was nothing she could do to protect them, even if she returned to St Vey right now. The damage had been done, and Stephen was a vindictive man. God help them. She could not protect them, but Lord Varington could. She was halfway across the yard when she stopped.

'Make haste, miss. We can't wait!' the guard shouted, reaching his hands down for her bag. 'Throw your baggage up to me!' The coach door swung open.

Over her shoulder she saw Lord Varington standing in the door frame that led into the inn. Beneath the light of the lanterns and with the dark coat moulded around his body he looked tall and muscular. He was watching her with a peculiar expression upon his face. One that she had not seen before. And in the line of his jaw and the press of those lips, in the sculpted straight nose and the stark pale eyes with their dark dark lashes, there was not one sign of weakness. The barely healed scar running down the side of his face emphasised his ruggedness. A strong man, in every sense of the word. Strong enough to stand up to the devil himself. Strong enough to save those she loved. The guard shouted again. Inside the coach a disgruntled woman shrieked, 'It's bleedin' freezin' in here. Take your time, won't you, love!'

She addressed herself to the guard. 'My apologies, sir. I fear I have made a mistake. I cannot travel today after all.'

'Bloody women!' the guard snorted, and slammed the door. Then the horses were clattering back out of the yard and the coach had gone, and with it any chance Helena had of leaving.

She did not look round, Just stood staring after the mail-coach with its lanterns and its luggage and the two men perched atop driving, until it merged into the inky blue of the morning. Until she was standing alone in the middle of the yard of the Crown Inn at three minutes past six on a November morning. And then she felt a warm presence at her shoulder and knew that it was Lord Varington. He took the bag from her frozen fingers, then gently tucked her hand into the crook of his arm.

'Come, Helena. It's cold out here. Let's go inside.'

Sir Stephen Tayburn lolled back against the bolsters and watched the grey gloom of the countryside pass by his window. His carriage rolled down the Kilmarnock road heading for Dumfries, from where he could travel to Gretna and the border that would take him into England. The team were fresh and pulling him at a brisk speed. Tayburn showed no sign of agitation; indeed, he showed no sign of any emotion at all. His face was one of calm indifference, a mask that hid the monster within. Only those that knew him would have seen the darkness in those narrow black eyes and realised the depths of his anger. He sat motionless, voiceless, expressionless, and yet within the confines of that carriage the atmosphere was heavy with suppressed rage. The woman sitting opposite him felt it, just as surely as she recognised when to hold her tongue; not that Lady Tayburn had any reason to fear her husband's wrath, not when it was so steadfastly directed against Helena. She adjusted the blanket that was draped around her legs. The movement drew Tayburn's notice.

He turned his dark gaze upon her, and even though she knew that it was not her that he would hurt, she could not help but feel afraid.

'Feeling cold, my dear?' he enquired in a voice that smacked of something other than sincerity.

'No, Stephen. I am fine, thank you.' She hid her hands beneath the blanket so that he would not see them gripping together.

The black eyes focused harder. 'Fine,' he repeated softly, and even though the words were innocent enough, slipping from Tayburn's mouth they seemed downright threatening.

Caroline Tayburn shifted uneasily in her seat.

Another silence erupted, but Tayburn kept his gaze fixed firmly on his wife, knowing full well that it made her nervous. Seconds became minutes. Minutes ticked by. He waited, and watched.

Eventually she could stand it no longer. 'Do you think that we shall catch up with them soon?'

He smiled, and even after ten years of marriage it was enough to make Caroline Tayburn blanch and look away.

'I'm not trying to catch up with them,' he said carefully, and his smile broadened.

Lady Tayburn made a show of fixing her blanket.

He struck quickly, like a serpent, snatching, then retreating. By the time he sat back, the blanket was in his hand. 'Do concentrate, Caroline. You know how much I dislike inattention.'

'Of course. Please forgive me,' she muttered and, winding her hands tightly together, stared at the carriage floor.

'I do not mean to waste my time stopping at every

damn coaching inn on the road. Why should I, when I know full well where he is taking her.'

Lady Tayburn said nothing.

'London.' He leaned forward, pronouncing the word as if she was a simpleton that would not understand it. 'I will call upon Varington when we reach London. And where Varington is, we shall find Helena. I am sure that she will be interested to hear my news of how matters in Ayrshire have developed.'

'I thought…' She let the words trail off unsaid.

'You thought what?' he sneered. 'That she was going to visit her aunt?' A short sharp laugh barked in the carriage. 'She has no aunt in London!' he spat. 'Don't you think I'd know about it if she did?'

Lady Tayburn nodded submissively. 'Of course you would.'

'Of course I would,' he repeated softly. 'Now what is her plan, I wonder?' he said as if asking the question of himself. 'Are you sure she did not speak of her intention to you?'

'S-she said nothing, nothing at all. Just as I told you before we left.' She shrank back against her seat.

'What *did* she tell you? Hmm?' He examined the nails of his left hand.

Lady Tayburn shook her head.

'I can't hear you,' he snapped.

'N-nothing.'

'Where would she go?'

'I do not know.'

'Where would you?'

It was a dangerous question, and Caroline Tayburn knew it. 'I would not leave in the first place.'

'Good. Helena would do well to learn from you, my

dear. But then again, she is so much younger and more foolish. I thought she had learned something in the years she has been with us. Evidently I overestimated her.' He smiled and it was the smile of the devil himself. 'Do you think that she will like what we have waiting for her at Dunleish?'

Lady Tayburn gave a slight shake of her ringlets.

'And if Varington has touched her...' His eyes darkened with the promise of murder. 'She belongs to me. She is mine. Mine,' he said again with conviction. 'And nobody takes what is mine, not even if he is Tregellas's brother.'

It was a full day before the hired carriage clattered into the yard of the Crown in Appleby, and only fifteen minutes later that it departed again with Lord Varington and Helena on board. Lord Varington's pace was reck-lessly hurried, especially for a carriage that had neither the quality of springs nor plush comfort of his own. Nevertheless Helena made no complaint. Indeed she was glad that she was forced to think of something else other than the presence of the man sitting opposite and what he now was to her. Protector, in name if not yet aught else. Last night he had kept to his own room and she to hers. Helena was torn between relief and disap-pointment.

'You are sure that returning to Ayrshire is the best thing to do?' Helena clung to the securing strap as she asked the question.

'Positive.'

'If you are mistaken, my lord...'

'I am not mistaken, Helena.' The corner of his mouth flickered up in that self-assured teasing manner so familiar of him. 'And you need not keep calling me "my lord". My given name is Guy.'

She blushed like some schoolroom miss. 'Guy.' His name sounded too familiar upon her tongue, reminding her of what she had promised this man in return for his protection.

His smile deepened.

As did the peachy hue upon her cheeks. 'I did not expect that we would turn around directly and head back to Scotland.'

'Neither will Tayburn.'

She hoped that he was right. 'What is your plan?'

'To ensure the transfer of your family to a place of safety.'

She watched him across the small space that divided them, confident that this man would do all that he had promised, knowing that she had made the right decision. 'Thank you, my lor…' She caught herself and then said, 'Thank you, Guy.'

'You're welcome, but it's no more than I agreed to do,' he said.

Her gaze dropped, all the more aware of exactly what her side of the agreement was.

'And we shall both rest a deal easier knowing that Tayburn cannot manipulate you through them.'

'Yes.' Such a little word to convey such a depth of emotion. Hope. Relief, A wedge of disbelief that in one fell swoop Sir Stephen Tayburn's power could be destroyed. 'It has been five long years since the nightmare started. I can scarcely believe that it will soon be over.'

'How has he held you to him all this time?'

'You evidently do not know St Vey. There is nothing on the island save Stephen's stronghold—Dunleish

Castle. It was my prison. He kept me locked in my bed-chamber for the first year. Thereafter, I was permitted access to various other specified rooms, such as the drawing room, and the dining room. Only in the last few years have I seen something of the outside, but always with a guard, never alone. There was little chance of escape, Stephen was careful of that.' She glanced away out of the window before adding, 'And I had seen only too well what befell those that crossed him.'

'Then how came you to escape at all?'

Some strong emotion flitted across her eyes before she closed them. And when she looked at him again she was quite composed. 'My father had little choice but to give me to Sir Stephen, but he sent his old servant Tam with me to Dunleish so that I might at least know one friendly face. Old Tam came to know of a man who could cut a key from a mere impression. Using the key to my bedchamber, he made just such an impression in a small slab of soap. The next I knew was a copy of the key being slipped beneath my chamber door. I stitched it into the hem of my dress and waited for an opportunity to make use of it.'

Guy slid his hand into his pocket and, producing the small silver key, held it out to her. 'It was found when your dress was being cleaned and repaired.'

'Thank you,' she said, and, taking it from him, she slipped it into the pocket of her dress.

'I take it the night of the storm was just such an opportunity.'

She nodded. 'Stephen was taken up with his guests and his celebrations for All Hallows Eve. It seemed the perfect time. We thought we would make it to the mainland before the storm started.' A pause. 'But we were wrong.'

Guy was sitting back as if the carriage seat was an easy chair in his club. He did not seem to feel the vibration from the road or the swing of the carriage as it rounded a corner.

She saw him reach across, let him take her hand. Warm fingers enclosed around hers. 'You're safe now, Helena. Tayburn will never hurt you again.'

'I can only pray that you are right.'

They stayed overnight in Gretna Hall coaching inn in Gretna Green. And Helena slept comfortably, soundly...and alone. She wondered when he would claim what she had agreed to give. The fact that he had not, only confirmed how different he was to Stephen, as if there could ever be a similarity between the two. Through the journey, rushed though it was, there was ample time for conversation, which was an art that Lord Varington conducted with ease. Helena, so used to guarding her words and suppressing any facial expression that might reveal her true feelings, found it wonderfully liberating. Just as matters had been before Stephen came into her life. She listened while Lord Varington told her of London, smiled at his stories of the intrigues of the grand ladies and gentlemen of the *haut ton*, and even gave a chuckle when he progressed on to the Prince Regent and the poor man's strange foibles. It seemed that Lord Varington did not take life too seriously. At no point did he make mention of their arrangement. If anything, he was less flirtatious in his behaviour than he had been prior to her revelation. Rather, he wanted to know her views on fashion, hunting, gardening, everything and anything—even politics. For the first time in years Helena voiced an opinion. Hesitantly at first, but then gaining in confidence with each hour that passed.

On the afternoon of the second day, she found herself telling him a silly tale from her childhood and could only wonder that the man sitting opposite her could so easily make her forget all that had passed in the last five years. Daylight was fading fast, but that made no difference to Helena. She could still see him. Indeed she did not need to look at him at all to be able to see every detail, for his image was etched upon her memory. That lazy sensual smile was never far from his face and his eyes crinkled when he laughed, which if the past two days' journey was anything to go by, was often. She had to conclude that Guy, Lord Varington, was indeed an extremely handsome man.

Chapter Nine

Sir Stephen Tayburn watched while the small plump serving woman placed the plate of roast beef next to the dish of potatoes on the table in the parlour. Sounds of the inn's other customers filtered through the half-open door from the public room. He picked up his knife and prodded at the meat. 'It's burnt. Take it away, and bring me another.'

The woman looked at the moist tenderness of the joint of beef and opened her mouth to disagree. One look at Tayburn's face was enough to have her hastily close it again and remove the plate with speed back to the George's kitchens.

Lady Tayburn sat at the opposite side of the table. She made the mistake of glancing in her husband's direction.

'What the hell do you think you're looking at?' he said softly.

Caroline Tayburn averted her face and murmured, 'Forgive me, Stephen, I had forgotten how overset you are by Helena's disappearance.'

'Overset?' The word almost spat from his tongue. 'I do not think so, dear wife. That would imply I have some kind of care for the woman. She is a possession, nothing more. She is pretty to look at and pleasant to use. But perhaps you are glad that she has gone. Perhaps you are jealous of the time I spend with her.'

Lady Tayburn gave no response.

It did not stop her husband from continuing. 'I had forgotten the pleasures of sharing your bed, Caroline. Last night was…' he paused '…almost enjoyable.'

Unable to help herself, Lady Tayburn shivered.

It was enough to bring a malevolent smile to her husband's face. 'Is that the real reason you tried to dissuade me from our trip? All your talk of bad weather and poor roads was nothing more than an excuse. You do not wish me to fetch Helena back to Dunleish because you wish me to lavish my attentions solely upon you.'

'No!' the lady gasped, then recovered some semblance of control over her emotions. 'No, indeed, you are mistaken. I hold Helena's company in high esteem.'

This time he barked a laugh. 'Do you, indeed?' And the smile on his face could have stripped rust from a paling.

'How magnanimous of you to say so, my sweet.' The acidic curve to his mouth intensified. 'Especially when you know full well that her presence stops me from visiting your bed every night.'

Lady Tayburn kept her focus firmly fixed upon the tablecloth.

'Take consolation in the fact that the longer it takes to retrieve Helena, the more time we may spend together.' He reached across the table and, with one finger beneath her chin, tilted her face up so that she had no choice but to look at him. 'Indeed, I begin to wonder if we should take the journey a trifle more leisurely so that we may better enjoy each other's company.'

The woman's face washed white.

'Perhaps I should leave the trollop to Varington and content myself with you…dear Caroline.'

Caroline Tayburn looked positively ill.

Tayburn cocked his head to the side and watched his wife. 'But then again, it would be remiss of me to abandon her, would you not say? In the meantime I shall not allow myself to fret. Until Helena is safely back within my fold, I'll take solace in *your* company, Caroline, every day…and every night.'

He let his hand drop and the sly smile upon his face revealed two yellowed incisors.

Where his finger had touched against Caroline Tayburn's delicate skin beneath her chin was the beginnings of a bruise.

It had been late afternoon by the time Helena and Guy arrived at the Star Inn in Ayr. It was a large stylish place, used to receiving the best of visitors. The staff were efficient and well trained. Guy was reminded of the quiet comfort of his club in London. No one commented upon the presence of a lady who, by the manner in which she was garbed and her lack of a maid, was quite clearly not Lady Varington. The Star appeared to be the height of discretion, even placing his lordship and the lady in adjoining rooms, much to Helena's embarrassment.

As they had neared the burgh of Ayr she had become quieter, more withdrawn. Although nothing of her demeanour betrayed her, from her modestly folded hands to the serene expression upon her face, Guy had sensed an underlying anxiety that was growing by the minute. Their arrival at the inn had not banished the worry from her eyes. He moved the curtain and peered down on to the street outside. Despite the dying light Ayr was still busy. The rumble of cart and carriage wheels, clatter of horses' hooves and buzz of voices carried through the paned-glass window. Guy twitched the curtain back into place and, moving silently towards the door that connected his bedchamber with the one in which Helena had been placed, stopped. He lifted his head and stayed very still, listening for any sounds that might reveal what she was doing. There were none.

Then out of the silence came a soft knocking at the connecting door. Guy caught his breath and stilled the sudden thrumming of his heart. He hesitated only for a moment before grasping the handle and opening the door.

'Helena.' He smiled. 'Please come in,' and stepped back to let her enter.

She made no move. Only stood there as if made of stone. 'Forgive me, Guy.' Her utterance of his name gave it a peculiarly intimate tone.

Her face was pale with fatigue, but the whisper of a blush touched to her cheeks. For one brief moment he wondered if she had come to him in the sense of a woman to a man. Excitement flickered at the idea, even as he knew it was not so. Helena might have been a mistress for five years, but she had a propriety about her that belied such a sullied past.

'I did not mean to disturb you.'

'Then rest assured I am not disturbed,' he said. 'You may come in,' he coaxed, and opened the door wider.

Still, she did not move. She stood in the same dark dress that she had worn for the past days, even though he had sent ahead to have a few new clothes awaiting them. The hem showed the dust and dirt of their travels. Her cloak had been discarded and her hair had been combed and pinned again. He could only be glad that her bonnet had been crushed in the carriage accident for Helena's hair was glorious to look upon.

'I know you planned to visit my family tomorrow morning, but I wondered if it were possible that we might go there this evening instead.' He saw the gentle rise and fall of her breast, knew how concerned she must be to come to knock upon the door to his bed-chamber to ask such a thing.

'If it is your desire, we may visit them immediately.'

The smoky green eyes widened slightly and the care-fully composed expression fell from her face. 'I would like that very much, Guy,' she said.

One corner of his mouth crooked up. 'Then fetch your cloak, Helena, and I shall organise a fresh team of horses.'

'There is no need. My father's house is in Straw-thorn Street, barely a mile from here. We would be quicker walking.'

'Very well.' He gathered up his new silver-topped walking stick, hat and gloves.

It had been a dry and frosty day and the cold snap seemed set to continue into the night. The sky was all pale blues and lavenders and pinks as the iciness of evening closed in. Throughout the air the smell of smoke tumbled with the scent of fresh air as the couple made their way down the main street in Ayr.

'It has been so long since I was last here,' Helena said, and the warmth of her breath clouded in the cold air. 'I thought never to see it again.'

Guy patted the small hand that was tucked through the crook in his arm. 'Then I am sorry to disappoint you.'

'No, never that,' she said softly, and gave him a shy smile.

Something warm expanded in Guy's chest. It was a most peculiar feeling and one that he had not experienced before. Before he could contemplate it further two small ragged boys ran up by his side.

'Please, sir, can you spare a farthing for the guy.' The thin-faced urchin's hand stretched out. His small friend did not look hopeful.

Guy dropped some coins into the child's hand. Judging from the exclamations that followed and the rather speedy departure of the two small boys, it was a much greater sum than they were used to. He looked up to find Helena watching him with a smile.

They continued on their way with Helena pointing out this building and that, and telling him something of the town. Yet all the while he could feel her impatience to reach their destination. If it had been at all acceptable, Guy did not doubt that Helena would be running full tilt. Then they turned off and she led him down a maze of narrower streets. The houses grew smaller, less expensive. With every step Helena's feet grew faster.

'It's just round this corner,' she said breathlessly. Her nose was nipped pink by the cold air and her eyes sparkled with anticipation and excitement and fear. She clutched his arm all the tighter.

They were barely into Strawthorn Street when he felt her suddenly grow rigid. She stopped. It was as if she ceased to breathe. She stared ahead down the street, her eyes wide and disbelieving, her cheeks suddenly blanched. Her lips opened as if to cry out, yet no sound was forthcoming. Guy followed the line of her vision to what it was that she stared at with such horror. Halfway down the road on the right-hand side between two houses that stood prim and quiet were the blackened remains of a building. Her hand slipped from his arm and then she was off and running, uncaring of the fact that she presented a most unladylike sight. The dark swirl of skirts was hitched up, exposing her ankles, and her hair, so neatly pinned and tucked, loosened and began to escape. Helena ran as if the flames were still licking round the door, as if she could hear the shouts of the occupants within. By the time Guy reached her she was standing before all that remained of her family home—a pile of charred timber and stone.

'Helena.' He touched a hand gently to her shoulder. She pulled back, dislodging his fingers.

Guy had never seen such shock or pain as flashed in her eyes.

'We're too late,' she whispered. 'Too damn late.'

'We must not leap to conclusions, Helena. Perhaps one of the neighbours can tell us what happened here and the fate of your family.'

'You were right. He has killed them.' And her voice held a quiet despair worse than a thousand shed tears. 'It's all been for nothing.'

'We do not know that,' he countered, but even as he said it he acknowledged the thought that she was most probably right. The stench of burning and smoke still clung to the place.

'Stephen is nothing but thorough. This is the work of his hand. I know now why he has not yet found me. He has been busy…with this.' She indicated the black-

ened mess that surrounded her. Then her focus fixed and
she stooped and picked up something that lay close to
her shoe: a large half-burned book. With tender care she
eased it open. The outer edge of the pages crumbled to
a sooty dust beneath her fingers. On the frontispiece
through the scorching the printed letters were still
legible—Family Bible. On the page opposite were the
faded scripts of her great-grandfather, and her grandfa-
ther and her father. Each birth, marriage and death in
the McGregor family had been recorded in neatly
flowing ink. She said nothing, just traced one finger
over each of the smoke-damaged words, locked in a
world of pain and remembrance.

The light was fading fast, the sky glowing a deep
crimson red amidst the blue and lavender hues.
'Helena.' He gently wrested the book from her fingers,
tucked it beneath his arm and steered her back out on
to the street. Her face was as pale as the day he had
found her so still and lifeless upon the shore. Yet she
did not cry, not as she had done after the carriage
accident. Her eyes were dry, her face impassive. Guy
had seen such reactions in the Peninsula, in men that
had watched the atrocities of war. He also had more
personal experience of such shock. Helena could not yet
believe the terrible scene she had just witnessed. It
would not take long before the truth permeated her
mind, and when it did he did not want her to be standing
here on a cold and darkening street. Where his fingers
pressed against her arm, he could feel the beginnings
of a tremor. She was so cold that it brought a chill to
his hand. Whatever had to be done here, it was clear that
Helena was in no fit state to undertake it.

'We must get you back to the inn.'

A shake of her head and the last of her pins dislodged, so that her hair flowed long and wanton over her shoulders. 'No. I must find the truth of this. Mr Robertson will know. I'll ask him how it happened…when it happened.'

'Come back to the inn,' he said. 'I'll return and discover all there is to know.'

'Mr Robertson…' she began, then stopped. Then tried again. 'He will not know the truth of where I went, of what I have been these last years.'

'Rest assured, Helena, he shall learn nothing from me.' He made no mention of the fact that the curtains the length of the street had been twitching since their arrival.

'Come,' he said again, and, leaning forward, pulled the hood up over her head, tucking the soft silkiness of her hair in behind the black wool. 'It's a cold night, and I would not want you to catch a chill.'

And with that he guided her back down the streets through which they had previously walked with such hopes.

Guy did not leave until he had watched Helena finish the whisky that he had ordered, and tucked her up in bed. He quelled the desire to climb in beside her, take her in his arms and offer her what little comfort he could. Instead, he pulled on a great caped coat and walked back out into the darkness of the night. Helena needed to know what had happened at the house in Strawthorn Street. She needed to know whether her family were alive or dead. And, more to the point, so did he, given that he had promised their safety. He set his face against the cold and strode out, wondering quite what he had taken on with the beautiful redheaded woman that lay upstairs in the inn.

'It was a terrible night, sir.' The old man nodded knowingly. He had been tall in his time, but the years had shrunk and bent him. He was thin to the point of being gaunt and his hair was a wiry grizzled grey. His cheeks were of wrinkled leather, his eyes stared fierce and blue and he wore clothes that were in fashion twenty years ago. The house was small and silent and cold. The maidservant had refused Guy entry when he first approached, but Mr Robertson had eventually been persuaded to relent—with the promise of a five-pound note.

Guy made all the right noises that he knew would prompt the man to tell him what he wanted to know. And it seemed that once the McGregors' neighbour started to talk, he had much to say.

'Happened nigh on a week ago. Smelled the smoke mysel' I did, but it was Bonfire Night and I thought it was just weans and another o' their fires.' He pulled a sour face. 'This time o' year it's aye the same. Fires and fireworks everywhere. I get nae peace for them. Bloody Bonfire Night.' He held on to the arms of the shabby chair. 'By the time I saw the flames it was too late. McGregor's house was well alight.'

'What of Mr and Mrs McGregor?'

The old eyes darted a look of surprise at him. 'I thought Miss Helena would have told you. It was her that you were outside wi' earlier, wasn't it?' He paused and waited expectantly.

Guy inclined his head. 'Indeed it was, Mr Robertson.'

'I thought as much.' He gave a knowing nod.

'You were about to tell me of Helena's parents,' Guy prompted.

Mr Robertson took a moment to think about this and then, as if making up his mind, continued with his words. 'Mrs McGregor, Miss Helena's mother, died giving birth to the youngest daughter, Miss Emma. It was McGregor himsel' that raised the family.'

'Forgive me, but I did not know,' said Guy.

'Four of them,' continued the old man, 'all lassies, more's the shame; no' a son amongst them.'

Guy suppressed the twitch of his jaw.

'The middle two were married off last year and the year afore, and no' afore time, I say. McGregor was too slow in gettin' them off his hands. He was still lumbered wi' Miss Emma.' He suddenly leaned forward in a conspiratorial manner. 'I aye knew that it wasnae true, you know.'

'What is that?' Varington asked.

He dropped his voice, as if someone would hear them within the confines of the house walls. 'The story o' Miss Helena's death,' he said smugly.

Guy waited for Mr Robertson to expand.

'They put it about that she had died o' scarlet fever, but I knew it wasnae true. I saw those men that took her. Alive and well she was when she climbed into Sir Stephen Tayburn's carriage.'

Guy raised an eyebrow, but only marginally. 'Perhaps you are mistaken, Mr Robertson.'

'No' me,' replied the old man robustly. 'His crest was clear as day on the door: a black deil on a red background. But I kept the knowledge to mysel'. I'm no' some gossipin' fishwife. Besides, I knew somethin' of what was going on afore. I had seen the way Tayburn looked at her. And when a man looks at a woman like that, it means only one thing. The lassie didnae stand a chance. Especially no' when Tayburn had McGregor set upon.' His thin lips tightened. 'What a beatin' that man suffered. Nigh on died, and that's no jest. He was never the same afterwards. Could barely run his business.'

'What was the nature of Mr McGregor's business?' asked Varington.

'He ran a company of weavers. Owned a factory down by the river. Tayburn invested in McGregor's business, that's how they came to know one another. Then the business hit a slow spot, and Tayburn demanded his money back—all o' it.'

'And McGregor couldn't pay.'

'No, indeed, he couldnae. Hardly a bean to his name by that stage. He didnae always live here. At one time the family had a house o'er in Wellington Square.'

Guy looked none the wiser.

'The mansion houses,' he said by way of explanation. 'Where all the rich folk live.'

'But with Mr McGregor's failing business they were forced to move.'

'Precisely,' said Mr Robertson. 'This is a fine street, is it no'?'

'Undoubtedly.'

'But no' when you're used to what they were. Bit of a comedown for them. Anyway…' he sniffed and dabbed a handkerchief to his nose '…Tayburn came round this way no' long after McGregor's attack. By that time, what wi' the doctor's bills and the like, they couldnae afford a single servant. It was Helena that kept house for her father, and Helena that Tayburn saw on his arrival. It doesnae take a genius to work out the rest. A pretty young lassie like that suddenly disappears and the next thing McGregor's business has an upturn in fortune. A new investor steps in to save him from ruin. Rumour has it that it was Tayburn, same rumour that says it was Tayburn behind the attack on McGregor in the first place, though it's no' for me to comment upon.'

'I see,' said Guy.

'So she's wi' you now, is she?'

Guy took out a five-pound note and sat it on the table in between them. 'About the fire,' he said, 'what became of Mr McGregor and his daughter?'

'They found the charred remains o' McGregor's body the next day.'

'And the daughter that lived with him?'

Mr Robertson sniffed again, and rubbed his nose.

Guy placed a second banknote on top of the first.

'McGregor had some visitors just afore the fire. Miss Emma, she went off wi' them.'

'Do you know who these visitors were?'

'Same ones as took Miss Helena, all them years ago. Tayburn's men. Robertson never forgets a face,' said the old man, and tapped a thickened nail against the side of his nose. 'You'd best watch your back, son. Tayburn's no' a man to be crossed. You mark ma words. Best stay clear o' the Deil o' St Vey, son, if you value your life.'

Chapter Ten

Helena heard the light knock at the connecting door. She was not asleep. The image of what her family home had become was lodged firmly in her mind. Nothing would shift the picture of that blackened shell of a house. She saw it when her eyes were closed. It haunted her when her eyes were open. Everywhere she looked she saw only those charred remains. She knew, of course, that her father and sisters were dead. Knew inside her head. That was the only logical conclusion that could be drawn. She had run, and Stephen had taken his revenge in the way he knew would hurt her most. She had underestimated him—again. But what she knew and what she felt were two different things. In her heart she could not believe they were dead…not after everything she had endured to save them. No matter how she tried to rationalise things, the knot in her stomach would not unwind. She lay rigid and un-yielding on the plush soft comfort of the bed. Alone. Disbelieving. Afraid.

The knock came again. He did not wait for an

answer. The handle turned and he walked into the room. She could smell the coldness of the night air on his clothes, feel the slight chill that emanated from him. She sat up, scrambled from the bed to stand before him, braced herself for what he would say.

'I spoke with Mr Robertson, your father's neighbour.'

'Yes?' She made no effort to quell the impatience in her voice. She wanted to shout out, 'Just tell me and be done with it!' but the look in his eye prevented her. She feared the worst and hoped for the best.

'The news is not good. Your father perished in the fire.' No doubt McGregor had been beaten and left for dead before the fire took hold, but Helena need not know of that. It was bad enough without embellishing the gory details.

A gasp sounded before her hand clutched to her mouth as if she would catch back the emotions ready to spill forth.

'I'm sorry, Helena.'

Her eyes closed momentarily and when they opened again all trace of the threatened hysteria had vanished. In its place was an unnatural calm composure. 'What of my sisters?'

He paused.

The façade did not last. He saw the shuttering of her eyes and the terrible shock that washed her face so pale that he thought she would swoon from the spot on which she stood.

'No, it's not as you think.' He moved forward, pressing his hands to the outer edges of her upper arms as if he would stop her from falling. 'Two of your sisters are married and no longer reside in Strawthorn Street. I cannot say for sure, but I believe them to be safe. But your youngest sister…'

She stilled in his arms. 'Emma,' she said, and it seemed that she held her breath, waiting for what he would say.

He guided her gently back and sat her down on the barely rumpled sheets of the bed. 'Helena, it seems that Tayburn has taken her.'

A silence followed his words. And it was pregnant with the most dreadful of imaginings.

'Stephen,' she whispered, and just the sound of his name brought a sinister feeling to the bedchamber. The candles guttered in the draught and the air seemed to chill. 'What have I done?' she cried. 'Dear Lord, what have I done?'

The mattress dipped as he sat down on the bed beside her. Very gently he took her hand in his. 'You have done nothing wrong, Helena. The fault is not yours.'

A sob escaped her before she could bite it back. 'I escaped, and so he has killed my father and taken Emma in my stead.'

'No.' Varington uttered the word with a conviction that carried to Helena.

'She shall not endure him,' she said. 'He will kill her.'

Again that single strong determined word. 'No.' Guy pulled her to face him. 'He plans to use her as leverage, to force your return. And as such, she is safe for now.'

She stared at him, wanting to believe him, but not quite doing so. Her eyes were awash with fear and guilt and shock and horror.

'Helena.'

But she had already turned her head away and was looking towards the fireplace with her usual air of fake composure. 'Then I shall go back to him,' she said in a quiet voice.

The thought of Helena returning to that villain

wrenched at Guy's gut. He understood only a little of what Tayburn had done to her: blackmailing her into being his mistress, subjecting her to a life that Guy could not bear to think about. God help him, but hell would freeze over before he let Tayburn harm one hair on Helena's head ever again. He knew what Tayburn would do, and so did Helena; he just had to make her face the truth, no matter how hard that might be. 'So that Tayburn may have you both?'

She shook her head. 'He will let Emma go.'

Guy took her hand within his, hearing both her longing and her guilt, knowing it was the echo of his own nightmares. 'Helena, you know that he will not.'

'Then all is lost,' she said. Her voice was filled with an aching desolation and it seemed that beneath Guy's fingers her pulse slowed and weakened, and he felt the extent of her pain.

Guy's face was grim. 'No,' he said, knowing that his strength must carry them both.

Her eyes swung to his. He saw the sudden flicker of hope.

He smiled and with gentle fingers stroked away a curl of hair that dangled close to her eyes. 'I will call him out.'

Helena gave a small incredulous laugh. 'You surely do not speak in earnest?'

One corner of Guy's mouth lifted higher, crooking his smile. 'I tell you I am deadly serious,' he said as if challenging Tayburn to a duel were nothing at all out of the ordinary. She needed to hear confidence, strength, arrogance even. He smiled lazily, betraying nothing of the emotions that raged beneath the surface.

'It is Sir Stephen Tayburn of whom we speak. He will kill you before you ever make it to a duelling field.'

He raised an eyebrow. 'I appreciate your confidence in my abilities.'

'It has nothing to do with that. Stephen has no honour. He cares nothing for the rules of engagement. If he wishes you dead, then that is what you will be, no matter how skilful you are with a pistol.'

'I'll call him out all the same.' And he knew that he wasn't only doing this for Helena.

'It's utter madness! You cannot hope for success.'

'Oh, but I can and I do, Helena,' he said with brutal honesty.

She stared at him as if she could not fathom him, puzzlement marring her brow.

'Why?' she asked.

He gave a casual shrug of his shoulders, playing it down, unwilling to betray the truth of the feelings that Tayburn stirred up. Memories from across the years of a man too like Tayburn. Memories of the darkness Guy could not forget. All the old pain that Guy had locked away was in danger of seeping back out.

'Why would you call him out over his abduction of my sister? You do not know her; she is nothing to you.'

'But you are,' he said. 'And had your father and sister been safe, I would call him out just the same.' It was the truth, he realised. He knew the damage that a man like Tayburn could do and, looking down into Helena's eyes, seeing the extent of her hurt, he knew that he had to stop him.

There was nothing but the softness of their breaths as their eyes clung together. It was Helena that was first to look away.

'Do you wish to be forever looking over your shoulder, never knowing when he might snatch you back? You are with me now and I will ensure that Tayburn knows it. If he has any grievances over his loss, he may settle them in the duel.' A steely determination settled in his eyes. He would not be swayed from his course.

'You would risk your life for my sister and for me. Yet you owe us nothing.'

'Have you forgotten my offer so swiftly, Helena? I offered protection for both you and your family.'

Beneath the flicker of the candle on the bedside table her eyes appeared to darken and soften. 'I know.' She bit her lip. 'I just did not think…' Her words trailed away unfinished.

They watched each other through the silence before she leaned in closer towards him, a wash of colour staining her cheeks.

'Helena.' There was a slight hoarseness to the word. The borrowed white nightdress gaped at the neck, exposing too much of the creamy white skin below. Guy could smell her sweetness, the clean pleasant scent he knew was her own. He wanted her now more than he had wanted her all along. Wanted to offer her the refuge that he had so often sought in coupling, a respite from the pain. And yet he knew that such a base reaction went against all decency. He reined in the urge, raked a hand through his hair. Hell, what was he thinking of? She might well be his mistress, but Helena had been brutalised by a monster, and she'd only just learned of the death of her father and abduction of her sister. Only a barbarian would bed her under such circumstances. Guy wrenched his gaze from hers and got to his feet.

'Guy.' She reached a hand towards him, resting her

fingers against the sleeve of his coat. In her eyes was gratitude.

His gaze sharpened. His hand moved to cup her face, and his thumb moved in a gentle stroking action. And in that moment he was tempted to kiss her, to touch her, to show her the way it should be between a man and a woman. But now was not the time. He wanted her, but not like this, not a coupling out of gratitude and pain. He dropped his hand before temptation could get the better of him.

His eyes were watching her with a hunger. She knew it was desire, but there was something else there too. There was nothing of Stephen's foul lust in him; Guy's eyes were as pale and clear as Stephen's were dark and murky. But for all that he wanted her, and Helena was in no doubt as to that, he made no move to take her. Indeed, he looked as if he were about to retire to his own chamber for the night. As if she were still respectable. As if he might have some care for her. This man who would risk his life to save both her and her sister. A fierce tenderness enveloped her heart. She rose without knowing that she did so and moved to stand before him.

'Good night, Helena.' And the smile he threw her made her heart skip a beat.

He was so tall that her head only came to his chin. She could look many men level in the eye, but not Varington. He was tall and strong, and instilled with a sense of decency. It had been a long time since any man had shown her such kindness.

'Thank you,' she whispered and, lifting her face to his, touched her lips to the edge of his jaw line. It was intended as a kiss of gratitude, a kiss in acknowledgement of all that he had done for her, a kiss between friends. But neither Helena nor Guy were prepared for the effect. Her lips fluttered like a baby's breath over his skin, resting with the briefest lightest touch upon his skin, but in the transience of that single moment awareness surged so strong as to obliterate everything. Blood coursed wildly through her body. Excitement spiralled deep in her stomach, spilling out in tingling surges that threatened to engulf her. She saw her own shock mirrored in his eyes, the blackness of his pupils expanding to fill the pale surround. She heard a gasp of breath and did not know that it was her own.

His head bowed and she felt the soft brush of his eyelashes against her cheek as his breath skimmed the column of her neck. Someone groaned, but she knew not whether it was Guy or herself who made the sound. Her head pulled back, exposing the vulnerability of her throat beneath. Her skin danced hot and dizzy with anticipation so that, when at last his lips closed upon its softness, she gave a sigh of relief. His mouth nuzzled hungrily against her throat, sliding slowly, steadily, up towards her mouth.

'Guy,' she whispered his name breathlessly into the room.

But he silenced her when his mouth at last found hers and their lips danced together in mounting passion. The smell of him, the heat of him, his proximity took her to a place she had never known. Her fingers entwined themselves in the black ruffle of his hair. He kissed her as she had never been kissed before, so that something of himself reached down into her and imprinted itself there. Her fingers traced the contours of his face, revelling in the roughness of the dark stubble that peppered his skin. It was as if he were the air and she were a woman suffocating for need of it.

He stroked her hair, caressed her spine beneath, pulling her in tight so that her breasts crushed against him. And all the while their mouths were locked in a hunger that she had never before known. His hands swept down to cradle the roundness of her buttocks. And then he lifted her up and into him so that, even through the layers of their clothing, she knew his arousal. Her arms clung to him, merging their two bodies as one.

From outside came a sudden flurry of bangs and explosions as if a volley of shots had been released from muskets. Guy stilled, stopped. Instinct and training kicked in. He set her down and moved quickly to the window, stealing a glance through the edge of the curtain so that his actions within the dimly lit room would not be visible to those on the street. In the distance of the night sky a spectacle of colour was exploding against the black.

'Fireworks.' An infinitesimal ripple of the curtain material and he was back by her side.

Fireworks outside, and fireworks of a different sort entirely within the bedchamber of the inn. Her lips were swollen from what they had shared. Helena stood awkwardly, unsure of what to say, what even to think. She wanted to feel his arms warm and strong around her, needed his lips to sear away all memory of the burnt-out house, all imaginings of her father and her sister, but something held her back. Stephen had called her a whore, and she had done nothing save endure his touch. But this man was different. With one kiss Guy had awakened a part of herself that she did not know had existed. And with its wakening she feared that Stephen had been right—for she wanted Guy never to stop. She wanted him to tumble her on the bed and make love to her.

Passion clouded by fear and guilt. Guy all too easily read the changes in Helena's emotions before the mask of impassivity slipped back upon her face. She made no move to reject him—indeed, she made no move at all, just stood there and waited. His blood raced hot and hard and he wanted nothing more than to strip the tent of a nightdress from her body, lay her back upon the bed and make love to her. He wanted it more than he ever could have imagined that a man might lust for a woman. He wanted her so much that it hurt. He moved his hand and caught the ends of her hair, rubbing the silken waves between his fingers. He caught the hank up, wrapping it round and round, the back of his fingers sliding up the cotton of the nightdress until they brushed against the hard pebbles of her nipples. Their gazes locked. He knew she would not deny him. They had an arrangement, after all. She was his mistress, and he, her protector. He had every right to take her body. He wanted her. She stood stock-still and let his knuckles stroke her, until he saw the darkening of her eyes. He moved forward. Her lips parted. Her eyes shuttered as he leaned closer to her face. With great self-control he placed a single chaste kiss upon her forehead.

'Good night, Helena.'

Her eyes flashed open in surprise. But Guy was off and walking towards the connecting door.

'Guy?' The word echoed with both relief and disappointment.

He turned and smiled his most devastating smile. 'Sleep well.' And then he disappeared into the chamber where his own bed awaited, before his resolve could weaken. Helena McGregor might be his mistress, but he had seen the fear and gratitude in her eyes. He would teach her that he was not like Tayburn, even if it meant forgoing his own pleasure.

Early the next morning Helena and Guy departed the inn in Ayr and headed north on the coastal road. The day was clear and bright with a glistening frost that had not yet vanished. Bare earth that had been sodden now stood frozen as if it had been churned in great chunks, the imprints of feet and hooves and wheels captured in some kind of sculpture that would last only until the thaw. Sheep, their coats long and unkempt and stained with mud, grazed seemingly oblivious to the freezing temperatures, jaws moving in rhythmic grinding as they chewed the cud and stared with suspicious pale Pan-like eyes. What had been deep muddied puddles across the surface of the road had frozen solid, the perfection of their opaque icy surfaces smashed by passing traffic. The carriage passed several burnt-out bonfires in fields. The blackened heaps were a constant reminder to Helena of the house she had witnessed yesterday and all that went with it. And something hard and heavy weighed upon her.

She sat very still. Beneath her feet was a brick and around her knees was tucked a blanket, both provided by Guy. Yet Helena felt neither the cold of the day nor the heat of the brick or blanket. All she was aware of was the terrible ache in her heart and of all that had been lost.

'Penny for them.' The deep melodic tilt of Guy's voice interrupted her thoughts.

She drew her gaze from the window and looked at

him, unsure of what he had said, afraid to admit that she had not been listening.

'A penny for your thoughts,' he said. 'You seem lost in contemplation.'

She didn't know what to say, couldn't tell him the truth of what she was thinking: that three people were dead and her sister imprisoned, and all because she had decided to flee Stephen. That all of it was her damn fault. That the pain of that knowledge was almost unbearable. She schooled her face to show nothing. 'I was thinking how fine the weather is today.'

It seemed that his eyes looked directly into hers and she knew that he did not believe the trite, silly answer she had given. She glanced away, afraid of how much was exposed, feeling awkward and foolish and confused. Almost desperately, she stared from the window at the passing winter landscape.

'Helena,' he said softly

She could feel the heat of his gaze upon her and, although he had not moved in the slightest, it was as if he was reaching out to her. At last she could bear it no longer and turned her eyes to meet his. The sun bleached his skin a marble white and added a blue lustre to the short dark hair that fanned feathers around his face so that there was something of an unearthly appearance about him. In the white winter sunlight his eyes were a clear icy blue, and his lashes a dark sooty black, and he beheld Helena with a scrutiny that seemed to reach into her very soul.

She felt two patches of heat warm her cheeks. 'I am fine.' Anything to stop him looking at her like that.

'It does not seem so.'

Her teeth nipped at her bottom lip, hard.

'We will get your sister back, and soon.'

She nodded, not trusting herself to speak.

'And Tayburn will pay with his life.'

More like Stephen would destroy Guy too. And all of her worry and all of her fear welled up so that she could contain it no longer and the tears spilled over to roll silently down her cheeks.

'Helena.' He sighed, and moved across the carriage to take her in his arms. He cradled her against him, murmuring quiet words of comfort in her ear. 'Do not cry. I promise you that he will never hurt you again.'

'He will kill you,' she said, and the breath was ragged in her throat. She felt the caress of his hand against her hair.

'No, Helena, he will not.' And in his eyes was such supreme confidence that, in spite of all she knew about Stephen, she almost believed him.

'It is all my fault, you know,' she whispered. 'My father, Emma, Agnes, Old Tam…' She refused to look away, forced herself to hold his gaze. 'Had I not run, then they would all still be safe.'

'You must not blame yourself, Helena.'

'Even if that is where the blame rests?'

'No!' he growled, and his fingers touched to her chin so that she could not look away. 'You are as much Tayburn's victim in all of this as the rest of them. Hell, you stayed with the villain for five years to protect your family. You have no reason to feel guilty.'

The pain was so bad that she thought her soul was being torn apart. 'And it was all for nothing, wasn't it? Five years with Stephen and now my father is murdered and my sister in his power!' And she began to sob.

He pulled her on to his lap, holding her tight against

him, rocking her, stroking her as if she were some small child.

'Sweetheart,' he whispered, and he held her until there were no more tears to be cried, and her eyes were dry and tender. The terrible tension inside of Helena had gone and in its place was a strange kind of exhaustion. There was only the rumble of the carriage wheels and the rhythmic clip of horses' hooves. She found she was clinging to him, and made to extricate herself from the intimate position. But Guy's arm only tightened around her. She looked up into his eyes, and she knew that he was going to kiss her, and, God help her, she wanted him to.

Guy lowered his face to hers. When their lips touched it was everything and more than Helena remembered from the previous evening. He kissed her with a warm gentleness that drew the breath from her body, and with it every last thought of Stephen and her father and Emma. His mouth massaged with a gentle insistent pressure until she melted against him, forgetting all else except the man whose lips were so giving to hers. Her palms lay flat against his chest, open, yielding, feeling the strong steady beat of his heart. The dark blue superfine of his coat was soft beneath the caress of her fingers. Cold heated to warm. Warm flamed to hot. Their lips were made to be together, their kiss to last a lifetime. In that moment there was only Guy.

When at last Guy drew away and looked down into her eyes with such tenderness, Helena knew that she was lost.

He lifted the travelling rug that had fallen to the floor and tucked it over her knees. His left arm draped around her shoulders with the lightest touch, but one that

imparted his warmth and comfort and protection.
Helena felt a strange kind of peace settle upon her and
something of her pain diminished and she knew that it
was because of the tall dark-haired man sitting by her
side.

They arrived at the Eglinton Arms Hotel in the small
town of Ardrossan, some five miles from the village of
Kilbride. The hotel was large and more than ready to
accommodate a member of the aristocracy. Indeed, it
had been established for just such a purpose by its
owner, the Earl of Eglinton. The Eglinton Arms was
luxurious and boasted a discreet and well-trained staff;
nevertheless, Helena could not help feeling uncomfortable when the manager was apprised of the fact that she
was not Lady Varington, nor was she travelling with a
maid. Guy's declaration that his valet and Mrs McLelland's maid had been delayed did not so much as raise
an eyebrow. She also knew very well why Guy had
chosen to stay in the hotel when not a week since he had
been a most welcome guest at Seamill Hall. Indeed, he
would undoubtedly still be welcome, but he could not
very well arrive there with his mistress in tow.

It was Guy's preference that they took a tray in their
room. He had not failed to notice that many of the male
patrons were finding it difficult to loosen their gazes
from Helena. It was hardly surprising given her
uncommon beauty. In the new expensive green travelling dress and fur-lined cloak and muff that Guy had
purchased for her in Ayr, Helena stood out from the
crowd. And Guy had reason enough to desire that their
presence in the area was not remarked upon.

The Scotch broth warmed them from the inside out.

In truth, Helena had no appetite for food, but she knew that she must keep her strength up for what lay ahead. For all of Guy's confidence she could not relax her fear. Helena knew Stephen. Guy did not. She, more than most, knew of what the man was capable. She worried if Guy understood what he had taken on by helping her.

'Finish your soup, Helena, and then I must visit Weir and Annabel.'

She glanced away, rosy embarrassment flooding her face.

'Helena,' he said, and, reaching across the table, laid one of his hands over hers. 'You know why I do not take you with me, don't you?'

She forced her chin up, and looked him in the eye. 'You need offer me no explanations.'

He raised an eyebrow.

'I do not expect to be made welcome in any respectable household,' she said. 'That is perfectly understandable…'

'Helena,' he growled, but she continued unabated.

'Besides, I would not wish to cause embarrassment to Mr and Mrs Weir.'

'I do not take you with me out of concern for your own safety,' he said.

'As I said, you need explain nothing.'

'Helena,' he said with a touch of exasperation, and his hand closed around hers. 'Tayburn, or his men, may be in Kilbride or the immediate area. For all we know, he may have discovered something of your visit to Seamill Hall. Until I know the lie of the land, it is safer that you stay here.'

Her face turned pale. She wetted her lips and looked away. 'Forgive me, I thought…'

'I'm not ashamed of you, Helena. Never think that.'
He gave her fingers a gentle squeeze of reassurance.
'Perhaps I should take you with me to Seamill Hall just
to prove my point.'

She smiled.

'Well?' he said. 'Shall you come with me?'

She laughed. 'No.'

'Why ever not?'

'You know why not,' she replied. 'You are teasing me.'

He smiled in all innocence. 'Am I?'

'Guy!'

His smile became suddenly roguish. 'You have not
answered my question?'

She gave a huff of exasperation. 'Guy, I am your
mistress.'

His eyes narrowed and darkened into a smoulder
and one corner of his mouth quirked in a most suggestive manner. 'Aren't I the lucky fellow.' He looked
pointedly at her lips and murmured, 'Lucky indeed.'
The dishes were set hastily on the tray and the tray
removed to the floor by the door.

He crossed the room back towards her at a faster pace
than she had seen him travel before. It was practically
a stride.

But before he could reach her, Helena was out of her
chair and backing away towards the window. Her heart
was hammering in her chest and there was a liquid
warmth deep in her belly at just the anticipation of his
touch. 'Guy, we have much to discuss.'

His smile was positively wicked. 'Indeed we do, but
it can wait a little longer.'

She knew she should not refuse him. He was, after
all, her protector in every sense of the word.

He stepped towards her.

Helena dodged to her left and, swinging round by the fireplace, inverted their positions. Now Guy stood with his back to the window, and Helena was facing him with her back to the bed and the door. He swept a brazen gaze over her body and began to move with a slow, determined stealth in her direction.

There could be no mistaking his intent. Helena gave a squeak, and, seeing that her path for escape was blocked in one way by Guy's advancing frame and in the other by the large double bed, made her split-second decision and made a bid for escape across the breadth of the bed. It was the wrong choice. The long skirts of her new dress impeded her progress across the mattress so that it amounted to an unladylike scramble. She had almost made it to the other side when something closed around one of her ankles and hoisted her backwards.

Helena gave a yelp of surprise and found herself being rolled on to her back with Guy leaning the length of his body over hers.

'Almost, but not quite fast enough,' he said, and there was a definite amusement in his voice.

She noticed that he did not lay his weight upon her, but took it on his own knees and elbows. Helena was not a fragile woman, but Guy was all lean hard muscle that would have crushed her had he not acted with such consideration. His eyes narrowed and darkened with desire. Helena knew that if he kissed her any semblance of resistance would be lost and there were things that must be said. 'Guy…' She tried to attract his attention from the road she knew his thoughts were taking. 'Guy, listen to me.'

'I'm listening,' he said, and lowered his face towards hers.

'You will have a care when you go to Kilbride, won't you?'

The dark sweep of Guy's lashes lowered as his gaze scanned down to her mouth.

'If he learns that I was at Seamill Hall…'

Something of the smile vanished. The pale eyes sent a spiralling of excitement down deep in her belly. 'Do not worry. I will warn Weir and Annabel of Tayburn.'

She shivered just at the mention of Stephen's name. 'Then you concede that he is a very dangerous man?'

'I never denied it,' he said in a lazy tone.

Helena's blood ran cold.

'But not as dangerous as me.' He smiled again and leaned down lower until their faces were almost touching, so close that when he spoke she could feel the warm moisture of his breath against her cheek and the tickle of his lips against her skin.

His fingers traced a light, teasing path from the hollow in her throat down to the edge of her bodice, his fingers caressing the creamy swell of her bosom. There was a tremor running through him as he unfastened her dress and pulled down the fine wool and the layers of flimsy materials that lay beneath it—a tremor such that he had not experienced since he'd been a green lad— until at last the fullness of her breasts lay exposed. He stared in awe.

'You're beautiful,' he whispered, and cupped his hands around her. She was smoother than satin, softer than silk, and he revelled in the feel of her. Beneath his caress her nipples beaded and he felt their gentle thrust against his hand. 'Sweetheart,' he murmured, and replaced his hand with his mouth to suckle her. Lord, but she was sweet, and he wanted her, wanted her with a desperation that he had never thought to feel. He lapped harder at the rosy bud and heard her soft gasps.

'Helena…' he raised his head to look at her, saw the passion darken her eyes '…I want to make love to you.'

She nodded.

His fingers brushed her nipples as his mouth made to claim hers.

'It is your right.'

Guy froze. 'My right?' And the thought that she was doing this out of duty, as she had done for Tayburn, curbed his desire. He touched the gentlest caress with one finger to the delicate skin beneath her ear.

'Do you wish me to continue?'

Helena was very conscious of the press of her naked breasts against the hardness of his chest, and of every other place that their bodies touched even by the slightest degree. She said nothing.

The finger stopped its motion, and everything about him was still. 'Was your flight across this bed from me in earnest, Helena?'

Her heart slid up her chest to thud in the base of her throat. Her chest was so tight that every breath seemed to come as a short sharp pant. She knew what any respectable lady should say. But then again she was not in the least respectable. 'We have an agreement. I will not renege on my side of the bargain.'

'That is not what I asked you,' he said.

The words teetered on the tip of her tongue, words that would tell him that she wanted him never to stop, words that would confirm her as a harlot. Pride would not let her say them.

Silence roared loud in her ears. Guy touched his lips against hers with a featherlight touch and then the mattress dipped and he was gone. Cold air filled the space where he had been.

'I must speak with the manager,' he said. 'I'll be back soon.' The lazy carefree smile was still on his face, but Helena thought that she saw the hint of something else beneath it. She closed her eyes against the sense of loss and lay where she was until she heard the door close.

Chapter Eleven

Helena did not go with Guy that afternoon to Seamill Hall. He left the carriage at the hotel, opting to travel on horseback. Half the distance to Kilbride he covered by road before turning down on to the beach and continuing along the firm caramel sand. Only when he was close to Weir's boathouse did he slow the beast, trotting him past the large faded shed and up the bramble-lined lane through which he had walked with Helena. Thus, Guy arrived at the stables at the back of Seamill Hall, left the horse with a surprised-looking stable-boy and gave the scullery maid a fright by appearing at the back door. Eventually he reached the drawing room and waited only a small time before Weir joined him.

'Varington!' Weir strode forwards and grasped Guy's hand in his own. 'Is everything well? You're back so soon, and Brown said that you came to the back door.'

'I took the horse for a canter along the beach. It was easier to cut up the back way.' Guy smiled and deliberately evaded the question.

'Sit down. Whisky?'

'That would be most welcome. What of Annabel and yourself? Are you both well?'

'Yes, yes,' Weir said with a touch of impatience. 'Perfectly well. But what has happened? Surely you cannot have returned from London already?' Pale golden liquid sloshed into two glasses, one of which was thrust unceremoniously towards the Viscount.

Guy accepted the proffered glass and downed the measure in one gulp. A satisfied blow of breath sounded and he relaxed back into the armchair. 'That stuff is damned good! You Scots have named it well *uisage bthea*—water of life.'

Weir knew better than to press Guy further. Past experience had taught him that Guy's stubborn streak meant he would offer an explanation only when he was good and ready.

'Had any interesting visitors in the past days?' The question was asked with a nonchalance that belied what Guy was really feeling.

The penny dropped with Weir. 'Hell! Tayburn didn't catch you, did he?'

'He's been here, then?' Guy said, passing his empty glass to Weir for a refill.

'Oh, he was here, all right. Arrived the day after you left… looking for his lady friend.'

'How very interesting,' drawled Guy, but there was a slight sharpening of his focus.

'Didn't I say that woman was bad news? To think I had her staying here in my house, chatting with my wife and children. She's the devil's mistress!'

'Not any more.'

'God in heaven! You didn't… You haven't… Tell me it is not so, Guy. Even you could not be that audacious.'

Guy sat back with what he hoped was an unfath-omable expression. He had no intention of telling Weir the truth of matters between himself and Helena. It was better to let his friend draw his own conclusions.

'I know you said that you meant to seduce her, but that was when we did not know who she was. Perhaps you've not heard of Sir Stephen Tayburn, but I can assure you he's infamous in these parts.'

'I've heard of him.' The revulsion rolled within him just at the thought of the villain.

'Then you'll have also heard that he's not a man to be crossed. My God, the man's a fiend. I do not jest when I say that you've signed your own death warrant if you've taken his woman.'

Guy raised an eyebrow. 'You're being a tad presump-tive. I did not say that my seduction of Helena was suc-cessful.' He thought of Helena weeping in his arms on that ledge with the carriage smashed far beneath them. He thought of her face, ashen with shock, as she stood before the burnt pile of rubble that had been her family's home. Hardly a seduction.

'But it was, wasn't it?'

He forced a laugh. 'It would be ungentlemanly of me to say.'

'You said that she's no longer Tayburn's mistress. Is she yours?'

'I will admit that she's under my protection.'

'Oh, hell, you'd better tell me all of it,' said Weir, rubbing his fingers against his forehead in nervous an-ticipation. 'You would not be back here sitting in my drawing room if there was not a very good reason. Nor,' he said with a snort, 'would you have descended to using the back door.'

'I could not be sure if Tayburn was having the house watched.'

'I take it by the fact you're still alive that Tayburn did not catch you?' Weir peered closer at Guy's face, noticing the newly healed cut running down the side of his face. 'Or did he?'

'He came after us, then?'

Weir gave a brief nod.

'When?'

'The morning after he was here. He owns a house near Brigurd Point. Keeps a four in hand there. Apparently he had his wife brought over from St Vey and was seen heading out on to the road like a bat out of hell. There's been no sight of him since. Hunter has the estate at Hunterston. There's nothing that gets past him; he knows everything that's going on. I spoke to him only yesterday: apparently Tayburn's boat is still moored at Brigurd Point, which means he's still on the mainland somewhere. If he were on the island, the boat would be on the other side. Tayburn knew the identity of the woman travelling with you, no matter what I said to the contrary.'

'I'll deal with Tayburn.'

Weir topped up the whisky glasses and pressed one into his friend's hand. 'Pray God that you do, Varington, pray God that you do.'

'The matter is already in hand.' The softness of Guy's tone belied the hardness in his eyes.

Weir glanced up, suspicion and the first inkling of fear upon his face. 'I do not like the sound of that.'

'Then you need not hear it,' said Guy simply.

'Damnation, Varington, I'll not just stand by and let you go up against Tayburn for the sake of a woman to warm your bed.'

Guy's eyes met Weir's and held. 'He has taken Helena's youngest sister out of revenge.'

'Good God!'

'I have no intention of allowing him to pursue Helena and neither will I leave her sister to his mercy.'

Weir rolled his eyes. 'Dare I ask you to tell me what you are planning?'

Guy smiled. 'Of course, old man. I was going to call him out—'

Weir waited.

'But now that I know Tayburn is on his way to London and not in his lair at all, a rather inviting opportunity makes itself known.'

Weir screwed his eyes shut in a cringing expression. 'I have a horrible suspicion where this is going. Please tell me that I'm wrong.'

Guy's smile deepened. 'How far is it between here and Tayburn's island?'

'Varington, you do not want to do this.'

'Oh, but I do, old chap, and I will. So let us discuss the details of just such a journey.'

And they did. By the time they had finished Weir had drained the whisky from his glass and was looking decidedly pasty about the gills. 'I wish to God that you'd never found that wretched woman.'

Guy wished no such thing.

'Let me come with you.'

'No. I've involved you and Annabel in this too much already and for that I'm sorry. I need not tell you to have a care over both your welfares when Tayburn returns.'

Weir gave a grim shake of his head.

'Besides, there's something else that I need you to do for me. And you aren't going to like it.'

'Then you had best tell me what it is.'

'I want to leave Helena here while I'm gone to St Vey. I know you'll see that she's kept safe.'

'You're right, I do not like it one little bit.'

'But you'll do it for me all the same?' Guy prompted.

A nod. 'You owe me, Varington. Hugely.'

'I won't forget,' said Guy grimly, and finished his whisky.

Helena stood by the window of the bedchamber in the Eglinton Arms Hotel and watched Guy ride into the yard. He was as strong a horseman as he was everything else. The sunshine and blue skies had faded to a cold white grey, against which Guy cut a severe swathe with the dark perfection of his tailoring. In his elegant dark blue jacket, hat and stylishly tied neckcloth, he looked rather out of place riding through the small Scottish town. She drew back as he passed through the stone gateposts, but not fast enough. The handsome face looked up, saw her, smiled and inclined in acknowledgement. Just the sight of him pushed her pulse up a notch and made her remember the heat of his breath against her breast. She whirled around and clutched at the back of the chair positioned close to the fireplace, so tightly that her knuckles shone white. Footsteps sounded coming up the stairs. Helena's stomach tightened. She tried to tell herself it was because he brought word of Stephen. In part she was right; but only in part. Helena knew full well the other reason that caused such sensations throughout her body; she just didn't want to admit it right now.

A polite knocking, accompanied by his voice. 'Helena.'

She moved towards the door, turned the key. A deep

breath, and then the doorknob twisted within her fingers and the door swung open. He stood there with just the faintest hint of a smile upon his face. He had looked handsome down in the driveway; he was even more handsome at close range, devastatingly so, and Helena was struck anew at how much his presence affected her. Lord, she barely knew the man! She lowered her eyes that he might not see the truth in them, and stepped back into the room for him to enter. That he locked the door after him was a testament to his caution. Stephen's shadow lingered around the periphery of both their minds.

'I trust that your visit went well?'

'Well enough,' said Guy. 'Weir and Annabel are both in good health.'

Helena retreated to stand behind the chair once more, resting her hands loosely on top of its back, taking refuge in the illusion of it as a barrier between them. 'Of that I am glad.'

'Annabel asked for you.'

She glanced up in surprise. 'She does not know? Stephen has not found them? Perhaps he believes me dead in the wreckage of the *Bonnie Lass*, after all.'

Guy did not move from his position in front of the fire, but she saw the compassion that entered his expression, and she knew that her hopes were in vain. 'No, I'm afraid that Tayburn knows both that you were at Seamill Hall and that you left with me.'

Helena's fingers stole towards her mouth before she checked the gesture. But she could not deny the sudden nausea that rolled in her stomach or the aridity of her mouth. Words escaped her. And in that moment she could do nothing other than cling to the back of the chair harder than ever. She was glad of its presence, for she did not know whether she would have been able to maintain her poise without it. She took a deep breath and her words, when they came, were calm and quiet. 'Then you are in very grave danger.'

'Oh, dear, what a worrisome discovery,' he said with irony.

'It's not too late to extricate yourself from this mess. If you go now, Stephen need never know anything more than you transported me to London. It was the gallant act of a gentleman, nothing more.'

'Have you forgotten that I came here to call him out?'

'How could I?' She stared at the handsome profile. 'But I can no longer let you do that.' And then, as if speaking to herself, she said, 'I shall throw myself on his mercy. Tell him that I came to my senses as soon as I arrived in London and returned to him as quickly as I could. He need know nothing further about you.'

'Tayburn has no mercy, and besides…' he turned away from the fire and came towards her '…we have an agreement.' He stopped directly in front of her. 'Unless you wish to change that, Helena? Perhaps you find my company disagreeable.'

She shook her head, unwittingly freeing a tendril of hair to dangle at the side of her cheek. 'You know that I do not,' she said softly, 'but he has Emma. And now he knows not only that Mr Weir and his wife gave me shelter, but that you and I travelled together.' She touched her fingers to the tight band of pain that was forming across her forehead. 'My father and Agnes and Old Tam are dead. And if I do nothing, then more will follow. Seven lives for my freedom. The cost is too high.' She let her hand drop and looked him directly in the eye. 'Had I known the price, I never would have left.'

'We've been through all of this, Helena. You did nothing wrong. And besides, you cannot go back—the die is already cast.'

Her brow creased. 'What do you mean? If I go back to him, it should temper his revenge against Mr and Mrs Weir…and you.'

'You know it will make not the slightest difference. Sacrificing yourself on Tayburn's alter shall not change what he has planned.'

She gripped the chair back so tightly that she thought it would snap beneath the pressure of her fingers. The terrible coldness was spreading through her again, bringing back with it all of the pain that she could not forget. 'Then God forgive me for what I have unleashed upon you all.'

He came to her then, stood behind her, covered her cold tense fingers with the relaxed warmth of his hands.

'What shall I do?' And for the first time in her five long years Helena was truly at a loss. It was one thing to endure the pain herself, quite another to stand by and watch it inflicted on others, knowing herself to be the cause. 'What shall I do?' she whispered again.

Guy gave no answer, just turned her slowly around in his arms, and tilted her face up to his, scanning her eyes as if he could see the torment in her soul, as if he understood exactly what it was that she felt.

'I know what he will do to her and I cannot bear it.' Her voice cracked.

'Helena,' he breathed, and the sound of her name upon his lips was as soothing as a caress. 'You need not bear it, for we shall stop Tayburn very neatly in his tracks.'

She stared up into his eyes, seeing the absolute confidence in them. 'There's nothing we can do while he has Emma.'

'Then we had better fetch her back.' And the smile that spread across his mouth was filled with deadly promise.

'How can we?' She stared at him as if he had run mad. 'He has her at Dunleish.'

The smile stretched deeper. 'Tayburn is not presently at home. I understand that he expressed an interest in travelling to London.' One eyebrow raised in a suggestive manner.

'London?' Her eyes widened. 'He is pursuing me!'

'He thinks he is pursuing us,' Guy corrected. 'Just as we knew he would…eventually.' He smiled a lazy smile. 'Thus leaving your sister alone in Dunleish. How very convenient…for us.'

'You cannot mean to…' Incredulity made her stare all the harder. 'You would not dare…'

'It is a simple enough solution, sweetheart. I shall be back tomorrow, hopefully accompanied by your sister.'

'No!' She gripped his arms. 'It is too dangerous.'

'I'm touched by your concern,' he said, and dropping his gaze to her lips, his smile became flirtatious.

'Do you think just to walk in there, take Emma and walk back out again?'

'Something like that,' he murmured, and slipped his arms around her.

She shivered, but whether it was from his touch or from the thought of what he planned to do she did not know. 'It is madness.'

His breath tickled against the side of her neck as he lowered his mouth to her ear. 'Madness that Tayburn shall not expect.'

She had to admit he had a point. No sane-minded man would venture willingly into Dunleish Castle. She chewed at her lip, feeling her skin tingle where his breath caressed.

'It is a good opportunity to rescue your sister.'

He was right, of course, if Emma was indeed still alive. She gave a little nod. 'It does not mean that I like it, but I suppose it is better than you calling him out.'

Guy did not correct her mistaken assumption. Instead he allowed the tip of his tongue to tease against her neck.

Helena released an involuntary gasp of pleasure and strove to keep her mind focused on their conversation. 'When…?'

His tongue traced a dance up to her jaw.

She tried again. 'When do you think to go there?'

He touched his tongue to the centre of her mouth, and as her lips parted and softened in response, he whispered, 'First light.'

She shivered at his words, but then his mouth closed upon hers, deliciously demanding, and his kisses silenced her questions.

Those that knew Sir Stephen were often heard to say that the devil looked after his own, and indeed Tayburn had an inordinate ability to come up trumps in the most tricky of situations. His flight to London in pursuit of Helena was no exception. For as luck would have it Tayburn happened to choose the very same coaching inn to rest overnight as Guy and Helena had used not so many nights previously.

Tayburn dispatched his wife to bed and spent the rest of the evening in the taproom, occupying a whole table to himself that not even the roughest of navvies dared to comment upon. Indeed, despite the crowd of bodies within the public room, it was as if there was a small exclusion zone around Tayburn. Men sensed something of the white-haired man's nature and were wise enough to give him a wide berth. It was a raw primeval power and Tayburn revelled in the fear that he saw in the faces around him. He drank his brandy and bided his time, letting the bodies become accustomed to his presence, like a wolf that sat within the heart of a flock of sheep, lulling them into a false sense of security by his inactivity and apparent inattention. It was not long before the buzz of conversation resumed around him. Tayburn sipped his brandy and listened to words of inconsequence spoken in accents that made the following difficult, but Tayburn had nothing else to do—for now. And so he continued to listen for an hour, and then another, until the drink had unguarded both tongues and suspicions. It was then that he heard it.

'That redhead he had with him was a tasty piece and no mistake.' The young man wiped the dribble of ale from his chin and continued to regale his friends with his thoughts on the woman. 'Well, it was that he had them sup in a private parlour. He was like the bloody cat that got the cream. No wonder he didn't want the likes of us to have a good old gander at her. Hell, but I'd sell my soul for a night with his missus.'

'She wasn't his wife,' said another. 'Harry there…' he indicated towards the landlord waiting behind the bar '…said she weren't lady to that lord.'

'Like that, was it?' leered the first man. 'Wish that I'd have known at the time. I gave her a friendly look and those green eyes looked right through me as if I were nothing. Right snooty she was. If I'd known she was his fancy piece, I'd have taken her down a peg or two.'

'And cross that aristo she was with? I don't think so, Frankie. You're all talk, you are. You'd have been scared shitless if he'd pulled a pistol on you.'

'Happen I've a pistol or two of my own. I'm no chicken-heart.'

A serving wench came over and dumped another pitcher of ale down on the bar beside them. 'Courtesy of the gentleman in black over there.'

Three pairs of eyes stared over at Tayburn.

Tayburn gave a nod of his head and raised his glass in their direction.

The man, Frankie, lifted his own in return.

'Who the hell is he?' his mate whispered.

'Cursed if I know,' came the reply. 'But free ale is free ale. Let the fool pay for our drink if he wants to. I'm not complaining.'

They laughed and worked their way quite merrily through the contents of the pitcher.

Tayburn bought them three further pitchers before two of the men decided they had best find their own ways home to their wives and their beds. Frankie was not wise enough to follow suit. He had no wife and he knew that his rented room would be cold. A glass of brandy appeared in his hand—courtesy of the same gentleman. The liquid was strong and seared a warmth in his throat. It was not often that Frankie had the chance to taste real French brandy. He decided to stay a while longer. And when Tayburn beckoned him, Frankie made his way somewhat unsteadily over to his table.

Another few glasses of brandy secured Tayburn all that he needed to know about the beautiful redheaded woman and the lord that had accompanied her. He had no further need of Frankie. Tayburn smiled at him and even in his drunken stupor the younger man quailed.

'No one calls me *fool*,' said Tayburn, and his smile was small and deadly.

Tayburn and his wife departed early the next day. The ostlers commented that it was strange that he headed back north when that was the direction from which he had arrived the previous evening, and in such a hurry. An hour later they found Frankie's body. His throat had been cut.

Chapter Twelve

That night Helena lay next to Guy in their bed within the Eglinton Arm's Hotel. Outside a patter of rain had set up, thrumming steadily against the glass of the large bow window in their bedchamber. A fire still burned in the grate, lighting the darkness with its orange glow. The smell of the candle that Guy had just extinguished drifted through the air. There was silence save for the pelting of raindrops and the run of water in the guttering outside.

Helena lay on her back, eyes open against the darkness, and waited to see what Guy would do. The expectation was obvious, but the previous nights had shown a different side to the man. She knew that he desired her, had known it almost from the moment they met. And yet he had not taken her, not fully as was a man's right to take of his mistress—not yet. She thought again of the way that his mouth had covered her breast, of the heat of his kisses and the aching wantonness with which her body had responded. And the way he had stopped so suddenly, even though his arousal was still firm and unsated. *Was your flight across this bed from me in earnest?* he had asked, as if her answer was so very important to him. She had wanted him, wanted him to touch her, to make love to her. The blush rose over her body at the memory and her thighs grew warm. The mattress moved and she felt Guy roll on to his side and lay his hand upon her stomach. She shivered beneath his fingers before lying completely still.

'Helena.' His voice was a husky murmur through the darkness and it seemed that he could feel the soft warm skin through the fine silk of the ivory nightdress he had bought for her. He heard the soft catch of her breath in her throat as he slid his hand slowly up to rest against her ribcage, close to her breasts. 'Are you cold?' he whispered, feeling the tension that surrounded her.

'I'm quite warm, thank you,' she said as if they were chatting politely over tea in a drawing room, instead of lying next to one another half-naked in bed.

He wanted to make love to her, to heal all the hurts that Tayburn had dealt her, but he did not know the depth of Helena's wounds. She had been forced to Tayburn's bed against her will and he'd be damned if he'd do anything similar. Despite his glib words to Weir, Guy knew that he would not attempt a seduction of any kind. He desired her with a force that gnawed at him night and day, but seduction smacked of bending her to his will, albeit in a more sophisticated fashion than the brutality Tayburn had used, and he could not do that to Helena, not after everything that she had endured.

'You are shivering.'

'No.' The denial was swift and adamant. 'You're mistaken.'

His fingers stroked against the base of her breasts,

feeling that which she could not hide—the harried thumping of her heart.

'You need not be afraid, Helena. I'm not Tayburn. I will not hurt you.'

'I'm not afraid.' The denial was uttered in a small tight voice as if her lips were as rigid as the rest of her body.

He gave a soft sigh of a laugh and dropped a kiss against her eyebrow. 'My poor sweetheart, you don't have to pretend any longer. I have no intention of letting Tayburn reclaim you. You're quite safe, and it's perfectly acceptable to show some measure of emotion. Indeed, ladies are positively expected to be having attacks of the megrims one minute and the vapours the next.' He smiled, feeling the soft silkiness of her hair against his mouth.

'You forget, Guy, that I am no lady.' She had not moved; she still stared up straight ahead towards the ceiling.

His hand moved from her body to her neck and then, gently cupping her cheek, he turned her face to his. He could see only the shadow of her features in the light cast from the glowing embers, and knew that she would see nothing more of him. Yet he lowered his face until their noses almost touched and stared into her eyes. 'You were a lady when Tayburn took you, were you not?'

She gave no answer.

'Were you not, Helena?' he said again, more forcefully.

'Yes,' came the whisper back.

'Then you are a lady still. No matter what happens, remember that.'

He felt the brush of her eyelashes against his as she closed her eyes. He ceased to think. As a matter of instinct his mouth lowered to hers and delivered a kiss that was both gentle yet firm, a kiss that both reassured and aroused.

She melted against him and returned the kiss in full.

It was almost his undoing. He groaned, as his tongue danced against hers, lapping and stroking and kissing in an ecstasy of delight. His arousal throbbed, seeking release as it pressed against her sweet softness. He felt her body answer his call, felt her heat, her invitation. His body clung to hers, striving for the coupling that his mind would not allow. Heaven help him, if he did not stop now he did not think that he would be capable of doing so until he had made her his own. And so, slowly, he forced his retreat, pulling gently back from lips that were everything that he wanted, easing his manhood away from such torturous temptation. He looked down into her eyes, seeing there a heavy-lidded desire that mirrored his own, and it was all he could do not to cover her mouth with his own once more and slide his length into her.

'Sweet Helena.' He gently stroked her cheek. 'Have you any idea of what you do to me?' There was silence save for the soft hush of her breath. He gave a sigh. 'When we free your sister, Tayburn will have no further hold over you.' He stared down into her face. 'Now we had best go to sleep. Tomorrow shall be a long day.' And with that he finally released her and turned over.

Helena looked at the strong broad back that Guy presented to her with mixed emotions. He was right, tomorrow would be a long day, a long and dangerous day. No matter what Guy said, Helena knew that there was a very real chance that he might not return from Dunleish. Many men had entered the castle; few ever left it alive. He was risking his life for her, to free her sister—a girl he did not even know. And all because he had taken her as his mistress—in name only. He had given her his protection and taken very little in return. Yet Helena knew that he wanted her; she felt his need as powerfully as if it were her own. None of it made any sense. He could have taken her at any time of his choosing, knowing that she would give no resistance.

And being bedded by Guy would be nothing of pain and everything of pleasure…the sweep of his hands, the ardour of his kiss… She still trembled from his touch…still ached for him. But for all that she longed for him, there was a part of her that dreaded to play the harlot, to confirm that that was all she was—a harlot, a whore. He was keeping his side of the bargain. Surely it was only honourable that she kept hers? And then she caught her line of thought—honourable! When could there ever be honour in that role? She raised herself up on her elbows and looked across the small distance that separated them. Warmth emanated from the dark shape facing the wall. His breaths came slow and even, as if he was already asleep. Helena knew that he was not.

'Guy?' she whispered his name through the darkness before she could think better of it.

She could see the change in his shape as he lifted his head and peered over his shoulder at her. 'What is it?'

A pause.

'You know that you risk your life in going to Dunleish?' Her voice sounded slightly breathless.

'Sweetheart,' he murmured over his shoulder, 'you have told me all I need to know. I have the map and all is prepared. Now, empty your head of such thoughts and go to sleep. Everything will be well tomorrow.'

'Do not underestimate him, Guy. I'm afraid that you do not know what you have taken on with Stephen.'

He rolled over and, gathering her into his arms, kissed the skin of her cheek beside her mouth. 'I know a lot better than you realise.'

'You do not know him.'

His fingers rubbed against the top of her arm. 'Men like Tayburn are all the same. Know one and you know them all,' and there was some emotion in his voice that she did not understand.

Her skin grew warm beneath his hand. 'No man is like Stephen. He is the very devil.' And she could not suppress the shiver that rippled down her spine. 'I fear for your life.'

Guy pulled her closer. 'Then do not. I have no intention of losing it and every intention of delivering Emma to you tomorrow.' He kissed her again; a small chaste kiss on her forehead. 'Now, go to sleep,' and started to move away.

Helena stayed him, resting her hand on his lean hard flank. 'Guy.'

He stopped. Beneath her fingers she felt him tense. 'Yes?'

Helena licked her suddenly dry lips. 'I am not tired,' she said, and felt a warmth flood her cheeks at her boldness.

'Are you saying that you want me?' His surprise was blatant.

She gave a little clear of her throat. 'Perhaps.'

'Perhaps?'

She felt his body come up against hers. Felt his breath upon her cheek. The pulse in her neck was throbbing so hard she thought she would not be able to speak.

'I know that you want to…that you want…' Her words trailed off. 'I will not resist.'

'It's not about what I want,' he growled.

She swallowed hard, not understanding, not knowing what to say. There was silence…and silence…and more silence.

His chest rose and fell in a slow steady movement. All else about him seemed frozen to immobility.

'You've given me your protection and taken nothing in return,' she said, unable to bear the silence any longer.

'What is it that you would have me take?' he asked, and she could hear the sadness in his tone.

'I…' Again the words escaped her.

'I told you, I'm not Tayburn, and I will *take* nothing from you,' he said, and there was an undercurrent that she did not understand through his words. This time there was no comforting caress, no kiss of affection. He turned on his side and went to sleep.

Helena lay where she was and thought over all that had happened. When she finally found sleep, it was not Stephen or Dunleish or even Emma that occupied her mind, but the enigma of the man that slept so soundly by her side.

It was still dark when Helena awoke to the sounds of splashing water. Over on the chest of drawers a single candle burned, casting a gloomy light throughout the bedchamber. Guy stood with his back to her, rinsing beneath his arms with water from the white china basin. Even within the dimness of the candlelight she could see the droplets of water glistening against the skin of his back. He had a sinewy musculature that belied his self-professed hedonistic lifestyle. Whatever he said to the contrary, Guy, Lord Varington, did some activity that kept his body lean and honed and fit. Helena found that she was staring. He leaned to the side, grabbed a towel and dried first his face and then his body. Helena knew that she should not have been watching him, but the knowledge did not move her eyes away, nor did she give him any indication that she was awake. She studied the broad line of his shoulders and the definition of each muscle until Guy turned round and glanced at her as if he sensed her attention.

''Morning, sweetheart.'

Helena had the grace to blush. 'Good morning,' she said, and rapidly averted her eyes.

He was smiling and she knew he knew that she had been staring. He rubbed a hand across his chin, testing the roughness of the skin, then, without even bothering to don his shirt, went to rummage in his bag.

'What time is it?' she asked

'A little after seven, I would guess,' came the reply from the vicinity of the foot of the bed.

'You do not need to look at your watch?'

'I always wake at seven. My watch is on the table. Check for yourself if you wish.' He rose and she saw that he held in his hand a razor and a small mirror. 'It's at times like these that I miss Collins.' So saying, he propped the mirror at the side of the candle and, wetting his shaving brush within the water, started to lather the soap on the brush's badger bristles.

'I can do that for you if it will make it easier.' The words were out before Helena realised that she was going to say them.

He stopped what he was doing and turned round to look at her. 'Have you ever shaved a man before?'

'Yes,' she said, then, seeing the dark expression that flitted across his eyes, added, 'After my father's attack he lost the use of his right arm. He did not trust anyone else to shave him save for me.'

He gave a soft laugh and held out his hand to the side in invitation. 'Then I put myself in your capable hands.'

She climbed out of the bed and came to stand by his side. 'I must tell you that it's been some time since my shaving practice. But I shall do my best.'

'I'm relieved to hear it.'

He manoeuvred the chair to the side of the chest of drawers close to the wash basin, and sat himself down. 'Here, take this.' He passed her the lathered shaving brush. Then he sat back and held his face up, ready for her ministrations.

Helena would rather have found a tie to catch back the curtain of her hair, but it was too late for that; her hands were already covered in soap from the brush. She moved to stand at his side, feeling the carpet rub against the bareness of her feet. Rather than meet his gaze, she started straight away, gently stroking the lather across the dark stubbled skin of his cheeks, lathering the soap up further to also cover his chin and throat. Beneath her fingers she felt the upward tilt of his mouth. She reached across, rinsed the brush and her hands in the water, dried them on the towel and picked up the razor. It opened to reveal a wicked-looking blade that glinted in the candlelight. A weapon by another name— one slip and a man's life could be severed.

'Are you ready?' she asked.

He raised his chin, exposing his throat. 'I trust that you shall keep a steady hand, Helena.' A corner of his mouth tugged up. 'I am completely at your mercy.'

Her eyes flickered from the blade in her hand to the soap-smeared skin of his throat and back again, realising the extent of his vulnerability and exactly what that meant. 'You trust me.'

The smile flickered again. 'Of course.'

Helena felt the response of her own mouth. Then she put all such thoughts from her mind and, with the blade in hand, bent lower over his throat.

Helena's touch was gentle. She shaved him with an efficiency that rivalled his valet's, but with a tenderness with which Collins could never have hoped to compete. The blade within her hand contacted his skin in short strokes, razing all trace of the beard's beginnings. She covered his throat, his cheeks, his upper lip, and even the contours of his chin without so much as a nick, leaning close so that she might see what she was doing within the dimness of the room, so close that he could smell her scent and feel the brush of her long tresses against the bare skin of his chest and arms. Having her so near was a taste of both heaven and hell. He wanted to cast the blade aside, take her into his arms and kiss her thoroughly before laying her back on the bed and making love to her. But he could not. He strove not to give rein to such thoughts and contented himself with watching her face.

Between her brows there was a tiny crease of concentration. The flicker of the candle flame caused golden lights to dance in her eyes. Her focus followed the blade across his skin, a soft scrape, left or right, up or down, following the direction of the hair growth, wiping the blade clean after each scrape. The small repetitive movements relaxed him, chased away all tension. And by the time Helena had rinsed his face, patted it dry and pronounced that he was all done, Guy was feeling strangely contented for a man about to embark on a hazardous mission.

He stood and rubbed his knuckles against her arm. 'I could get used to that.'

They shared a smile.

'Now you had best get dressed and quickly.'

She looked at him with a start of surprise. 'You wish me to come with you?'

He looked right back at her with a twinkle in his eye. 'Only as far as Seamill Hall.'

'What do you mean?'

He bent, retrieved his shirt, and pulled it on over his head. 'I have arranged with Weir that you will stay there today.'

'I cannot.'

'Make haste, Helena. We do not have much time.'

'I am…' She hesitated, blushed and forced the words out. 'I am your mistress, for pity's sake, Guy!'

He stopped fastening the buttons and cocked an eyebrow. 'And don't I know it.' He smiled a warm seductive smile and looked meaningfully into her eyes.

'I cannot embarrass Mrs Weir so by arriving on her doorstep.'

'Helena, I shall feel better for knowing that you are with Weir and not here alone while I am gone for such a time.'

'But if you are certain that Stephen has departed for London…'

'And left behind men who are loyal to him.'

There was a small silence between them, and then Guy resumed his buttoning once more. 'Will you go to Seamill Hall as I ask?'

'Very well,' she said, confused by what she saw in his eyes.

'Good.' He seemed relieved.

'You have the map that I drew?' she asked.

'Safe in my pocket. If Emma is not in the chamber you marked, is there anywhere else he might have hidden her?'

She looked at him. And he saw the flit of fear in her eyes. 'The dungeon. But pray God he has not resorted to that. There are sights there that would turn Emma's mind.'

'Never fear, I will bring her back to you.'

She mustered a small brave smile at that and rushed to make ready for the journey. They completed their *toilettes* in a comfortable silence. She did not speak again until the cloak was wrapped around her shoulders and they were ready to leave. The baggage was already packed upon the coach. It was now or never. She did not think that she would have a chance to speak to him at Seamill Hall.

'You will have a care, won't you, Guy?'

The lopsided cheeky smile was back on his face. 'No, I intend to be completely reckless.'

She shook her head and gave a sob of a laugh.

And then his arms touched to her shoulders. One hand moved up and his thumb touched lightly against her cheek. It seemed that he was about to say something, something that Helena instinctively knew was of the greatest importance. With great tenderness he brushed her hair from her cheek. 'Helena, there is a purse and a letter tucked down the side of my small travelling valise. If things go awry and I do not come back from Dunleish by tomorrow night, then I want you to take the money from the purse—'

She interrupted him with a gasp. 'No, please do not—'

But his arms wrapped themselves around her and he

captured her to him. 'Hear me out, Helena. There is not much time left and it is important that I say this.'

A nod and she caught back what words she would have said.

'Take the money from the purse,' he repeated, 'use it to travel post-chaise to Cornwall and seek out my brother. Hand the letter to him in person, no one else. His name and direction are penned upon the paper. Lucien will ensure your safety. Give me your word that you will do this.'

'I would not just abandon you in Dunleish!' she exclaimed.

'Promise me, Helena.' And his eyes stared down into hers with a determination that she had not seen before.

She nodded.

'Say the words,' he insisted.

She sighed, and looked at him with a great weight around her heart.

'Helena?' he prompted.

'Very well,' she said at last. 'I promise.'

He seemed to relax at her words. Then his face lowered to hers and she saw the closing of his eyes before his mouth slid against hers.

Too soon he moved back.

'We had best be gone before Tayburn realises the error of his call and decides to head for home.' Guy laughed. One last kiss from her mouth and they moved towards the door.

The knob was turning beneath his hand as she said his name, 'Guy.'

He paused, looked down at her.

'Thank you,' she said, and meant it with every fibre of her being.

The smile that he gave her showed that he understood. Sensuous and caring and reassuring all at once.
Helena's heart squeezed tight. And then they were off
and walking along the thick pile of the carpet and down
the broad expanse of the staircase. Outside the early
morning was still thick and dark.

When he left her at Seamill Hall the sky had lightened
to a charcoal grey with the first hint of dawn. By the time
that daylight surfaced in full, she knew that the rowing
boat would be well on its way across the Firth of Clyde
to the island of St Vey, carrying Guy towards Dunleish.
No matter how hard she tried to stop, she could not help
but hear Guy's words play again and again in her mind:
*before Tayburn realises the error of his call and decides
to head for home*. And the chill made the blood in
Helena's veins run cold with foreboding.

Pine creaked against oak as the oars swept their
rhythmic circle, pulling them through the cold grey
seawater. The small wooden boat slid forwards as easily
as a warmed knife through butter and Guy supposed that
the current must be in his favour, aiding his progress
towards the island. He scanned the distance ahead. It
seemed close enough to swim. One look at the chilly
water was enough to banish any such notions and he
was glad that he had worn the caped overcoat and
gloves. The sky was lighting from the east, washing out
the darkness, turning night to day. Wind ruffled his hair
and nipped at his cheeks. Not for the first time he
wondered if Helena's sister was still alive. He set his jaw
firm and turned his mind from such speculation. He did
not want to think what it might mean for Helena were
she not.

Helena. A vision of her face swam into his mind. Fixed in concentration as she shaved him, the perfectly shaped brows, the beautiful smoky green eyes, the slope of her small straight nose and the ripe fullness of her lips. Within the candlelight her skin had glowed a smooth golden cream and her hair was as red and long and riotous as any beauty from a Pre-Raphaelite painting.

She had wielded the razor with such gentle competent strokes, such steady hands. No woman had ever done such a thing for him before. She had smiled at him, with no sign of the mask that hid her emotions from the world. And Guy had never seen a more beautiful sight than Helena's smile, nor heard a better sound than her laughter. Just the memory gladdened his heart and turned his own mouth up into an arc. Thank you, she had said, and Guy had known that those two small words covered a multitude of emotion. It was as if all barriers between them had fallen away and he had seen the real Helena, the woman she had hidden from Tayburn. In the sharing of that moment something had bound them together. Guy felt it still, and he knew that it could not be undone. He knew too that he would do whatever he had to, to free her from Tayburn. A gull appeared overhead, gliding on a current of air, precarious in the wind's buffeting. He pulled harder at the oars and the boat moved silently on towards St Vey.

Helena had dreaded it but her reception at Seamill Hall had not been as bad as she had imagined. Mr Weir had been polite and stiff; his dislike and disapproval no worse than before. Of his wife there had been no sign, and that hurt more than all of Mr Weir's censure ever could.

The morning wore on with a creeping slowness; every passing hour only adding to Helena's anxiety. The book that Mrs Weir had sent for her to read lay opened upon her lap. She read the same page again, the black print of words meaningless again. A sigh, and she gave up the pretence, snapping the book shut with agitated fingers. She tried to reason with herself. Stephen was not at Dunleish. Guy knew what he was doing. He had her map. She had told him everything she knew of the place: where Stephen's men would stand guard, the day's routine, who was who in Stephen's little empire, right down to descriptions and names. So why could she not rid herself of this feeling of dread?

The book tumbled on to the bedcovers and she rose from where she was seated on the comfort of the mattress to wander to the window. It was not the cosy yellow chamber in which she had stayed before. This room was larger, colder and decorated in a range of chilly blue hues. The view from the window was not of the sea, but of the front garden and the main road that passed before the big house. Dove-grey clouds drifted over a cold pale sky. Rain drizzled, adding steadily to the puddles that remained from last night's deluge. The road was quiet. No passing traffic. Helen's fingers tapped impatiently upon the window ledge. She chewed at her lip, then nibbled at her thumbnail. A group of sparrows hopped near a crab-apple tree. Nothing else moved. Another sigh, and she gave up her place at the window and wandered over towards the fire.

The fingers of her right hand slipped into the pocket of her dress and touched absently the silver key that she had placed there on impulse before leaving the Eglinton Arms Hotel that morning. She wondered where Guy was precisely. He must surely have reached the castle by now. Had he found Emma? She placed another log from the box on to the fire and moved the guard back into place. Please, God, let them be safe, both Emma and Guy. She turned away and caught sight of the portmanteaux and bags tucked neatly in the corner of the room. Her eyes were drawn to Guy's small valise at the top of his pile; just one part of the matching set that he had bought in Ayr during their recent stay in the town.

The wrecking of the *Bonnie Lass* and Helena's subsequent journey south was a lifetime ago. Days had stretched to years. Had she really only known him for little under a fortnight? It seemed to Helena that they had always been together. Her life with Stephen was like some horrible nightmare that had faded in the daylight. Five years of nothing. Only now was she alive again. 'Guy,' she whispered the word aloud and the soft catch of his name seemed to resonate in the room around her. *If I do not come back from Dunleish…* The hairs on the back of her neck prickled. Pray God bring him back safe. *There is a purse and a letter tucked down the side of my small travelling valise.* She did not want his money, she wanted him.

Helena walked slowly forwards until the pile of dark brown leather baggage lay at her feet. A purse and a letter. The straps of Guy's valise were not buckled. The valise opened easily. Her hand swept lightly over his neatly folded clothes. She lifted the uppermost shirt and raised it to her face, until it met with her nose. Her eyes closed as she inhaled the clean scent of him, feeling the cotton soft against her cheek, softer still against her lips and the kiss that she pressed to it. She remembered the feel of his hands upon her, the magical touch of his mouth, and when she laid the shirt carefully back in its place there was an ache in her heart. It was a small pain that was both joyful and sorrowful. Helena had felt it before during these past days. Only now did she understand what it was. And the knowledge made Guy's trip to Dunleish all the more worrying.

She stopped where she was, letting the revelation sweep over her, letting it fill every pore. It was a glorious feeling, and one that made her heart sing. She smiled, and let her hand wander down the side of Guy's valise, until it found the purse and letter. The purse contained a pile of gold coins and a roll of white banknotes. She tucked it back down out of sight. The letter… The smile was wiped from her face. Her eyes opened wide and the breath rushed from between her parted lips. Happiness cracked in a sudden explosion of shock and splintered into shards around her. In the ensuing silence everything stopped: Helena's heart, Helena's breath.

The hurriedly penned script upon the letter's front was bold before her eyes. It taunted her with her own foolish trust. For Helena recognised the name written upon the paper, the name of the man Guy had said was his brother: The Earl of Tregellas—the so-called Wicked Earl, a man of whom Stephen had spoken, a man whom Stephen admired. Her eyes pressed shut and then opened again as if by doing so the name would have changed to something more palatable. Tregellas. It lay there, written in Guy's own hand. *Lucien will ensure your safety*, he had said. Helena set the letter down on top of Guy's folded shirt and backed away towards the bed. *I have known a man like Tayburn*. His words played again in her mind. Helena shivered and suspicion hung heavy upon her, smothering all else that had gone in its path.

* * *

The trek from his landing point upon St Vey to Dunleish was much as Guy had expected. The small sandy bay where he had moored the boat was located on the south side of the island; Tayburn's castle was on the northernmost coast. The rocky terrain near the landing bay forced him to keep to a coastal route initially. None of that had been unknown to him. So far Helena's words had proved accurate. Sand clung to his boots as he walked steadily on across the firmness of the shore. She had told to him to follow the line of the beach for the first part, and so he had. It increased the distance greatly, but the ground underfoot was easier and safer than scrabbling over the huge rocks.

He cut up on to the hills as soon as he was able. Everything of the place was coarse and sparse and tough. Even the grass beneath his feet was short and scrubby. The few trees that clustered here and there were bare and bent, lichen patterning their grey spindles of branches. There were great clumps of gorse that looked as if they had been ravaged by the worst of the weather, their small spiny leaves as hostile as everything else on the island. With great loping strides he paced himself to cover the ground. The compass in his pocket confirmed his direction, Helena's carefully drawn map told him the rest. He headed on, oblivious to the smir of rain that wetted his skin and clothes and hair, his eyes watchful, ever alert for the presence of danger. He knew that there was little else on the island except the castle, but caution cost little and saved much. The past had taught him that much.

In less than an hour he had reached the ledge hidden above the shore. He dropped to his haunches, lay flat on his stomach and crawled out towards the edge of the rocky platform. Leaning out over the precipice, he peered round past the sheets of sheer rock…to the castle that lay beyond.

Cut from the red sandstone that filled the hills beneath his feet, Dunleish Castle was more of a large fortified keep. It was tall in design, with such small narrow windows that Guy knew it would be dark within the thickness of those walls. The tops of the walls were crenellated in the fashion of castles of old and in each of the four corners, adjoined to the main body, were tall thin towers. It was from one of these that a flag hung at half-mast—proclaiming that the castle's master was not presently in residence. He scanned the other towers, saw a figure leaning against the wall in one—the lookout. Tayburn must have a lot of enemies to keep a man permanently in such a post. Guy looked for only a moment longer. Then, still on his stomach, he wriggled back from danger, retreating to the safety of the ledge. One last glance around, then he turned and disappeared into the rocks behind him.

The cave was dark, but Guy had come prepared with a candle lantern and tinderbox. With the tiny lantern held before him, he moved towards the back of the cave and stepped through the narrow gap into the tunnel. The small flickering light revealed only a few steps ahead, but Guy knew where the tunnel would take him. The leather of his soles sounded loud upon the gritty stone beneath. The air grew stale. Water dripped down the dark hewn red walls. He followed on, until at last the passageway ended and before him lay the two wooden crates used by Helena and her servants in their escape. He took what he needed from his pockets before shrugging off his greatcoat on to the floor. At last he looked up to the small wooden hatch overhead. And the smile on his face was grim and determined. Guy stood up on the first crate and prepared to enter the south-west tower of Dunleish Castle.

Helena paced the blue bedchamber in Seamill Hall for the hundredth time. The book lay abandoned on the bed. She could not stop thinking about Guy and Emma and Dunleish. And neither could she banish the name that she had seen written upon that letter. Tregellas, the Wicked Earl, a man like Stephen by all accounts, a man to whom Guy would send her, a man who was his brother. It didn't make sense. Intrinsically she trusted Guy, could not believe there was anything sinister about him. He had treated her well, with respect, with kindness. He wanted her, yet he did not take her. Had said he would *take* nothing of her.

She closed her eyes and could see the strong lines of his face, the piercing paleness of his eyes, the playfulness of his smile. Even now he was on his way to a monster's lair to save her sister. She did not doubt that he would give his all to do it too. Could he rescue Emma from Stephen, just as he had rescued her?

There had to be some other explanation about his brother. Maybe Stephen had been wrong. She doubted that: Stephen was never wrong. She sat down by the window, mulling the matter, barely seeing what was before her. A small red-breasted robin hopped along the garden wall to perch upon the gate. Black birds scurried beneath the russet-leaved bushes. Three women walked past up on the road with baskets hung over their arms. A horse trotted by. Helena decided she could do nothing other than ask Guy of the matter when he returned…if he returned. She tried to push the fear from her mind, to stay positive.

Guy was right. It was a risky venture, but the odds were stacked in his favour. Stephen was not there and that alone meant there was a good chance of Guy's success. And it was better surely than Guy calling Stephen out. Or so she tried to convince herself. But her hands grew as cold as ice and a ripple of foreboding snaked down her spine. She glanced uneasily around the bedroom. Nothing was out of place. A clock ticked upon the mantel. Flames licked lively in the fireplace. But the air was growing colder. Helena knew she was not a woman given to fancies. She had spent the last five years deliberately deadening all feeling. And yet now… She scolded herself for being foolish. Daylight dimmed. She glanced out of the window, looked up to the sky. The clouds had darkened, rendering the day sinister and gloomy. Helena shivered. She was becoming like those women Guy had spoken of—fanciful, hysterical. She would sit by the fire, quietly read Mrs Weir's book and wait for Guy to return.

But Helena made no move. Indeed, she found that she could not draw her eyes from the road at the top of the garden. She stared as if transfixed by the sight. Her scalp began to prickle. The hairs on the back of her neck stood on end. Her stomach clenched tightly. Still, Helena could not take her eyes from the empty road. Then she heard it: the distant gallop of horses, the far-off rumble of carriage wheels. The noise grew louder, and louder still, until a carriage appeared, its dark body swaying with the recklessness of its speed. The mouths of the four black horses that pulled it were foam-flecked and bloodied, their coats gleaming with sweat, but Helena was not looking at the horses. Her mouth gaped open. The blood drained from her face. Her heart plummeted into her stomach. She whirled and ran for the bedroom door, the wood hitting hard against the wall as she threw it open, the sound of her running footsteps echoing along the corridor. The coach sped off into the distance, its crest still visible upon its mud-splattered doors—a black devil on a red background.

Chapter Thirteen

'Mr Weir!' Helena burst into the drawing room to find only his wife sitting by the window, stitching her embroidery.

'Helena?' Annabel Weir's face contorted with shocked puzzlement. 'What on earth are you doing up? John said you had some sort of contagion and that I mustn't go near.'

Helena would have laughed at the crudity of John Weir's lie had she not been so desperate and determined to save Guy. Every second was critical. 'Where is your husband, ma'am?'

'Where he usually is—in the gunroom. But what is—?'

'Sorry,' shouted Helena over her shoulder as she sprinted to the door. 'No time to explain.' She threw open the door and almost collided with Mr Weir, who had heard the running footsteps and Helena's shouting.

'What in heaven's name!' His face scowled his anger. 'You were to stay within the bedchamber. That was the agreement. Guy shall hear of this.'

She was breathing hard from exertion and anxiety. 'Guy is in danger,' she panted. 'Stephen is back. His coach has just passed along the main road, travelling at speed.'

'Don't be absurd,' snapped Weir. 'Tayburn's in London.'

'He has returned.'

'It's not possible. He couldn't be back so soon, there's not enough time—'

'Mr Weir, we must warn Guy.' Her voice raised in frustration.

'Calm down, madam. You cannot even be sure that the coach was Tayburn's.'

It was all Helena could do to keep from yelling at him. 'Do you doubt that I know Sir Stephen's crest?' she demanded. 'Need I tell you what it stands for? You may stand here all day speculating on whether I have the right or wrong of it, and let Stephen catch Guy at Dunleish, but I, sir, will not.' She saw the subtle shift in his expression.

'We cannot stop Tayburn,' he said.

'We can try,' she countered. 'Will you help me or not, Mr Weir?' An idea was forming in her head. 'Guy took your rowing boat, but you have another, do you not?'

'I have a small sailing boat moored at the jetty.'

Then there was hope. 'Send one of your men on horseback to Brigurd Point. Have him hole the bottom of all boats there. We can sail from here, cutting up and landing at Dunleish.'

'They will see us. The waters all around the castle are exposed; that's why Guy took the route he did.'

'It does not matter,' she said. 'There is no time to do aught else. We can concoct a story to satisfy the guard.'

'He leaves a guard?' Weir's eyes squinted.

'Oh, yes,' she said grimly. A calm determination overrode her panic. Helena knew what she must do. 'There is always a guard.'

And then the pair of them whirled into action. Mr Weir barked orders to have a horse saddled with speed, then ran to the gunroom. Helena raced back upstairs, grabbed the dark fur-lined cloak and was back downstairs outlining a semblance of an explanation to his wide-eyed wife by the time Weir returned.

'Annabel, take the girls and the carriage to your parents' house. You must leave here immediately. Stay there until I come for you.' Mr Weir dropped a kiss to his wife's cheek.

'But, John…'

'Do as I say, Annabel. I do not want you here for Tayburn or his men to find.'

Mrs Weir's face was white and petrified, but she nodded at her husband's words.

There was no more time. Helena and Weir turned and began to run, leaving the back door to slam in their wake. The groom had already left, a small wood axe tucked neatly in his pocket. One horse stood ready, a boy holding the reins. Mr Weir stepped up in the stirrup, pulled Helena up before him. The beast sensed the tension, whinnied, reared up. Mr Weir steered him down the narrow briar-clad lane to the shore and then they were off, galloping across the ripple-marked sands, taking the short cut to the jetty. And with every drum of the hooves, every thrust of the saddle, Helena silently shouted his name: *Guy!* Again and again, *Guy! Guy! He is coming,* until it formed a mantra that obscured all else from her mind. Willing him to hear the silent message across the miles.

* * *

Guy ceased his tread upon the stone spiralling stairwell and listened. The distant hum of noises. The faint bang of a door. Nothing close. Yet he felt the sense of danger all around him, stronger now than ever before. He carried on up the stairs, tried to shrug it off, ignore it. The feeling persisted, growing in strength. For some reason he thought of Helena, Helena with her red hair flowing long in wild wanton waves. Helena reaching out to him. Lord, but he was growing soft. But he smiled all the same. He found the top of the stairs, stole quickly and quietly along the corridor. And then he was at the chamber marked with an X on the map. There was no key within the lock. No guard at the door. Guy's eyes narrowed. The doorknob twisted beneath his hand and the door swung open. He pushed it right back in case anyone was standing behind it, then stepped across the threshold and no further. The room was dim, lit by neither candle nor firelight. The tiny narrow window looked out at a sky that had darkened to a charcoal grey. He scanned the space, eyes moving quickly, taking in the small bed in the corner beside the blackened hearth and the pile of thin blankets. There was not another stick of furniture within the room. He sensed the movement rather than saw it.

The girl was standing in the corner along from the door and furthest from the window.

He stepped quickly forwards and whispered her name. 'Emma?'

She stared at him in defiant silence, fear blatant in her eyes.

'Helena has sent me to rescue you.'

Still, she gave no response and he wondered if Tayburn's treatment had rendered her senseless.

'Emma,' he said again, reaching a hand slowly towards her. 'We have not much time. Quickly. Come, I will help you.'

'Helena sent you?' she whispered at last.

'Yes.' His fingers beckoned her forward.

'Then she really is alive?'

'Very much so when I left her on the mainland.' Guy flashed the girl a reassuring smile.

She made a funny little noise, half sigh, half sob, and then her hand found his.

'My name is Varington.'

She nodded.

Keeping the girl behind him he turned to leave the room.

'Wait!' she whispered.

He turned with impatience.

'We cannot leave Agnes and Old Tam. I heard him say what he was going to do to them. He is saving them to make her watch.'

'Helena's servants? The ones she believed had drowned the night of her escape?'

Emma nodded. 'They helped her get away.'

'Where are they?'

'In the dungeon. He said he would send me to join them if I tried to leave this room.'

'So you stayed.'

Another nod. 'You don't know what he's like. I don't know how she could have stood it all those years. He hasn't even touched me and I cannot bear it.'

Guy's voice was grim. 'Then we had best make our way to the dungeon.'

* * *

The black carriage bypassed Kilbride village before drawing up at the house near Brigurd Point. Tayburn barely waited for the carriage to stop before he leapt down. The front door of the house was already open, the manservant waiting in the hallway, silver tray in hand with a crystal glass of his master's brandy upon it. Tayburn snatched the glass, drained its contents and clattered the empty glass back down on the tray. Then, without so much as a word in the direction of his wife who stood silent and unsure in the hallway, he turned and was gone, back out of the house, on to the fresh horse standing ready for him, galloping towards Seamill Hall.

Caroline Tayburn's respite was short, for her husband returned less than half an hour later, slamming the door in his wake, his face ruddy with rage.

'Ready my sailing boat this instant!'

The house sprang into action. Bodies ran this way and that, voices murmuring quietly.

'Caroline!' he roared. 'Caroline, where the hell are you?'

She appeared in the doorway to the drawing room.

'About bloody time! We leave for Dunleish—now.' His eyes were dark and devilish, the snarl on his lips promised violence.

Lady Tayburn's gaze slid to the girl whose arms were imprisoned in her husband's grip. She saw the maid's clothing and guessed that Stephen had brought the girl back with him from Seamill Hall. 'What…what has happened?' asked Caroline, and then regretted it.

Tayburn turned the full force of his gaze upon her and

she shrank back. 'While I have been chasing the length and breadth of the country, Varington has slipped across the water to Dunleish. I'm sure that Weir's maid here will be only too happy to relay the details of the matter to you once we are aboard the boat.' He threw the girl at his wife. 'Keep her safe. If she escapes, I'll kill you both.'

The maid, Senga, stumbled and fell her length along the floor.

Tayburn turned at the approach of his manservant.

'Well?' Tayburn moved towards him.

The man retreated. 'Sir.' His voice shook and his face was white.

Senga started to scramble to her feet.

'Stay down!' barked Tayburn at her, then turned his attention back to his man. 'What have you to tell me?' he demanded in a quiet, deadly voice.

His servant swallowed hard and in a hushed whisper told the news that Sir Stephen would not want to hear. 'The boats have been holed.'

Not one muscle on Tayburn's face shifted. There was silence. Three faces with horrified anticipation stared at him. Nobody moved.

'Take the large sailing boat from the boathouse. If it is not ready to sail in ten minutes, you will find that your head is no longer attached to your body.' He hunkered down on his haunches and looked directly into Senga's eyes as she lay on the floor. His fingers moved to grip her face. 'You did not tell me of that little detail, my dear.'

'I didnae know,' the girl sobbed, 'honest, I didnae.'

'That's what they all say.' The pressure of his fingers increased against her cheek. 'You'll be pleased to know that both the wind and tide are in our favour.' The fingers pressed harder still. 'And *Cerberus* can outrun any boat in these parts. You had better utter a prayer for your master.' And then he released her, and, stepping over her prostrate body, disappeared up the staircase of Brigurd House.

Helena's eyes were still closed when she heard the thud of the heavy studded door swing shut behind them, and she knew that she had returned to Dunleish. The ruse had worked: Weir's pretence of dragging her back here against her will, returning Sir Stephen's woman in hope of currying favour. The familiar smell of the place filled her nostrils and she feared for one horrible moment that she would not be able to go through with their plan. And then she thought of Guy…and of Emma, and knew what she must do.

Weir was talking with them again. She even heard a laugh, the chink of glasses, the pouring of liquid, the smell of brandy. And then she felt herself passed to another and willed herself to stay limp and fluid-like as she was. Her head lolled against the man's arm and she stoppered her nose against the unwashed smell of him. The opening and closing of doors, and then they were climbing, his feet heavy, almost slovenly against the stone below, hers brushing lightly against the walls as the stairwell wound round to the right. Up to the first floor. Her eyes were still closed as he laid her clumsily down on the bed. She did not need to open them to know where she was.

A jangle of keys sounded, then the mumble of Rab's voice, as he spoke almost beneath his breath, 'No escapin' for you this time, hen. Just wait till his lordship sees what we have for him.'

Footsteps and the thump of the door. Scrape of key in the lock, shutting her in securely; there was, after all, no way out of the room except through the door. The footsteps receded and the jangle of the keys grew faint. She opened her eyes and saw the damp plaster-moulded ceiling above. Helena smiled and knew she was exactly where she wanted to be—locked alone in the room that Stephen had given over to be her bedchamber.

She sat up quickly, swung her legs over the side of the bed and stood up. From the wooden chest in the corner she retrieved a pile of clothes, which she posi-tioned to loosely resemble the sleeping form of a body beneath the blanket on the bed. Then she slipped her fingers into the pocket of her dress and produced the silver key. She stared at it for a moment, praying that Weir would be able to keep the men distracted. She pulled her fur-lined cloak more tightly around her and, forcing herself to stay calm, she stepped towards the door. The click of her shoes sounded loud against the floor. She stopped, listened, heard nothing. The shoes slipped easily from her feet and were quickly hidden beneath the bed. And when she stood again she knew that she was ready. The stone floor was chilled against her bare feet. Noiselessly she padded across to the door, inserted the key into the lock and turned it.

The corridor outside was empty; there was no moulded plaster out here, no painted or papered walls or furniture. The walls were the bare red sandstone blocks laid by men three hundred years ago. The floor comprised great slabs of stone. The whole passageway was lit by a single old-fashioned flambeau positioned at a midway point, its unsteady flicker of flames casting deep shadows. Helena knew where she was going. Quickly and quietly she hurried further along the corridor towards the room over which she had marked an X on the map, knowing that, if Emma and Guy were not there, she would have to go down to the dungeon.

Having freed Old Tam and the maidservant Agnes from the dungeon, Guy led their exit from that dismal place. The little group hurried along the flambeaux-lit damp corridor, heading towards the south-west tower and its secret escape.

From up above came the almighty slam of the front door, the echo of the thud reverberating throughout the castle. Everyone halted.

'What was that?' The words were Emma's, although everyone thought them.

Foreboding prickled across Guy's scalp. And the answer that whispered through his mind was not what he wanted to hear. It was not possible. Tayburn was in London. He could not be here. Yet the sensation of danger persisted through the blanket of logic. 'It's nothing. Keep moving and keep quiet.' His voice was steady and confident. He gestured them to keep walking. The light of the flambeau high on their left-hand side glittered and danced upon the blade of Guy's knife. No one in the little group noticed that his grip around the handle had tightened.

A scream sounded. A haunting shrill cry that carried down from the floors above. A cry that pierced their ears and was no more. The ensuing silence seemed only to heighten the horror of what they had heard.

'It's him. He's back.' Fear made the words shake as they slipped from Emma's mouth.

The maid gave a whimper and clutched at the wall. 'May God have mercy on our souls.'

'Keep going,' Guy said grimly, and forced them onwards.

* * *

Helena was in the dungeon when she heard the scream and her stomach turned upside down. She had heard such screams before and knew very well what it was and who had caused it. The retch forced its way up to her mouth. First one and then another, until she thought she would vomit the contents of her stomach upon the floor. Her legs began to shake and the over-whelming rush of fear paralysed her so that she could not move or speak or even breathe. She stood there in the dank dismal room with its ripe stench of death; no matter how much she willed her feet to move, they remained frozen. And then, in the dark horror of what surrounded her, she thought of Guy. Guy, with his all-too-perceptive gaze. Guy, with his smile that moved so readily to his mouth. Guy, who had risked every-thing…for her. And as the warmth in her heart thawed the fear, Helena's eyes fastened upon the glint of the small metal tool that lay amidst the filth of the floor close by the opened manacles. She moved forward, stooped, and as her fingers closed around it the courage rose within her, for she knew that Guy had been here and that he had not left alone. Over in the corner the rats were squeaking, but Helena did not hear. Nor did she notice the damp stinking straw beneath her feet as she ran towards the door. For Helena knew Guy's plan. There was only one way he would leave the castle. She began to make her way towards the south-west tower.

They were treading down the stairs of the south-west tower, only yards from the room with the secret tunnel. Guy stepped off the last of the stone stairs, rounded to the right. And stopped. The smile wiped from his face. His grip upon the knife handle tightened instinctively.

'Get back!' he yelled behind him. But it was too late. He looked ahead into the blackness of the man's eyes. Saw the white hair drawn back and tied with the black ribbon and he knew the name of the man he looked upon without any need for an introduction: Tayburn.

Chapter Fourteen

'Varington,' Tayburn said with a slight sneer. 'Come to steal more of what is mine?' His eyes looked from Agnes, to Emma and back to Guy. 'It seems that we share the same taste in women.' Tayburn stood, relaxed in his manner, almost leisurely. His gaze flickered momentarily over the old man in the background. 'But then again, maybe you have quite a different reason for stealing this particular choice of…possessions.'

A ripple of fresh air fanned across the still dankness of the passageway as Guy looked into the darkness of the man's eyes and knew he was in the presence of evil. There was something about Tayburn that did not need the man to speak or move or even make so much as an expression upon his face. Just his presence seemed to foul the air.

'What, nothing to say to me in return, Varington? Cat got your tongue?' His black eyes glanced away. 'It soon will have,' he said in a much quieter tone, but still loud enough for Guy to hear.

Guy retreated, one step and then another, until the

women and old man were backed further up the stairs, then he jumped back down to the lowest stone-carved step so that his body blocked Tayburn's route to Emma and Agnes and Old Tam. 'Your argument is with me. Let the others go.'

Tayburn laughed and the sound sent a shiver to the depths of Guy's soul. 'I find myself attached to these particular possessions. I am loath to let them go.'

'They are no man's possessions.'

The laugh diminished to a smile, and it was a truly horrific sight to behold. Guy heard Emma's gasp from behind him. 'They are what I deem them to be. Besides, you have nothing with which to bargain.'

'Really?'

'You're in my castle. And now that you're here you shall never leave, not even when the flesh has been stripped from your bones. As I said, you have nothing with which to bargain.'

'He has Helena!' Emma shouted with false bravado from her perch up on the stairs behind Guy. 'If you kill us, you shall never get her back.'

Tayburn raised one dark slanting eyebrow so that it touched against a lock of his colourless hair. 'Really, my dear, you are misinformed. He has not even that. Helena is back here where she belongs…with me.'

'No!' Emma shouted.

Guy could hear the vehemence in her denial. 'It makes no difference. I will not bargain with Helena's life,' he said.

'Then we will all lose ours,' sobbed Emma.

Tayburn smoothed back a strand of hair that had freed itself from his ribbon. 'She saw my carriage pass, you see.' He turned his attention to his middle finger of

his right hand and picked at a nail. 'And had some
foolish notion to warn you of my return.' He glanced
up at Guy. 'Weir brought her here.'

Guy betrayed nothing by his face. Helena would not
come back to this place, a place she had risked all to
leave. And he had her promise that she would seek out
his brother if the plan went awry. But then he heard
again the words she had uttered during their conversation that morning. *I would not just abandon you in
Dunleish!* And he knew that Tayburn was telling the
truth. In that moment he saw again the sweetness of her
smile, and heard again the softness of her voice, and
something contracted in Guy's chest. Helena. He had
seen her hurt and her sadness, her fear and her fury, her
passion…and her love. And Guy knew what it was that
he felt as he stood there in the depths of Tayburn's lair.
He recognised the emotion even though he had never
felt it before. And he almost laughed that he could suffer
such a revelation right here, right now, with Tayburn and
his men armed and before him and with those he had
tried to help frightened and cowed behind him.

'And in return I have brought him one of his maid-
servants. She proved most co-operative after a little
persuasion.'

Still, Guy did not speak. Outnumbered. Out-armed.
Unwilling to abandon those he had come here to rescue.
Guy's army training kicked in. Emotions shut down.
Eyes scanned relative positions, distances, potential
exits. Brain measured strengths and weaknesses. Mouth
played for time.

'He's lying, isn't he?' Emma's voice wobbled with
uncertainty. 'Isn't he?' and there was a helplessness in
her pleading.

'I never lie,' Tayburn said in a good-natured tone. 'I have no need to.' His eyes gleamed black and deadly.

'I find that hard to believe,' muttered Guy.

'Which? My unparalleled honesty or the fact that the trollop is back here under lock and key, returned to me?'

Guy gave a disparaging laugh. 'Both.'

'You'll see for yourself, Varington, soon enough.'

The corner of Guy's mouth flickered. 'Really?' He raised his eyebrows in mock surprise. 'Somehow I don't think so.' From his vantage point he had clear views down each of the passageways that led to the stairwell, but Guy had seen enough. He kept his eyes fixed upon Tayburn.

Tayburn's upper lip curled by just the slightest degree, exposing eye teeth that were too long and pointed to have been fashioned by nature. 'What can you mean, Varington? I hold all of the cards, I believe: Helena, the poxy servants that aided her escape, her sister, Weir…and, of course, you. And you, you hold, let me see…' He pretended to think, scratching a finger against his chin. 'Mmm, that's right, you, Lord Varington—' the finger spun off his chin to point condemningly at Guy '—hold precisely nothing.'

Guy shrugged, as if it were of no consequence. 'Perhaps,' he admitted. 'But then again, it may be that your vision has been somewhat obscured.'

'What the hell are you talking of?' Tayburn scowled.

'Merely a matter of the wool being pulled over your eyes. You did not think I would come here to Dunleish without a card or two of my own up my sleeve, so to speak.'

The black eyes narrowed to a slit and Tayburn stepped forward, revealing for the first time the long sword in his left hand. 'Nothing remains hidden from me,' he said. 'I know everything.' And each word was enunciated with meticulous care. He touched his right index finger slowly, meaningfully, to the centre of his forehead—the third eye. Guy felt the fear that rippled through both Tayburn's men and the little group that huddled on the stairwell. And he understood something of the villain's power.

Tayburn raised the sword and pointed it directly at Guy.

The smile that broke across Guy's face infuriated Tayburn just as Guy had intended it to. 'Do it now,' he said, and never for a moment did the pale gaze waver from the dark one of Tayburn. Tempting death. Facing evil. The smile did not falter. 'Now,' he repeated, 'if you dare.'

And it seemed that Sir Stephen Tayburn was only too happy to oblige.

Helena's bare feet made no sound upon the stone floor of the passageway. The voices ahead told her precisely where she must go. She heard the short panicked scream of a woman and knew it was Emma. Quickly and quietly she made her way on, following down the passageway, just another shadow that moved beneath the flickering of the flambeaux, the long fur-lined cloak pulled around her. A slight dark shape.

She was close enough to discern the words. The voices were no longer just a hum or babble. Her feet carried her closer and closer still, until she reached the small dark alcove in the wall and slunk into it. Twenty paces at most to where Stephen and his men stood by the recess of the stairwell. Guy was there, backed up against the stairs, the knife in his hand holding off Stephen—for now. She could not see Emma and guessed that her sister must be somewhere up on the stairs.

The voices carried clear enough: Stephen's taunting, crowing, making her blood run cold, telling Guy that she was here, ensuring that he knew she was lost. Her stomach churned and the thought of Stephen raised the nausea to the back of her throat until she feared it would betray her presence. She pressed herself against the wall, clinging to the damp rough stone, fearful to let go, knowing that he was round there, knowing what he would do to her. And across her mind the thought flashed that she could just run away while Stephen and his men were distracted.

Then she heard Guy. 'I will not bargain with Helena's life,' he said, and his voice was firm and resolute. She felt ashamed of her fear and of its selfishness and most of all of the tempting little thought that had beckoned her and which, albeit for the tiniest second, she had contemplated. *I will not bargain with Helena's life.* Somewhere deep inside the small flame of determination within her roared to a fire. And she would not risk his life. Not against Stephen. Not Guy. Not the man she loved. She had no weapon. She had no one other than herself. Neither fact mattered. Stephen meant to kill Guy. And Helena meant to stop him. She stepped silently into the passageway and began to walk, step by noiseless step, towards Sir Stephen Tayburn.

Even as she walked she did not know truly what she meant to do. But she could see Guy quite clearly now and her soul was filled with a fiery determination to save him. He spoke with Stephen as if the two were seated across a gaming table and not facing one another across the dim passage deep in the monster's castle. Without fear. Holding off Stephen and his men. The knife blade glinted within Guy's hand and Helena knew that Stephen would have his sword. She wondered that none of them heard her. Expected with every footstep, with every breath, that they would look round and discover her. But they did not.

Curiously, now that she was out here and moving to face him, her fear was less than it had been skulking behind the corner. Step by step, closer and closer, creeping ever forward. Her hands were open and by her side. The cloak hung useless across her shoulders. Still, she walked on, her sole purpose to give the others one last chance, to save them from Stephen. Not once did Guy look at her, not once did he see her. She wondered, within the madness of the moment, if she had faded to invisibility. Until she heard Guy's words…

'But then again, it may be that your vision has been somewhat obscured.'

'What the hell are you talking of?' She heard the scowl in Stephen's voice.

'Merely a matter of the wool being pulled over your eyes.'

And she knew then what to do, for she understood Guy's message.

Her feet stepped and her fingers were at her collarbone, unfastening the heavy weight of the cloak. Step. The cloak unfurled, a silent sail upon the mast of her body. Step.

'Do it now,' he said, and never for a moment did Guy's gaze waver from Stephen. 'Now, if you dare.'

Too late Stephen sensed her presence. Too late he turned. Helena threw the cloak over his head and all hell broke loose. With an almighty roar he fumbled with the material that blinded him, struggling to pull the cloak clear. But the sword was heavy and unwieldy in his hand and the material thick and copious. A string of curses and obscenities flowed from beneath the cloak. Stephen's minions stood as if frozen, shock etched upon their faces at the unexpected drama unfolding before them. Stephen roared for their assistance, but his sword was flailing around him, desperate to prevent Guy from getting near, and no man there was foolish enough to brave it. One of them shouted, 'Drop your sword, sir. We cannae get near!'

Tayburn's sword stayed firmly in his hand.

It took a woman to face it. Helena did not hesitate. One small window of time, and then it would be gone. All that separated her from Guy was the long whirling blade in Stephen's hand. She ran, dodging Stephen's violent movements as best she could across the small space of flagstones.

'Guy!'

Then she was in his arms and pushed behind him in one swift flowing move. And even though the cloak was being ripped from Stephen's eyes as she watched, she was filled with relief.

Guy moved fast, striking just as the fur-lined material landed in a pile on the floor. One hand yanked at the snow-white hair, pulling the head back, exposing Tayburn's throat. The knife in his other hand was small but exceedingly sharp. Its blade touched against the stretched skin of Tayburn's throat.

'Tell your men to drop their weapons or you're dead.' Guy stood tall behind Tayburn.

'I'll see you in hell first,' Tayburn sneered.

The smile upon Guy's face was tight and grim. The

pressure of his right hand increased. A thin red edging appeared along the length of the knife blade where it contacted Tayburn's skin. 'God knows how much I've dreamed of this moment. Go on, give me an excuse to slit your throat open and watch the lifeblood ebb from your veins. It would not atone for all you have inflicted upon Helena, but it would be a start.'

Tayburn's eyes, as black and hard as polished jet pebbles, stared at his men, and still, the words did not come from his mouth.

Guy's right hand moved infinitesimally and a tiny rivulet of blood dribbled down Tayburn's neck.

Tayburn's men stared with unease at what was unfolding before their very eyes, trapped in a dilemma to which there was no right outcome.

'Do as he says. Drop your weapons,' Tayburn ground out.

'Pity,' said Guy with sarcasm. 'I was looking forward to dispatching you.'

Tayburn said nothing, but his malice was palpable, a living breathing thing.

Three knives, two pistols and a cudgel clattered to the floor.

Helena made to move forward to collect them.

Guy stayed her with a word. 'No.' He would not have her stray too close to any of Tayburn's rabble. He shouted the instruction over his shoulder, 'Tam, take their weapons and distribute them amongst the women. Keep the cudgel for yourself. And take the rope from my left pocket and bind each man's hands.'

Helena's eyes widened as the old man came out of the darkness of the stairwell. 'Tam?' The word was filled with disbelief.

'Miss Helena…' the old man sighed '…I was so feart for you. We both were.'

'Tam.' Guy gestured towards the pile of weapons. 'It would be better to save the reunion until we are elsewhere.'

Tam nodded and did as he was bid.

Guy spoke to Tayburn's men. 'You lot, get in front of me where I can see you, and take us to the front door. Do as I say and no one gets hurt.' Only when they were in front of him and facing away up the corridor did he speak to Helena. 'Helena, you know the way out of here. Stay at my shoulder and let me know if they are playing me false.' Guy kept his voice curt and to the point. He allowed his eyes to meet momentarily with hers, willing her to stay strong, and then it was back to the task in hand. The situation was precarious and it would take only one slip for the advantage to fall to Tayburn. One sign of weakness and all would be lost. And Guy had no intention of losing Helena, not to Tayburn, not to anyone.

A soft murmur of assent.

'If you think that you can just walk out of here, then you are grossly mistaken, Varington.' Tayburn's voice was strained against the blade. 'Escape is impossible. Just ask Helena, she'll tell you, won't you, my love?'

Guy felt Helena stiffen by his side and when she spoke her words were low and filled with loathing. 'I am not your love,' she said. 'I was never your love.'

'But you are mine all the same, Helena McGregor. And you'll never escape me.'

'Quiet!' Guy jerked Tayburn's head back harder. 'We'll all escape you, Tayburn, because you're going to take us to the front door. Now, start walking before I change my mind and slit your throat.'

'Very amusing, Varington; I've men everywhere. Kill me and you'd not make it two paces out of here before they'd cut you down.'

'Really?' Guy raised an eyebrow. 'Loyalty bought through fear and brutality is a shallow thing. Do you honestly think that your men would act to stop me once you are dead? Why would they risk their lives once the threat you hold over them is gone? Face it, Tayburn, with you dead there's not a man present that will lift so much as a finger to stop us walking out of here.'

Tayburn's mouth tightened. 'Liar!' But the word had a hollow ring to it.

Slowly the motley group moved off towards the north-west tower, making their way beneath the flickering flambeaux that lit the way along the corridor.

Helena could scarcely believe that they would make it. It seemed an audacious plan. And yet they edged their way, step by step, inch by inch along one damp redstone passageway after another, ever closer towards the great blackened front door. The tension within the group was almost unbearable. They moved in silence, only Guy's voice sounding every so often in caution. Tayburn's men led on, unarmed, hands bound behind their backs. Next came Tayburn, hands tied, knife held to his back, an unwilling hostage, being frog-marched by Guy. Helena walked by his side, the pistol heavy in her hand. Behind her, Old Tam, Emma and Agnes provided a rearguard.

They were on the stairwell, heading up towards the front door via the north-west tower. She was under no illusion to the danger. She didn't need the warning that flashed in Guy's eyes to know. The stairs were narrow, too narrow to let Guy keep his hold upon Tayburn. He

shifted the knife to prod against Tayburn's back, kept a
grip of the rope that bound the villain's hands in his own.
The stairwell was dimly lit, making it all too easy to
stumble, to fall. It was here that Tayburn's chance of
escape was greatest. One slip. One mistake. That's all
that Tayburn needed. Helena prayed that he would not
get it.

Her left hand leaned against the dampness of the
wall, following the curve of the stairwell, ensuring that
she did not miss her footing. They moved onwards,
upwards, stair by stair, and gradually the staleness of the
air that had hung around the dungeons faded. They
passed a window, nothing more than a slit in the wall,
and fresh sea air filled their nostrils. Even though the
whole place was damp and cold, Helena could feel the
sweat prickle against her back. And still, they kept
going. The pistol pulled heavy at her wrist, yet she kept
it levelled, ever ready to meet the challenge she was
convinced would come. Tayburn moved without resistance, hands tied, Guy's knife pressed against his back.
So why did Helena have the overwhelming conviction
that something would go wrong? It was as Tayburn had
said—they could not simply walk out of Dunleish.
Could they? Helena's feet moved ever up, and not once
did her eyes cease their scanning, not once did her
fingers slacken their grip against the pistol's handle. The
paltry light dimmed. The flambeau that should have
burned to light the stairs stood black and cold. And in
the air hung the scent of its dowsing.

Helena felt the hairs on the back of her neck stand
on end. The entirety of her scalp prickled. Tension
stretched the air until it was tight and thin. Guy could
feel it too. She watched him slow, pull Tayburn back in

closer against his body. Tayburn emitted a small breathy groan. She couldn't see Guy's knife, but she suspected it prodded all the harder at Tayburn's flesh. And she was glad. *Be careful*! she wanted to shout to Guy. *There is something amiss*! But that would only distract him and she could not risk such a thing. Besides, she had no basis, other than her own instinct, for the sudden resurfacing of her fears.

Beneath the blackened stump of the expired flame the air seemed to chill. There was only the sound of their feet treading upon worn stone. Anxiety wound Helena's body so tight that she could almost feel the constriction around her chest and throat. She tried to shake it off. Willed herself not to think upon it. If they could just make it out of the stairwell, then it was a straight passage to the door… and escape. So close. A shaft of light beckoned ahead. Nearly there. They were going to make it. Lord above, but they were going to make it.

It was the last thought that passed through Helena's head before Tayburn suddenly twisted around and levelled a hard kick at Guy, the force of which propelled him against Helena. Her hand grasped at the wall, but there was nothing to grip on the bare curve of stone. She felt her feet stumble beneath her, could not catch her balance, shouted a warning to those below as she began to topple backwards towards the long spiral of the stairs.

The fall did not come. Helena found herself jerked back up. Someone was pulling hard against her outstretched arm, hoisting her back to safety.

'Helena!' She heard his voice beside her ear, felt herself pressed momentarily against the warmth of his body. Only when he was sure that she was safe did he release her. But it was too late. Tayburn was gone. They could hear the clatter of his boots up the last of the stairs out on to the passageway above; could hear too the roar of command to his men. In that single moment of decision Guy had chosen to loose his grip upon Tayburn's rope in order to save Helena. And Helena knew it. She knew too the price that his sacrifice would cost. She could hear it in the gleeful urgency that filled Tayburn's voice.

'No!' she whispered. 'Oh, God, no,' and the gaze that she raised to Guy's was full of anguish. 'We must head back down!' She grabbed his hand and whirled.

'No.' Guy touched her shoulder.

She turned, plucked at Guy's coat, trying to pull him forward. 'Quickly, come on!'

'Helena, we cannot reach the tunnel before him.'

Tam and the two women stopped where they were. Emma and Agnes's eyes bulged with fear.

'You might without me. Go on without me, ma lord.' It was Tam that spoke.

'It is a fine thing you offer, Tam,' said Guy, acknowledging the old man's bravery, 'but I need you to look after the women. Find the tunnel, get them to safety. I'll delay Tayburn as best I can.'

Tam gave a nod.

And then Guy's hand found Helena's and pulled her up the stair that separated them, so that she was close to him. His fingers brushed against her cheek, his touch so light she was not sure that he touched her at all. His head lowered to hers and his mouth found hers. The kiss was swift and fierce and concentrated, as if he had condensed a multitude of feelings into that one sliver of contact. He moved away, but not before the whisper of his words had found her ear. She stared at him in disbelief and felt the tears prick against her eyes. It did not matter that Stephen was above. It did not matter that she would die. She had heard his words and in comparison all else seemed small and inconsequential. *I love you, Helena McGregor.* Then he crept stealthily up the stairs, knife in hand, ready to face Stephen.

Guy heard their footsteps recede as Tam led the women down the stairwell. He did not look back, just kept his gaze focused ahead, ready, waiting for the attack that he knew would come. Helena's scent filled his nose, blocking out the damp smell of Dunleish. The heat of her lips still lingered on his, warming him from the cold. The imprint of her soft body was a barrier to all hurts. And he was glad that he had told her the truth before it was too late to do so. He prayed that she would reach the tunnel, but he suspected the worst. Tayburn's men would no doubt be scuttling towards the bottom of the south-west tower, intent on blocking Helena's route to freedom. Even so, Tayburn would never have her. Guy swore it on all that was holy. Death was in the air. Tayburn had been right about one thing—Guy would never leave Dunleish alive, but then again, neither would Tayburn. Tayburn would never touch Helena ever again; Guy would make sure of that.

Helena followed the others only as far as the next floor down.

'Emma.' She pressed a kiss to her sister's cheek. 'Forgive me for bringing all of this upon you. Did Tayburn…?' She could barely bring herself to ask the question. 'Did he hurt you very badly?'

Emma gave a sigh. 'He kept me locked in a room, but that is all,' she reassured her sister. 'He did not touch me. You are all he thinks of, no one else. Not even that poor creature who is his wife. She sent me food and blankets. She knew I was here and yet she spoke not one word against him.'

'Poor Caroline. Her fear and pride are too great to do anything else. Do not judge her so harshly, Emma.' She pulled Emma into a hug. 'Thank God, you are safe.'

Emma drew her a wry smile. 'I do not think any of us are very safe at this minute.'

'Come on, Miss Helena, Miss Emma, this is no time to be bletherin'.' Old Tam waved them on with gnarled old hands.

Helena released her sister and caught hold of Agnes's hand. 'Dear Agnes, you are as a ghost come back from the dead to me. I thought that you and Tam had perished in the wrecking of the *Bonnie Lass*.'

'No' us, miss. We had the misfortune to be washed up at Brigurd Point. They soon had us sent back here.'

'I'm so sorry.' Helena squeezed the maid's hand.

'Lassies!' Old Tam admonished.

Helena dropped her voice to a whisper. 'Go on ahead. Get Tam out of here. There's a rowing boat beached down near Gull Point; keep to the shoreline and head for that. I'll meet you there.'

'But we can't leave without you. Where are you going?' It was Emma that raised the protest.

'Don't worry, I'll be there,' lied Helena. 'There's something I have to do first. Now, get going or none of us will make it out. I'm counting on you to ready the boat.' And then she slipped away along the passageway before anyone could protest further.

* * *

Guy's back hugged the wall close to the top of the stairs. He shifted the knife into his left hand and slipped the right into his coat pocket.

'You might as well come out, Varington. Or would you rather I had my men fetch you like a rabbit from its hole?' Tayburn made no effort to disguise the excitement in his voice.

'Afraid to face me yourself, Tayburn, that you must have your minions do your dirty work?'

'I'm afraid of nothing,' came back Tayburn's voice.

There was a pause, a silence. 'We both know that is not true,' said Guy.

Tayburn laughed, and the sound was grating and cruel.

'Which of us do you think Helena will choose? You or me, Tayburn?'

Tayburn's laughter stopped. 'She's mine, whether she wills it or not.'

'She was never yours.'

Tayburn grabbed a pistol from the man nearest him. 'You think to just steal her from me? Nobody takes what is mine and lives. And know this, Varington, I'll make her sorry for running to you, more sorry than she could ever have imagined.'

Guy gritted his teeth and blocked out the image that Tayburn sought to sow.

'Shall I let you watch? Watch while she writhes beneath me in my bed? Watch while I touch that creamy soft skin?' Tayburn's voice was creeping closer.

Guy's jaw clamped tighter. His right hand slipped from his coat pocket and in it was a pistol.

'Come on, Varington, you know that you want to.'

Guy listened to the voice rather than its baiting words, pinpointing that Tayburn was almost centrally located perhaps fifteen feet from the top of the stairs. Close enough. Guy's feet pushed hard against stone and he rounded the last few stairs to the top two at a time, propelling round the corner and out of the stairwell at full force. The pistol aimed at the spot from which Tayburn's voice had sounded. His finger moved over the trigger, tensed to squeeze the metal lever that would send the lead ball into Tayburn's heart. Something knocked Guy's legs from beneath him, sending him sprawling face first in the filth of the floor. The pistol clattered to the ground, its bullet knocking a shard of stone from the wall, before landing misshapen and useless. He felt the weight of a man drop on to his back and then his arms were wrenched behind until they were almost clear of their sockets. A hand ripped at his hair, forcing him up to his knees while his wrists were bound so tight that the blood ceased to flow there. Someone pulled his head back hard, jerking his face up until his eyes focused upon Tayburn.

'Didn't hear Wylie coming up behind you, did you, Varington? You're not as good as you think.' Tayburn smiled. 'You should have killed me while you had the chance; I won't be so obliging with you.' He drew back his arm and landed his fist against Guy's jaw.

'Stop!' The voice rang out from the other end of the passageway.

Tayburn stopped. Looked around. And his eyes glittered with greed and lust and disbelief at the sight that met his eyes. 'Helena,' he said, 'how good of you to join us.'

'Let him go, Stephen.' Helena walked slowly forward. Tayburn's men started to move towards her, but he gestured them back. 'Why would I want to do that? He's had you, tasted you, *my* woman. There's a choice of options, but release is not one of them.' His eyes swept over the contours of her hips, following up to where the fine wool of her bodice curved around her breasts.

The sway of her hips ceased. She paused. 'Then you are not prepared to negotiate?' she asked.

'As I told *him* a little while ago—' Tayburn's foot dug against Guy's thigh '—one can only bargain when one has something worth bargaining with. Enlighten me as to what you have, Helena.'

She stood, her back very straight, her shoulders squared, her head held proud. 'I have myself,' she said.

He gave a grunt of amusement. 'You stand there as if you're some fine lady. Let me remind you that you're my whore, Helena,' he said, and enjoyed the cruelty of his words. 'You are mine to have when I wish. So I ask you again, with what do you bargain?'

Several tendrils of hair had escaped their pins to snake down her cheeks. She stepped closer until she was level with the window just beyond the great studded front door of Dunleish. His men's eyes swivelled between their master and herself. 'There is a difference between what is taken and that which is given.' Her gaze flickered fleetingly to Guy's, held for a second and swung back to Tayburn. She understood now why Guy had not bedded the woman he had made his mistress.

'No, Helena!' The words spilled from Guy's mouth.

Helena forced her face to remain impassive. 'Set Lord Varington free and I shall give you what you have only ever taken.'

'Do not do it, Helena!'

She could hear the anguish in Guy's plea, and, for all that her strength held, a single tear spilled from the corner of her eye and traced a solitary track down her cheek.

Tayburn looked from the pain and anger on Guy's face to the pale fragility of Helena's. And it was everything he could have wanted. 'You will wait until he's free, then you will refuse me.'

But she heard the desire in his voice. Tayburn was tempted. 'No,' she said. 'I give you my word.'

'Your word!' he spat. 'What does that mean? Nothing!'

'Helena, no. This is madness. He will kill me regardless. Do not do this thing. I am not worth it.'

But Guy's words only strengthened her determination. The price was small to save the life of the man she loved. Her hand slipped to her head, plucked out the pins one by one, and the deep red waves uncoiled to fall as a long heavy cloak over her shoulders. And as she did so a shaft of sunlight pierced the thick wall of sandstone, passing through the high slit of a window to bathe Helena in its spotlight. The light was soft and bright, its timing magically illuminating Helena's ethereal beauty, so that she seemed an illusion against the darkness surrounding her. Every man there turned to stare, entrapped in the spell woven by the simple action of the sun slipping from behind a cloud. And at its centre Helena remained oblivious to the effect that the sunbeam had wrought.

The rope bit into his skin as Guy strained his wrists against the binding. Blood trickled down from the wound to wet his fingers, but he did not slacken his effort. Helena might think that Tayburn could be held to a bargain, but Guy knew better. His life was forfeit;

Tayburn would never let him leave the island alive despite Helena's bargain. The fiend would take what she offered and give nothing in return. And Guy had no intention of letting Tayburn take anything from Helena ever again.

The sunlight flooded the single spot where she stood, streaming through the narrow hole in the wall as a beam straight from heaven, and everywhere else stayed dim and dank and shaded. Within the light her hair glowed a long burnished red, her skin was a soft velvet of cream and her smoky green eyes seemed to smoulder. A vision of Venus. A sight to enchant any man's gaze. But Guy saw that she had hidden every emotion from her face and he knew that she wore her mask, as he called it. Beneath it was a different woman altogether, a woman only Guy had seen, and she was more beautiful than the physical perfection that showed on the surface. And, despite the desperation of his situation, he felt his spirit soar with love. Love filled every pore of his being, until at last his gaze fell away into the darkness. Guy bided his time, waiting and watchful. His chance would come. Death was inevitable, but he'd damn well take out Tayburn in the process…and Helena would be safe.

She saw the men's faces and the way that they stared. She saw the lust and greed that Stephen could not hide. And she looked into the pale blue eyes of the man that knelt upon the floor and saw love and torment and guilt and anger. They did not need words. They did not need touch. Their love reached out and bound them together. Helena deliberately turned her face away and did not look again at Guy. She focused on Stephen. 'When Lord Varington's boat is clear of the shore, then I will go with you.'

'You ask a lot,' said Stephen.

She said nothing, just waited, the expression of sensual serenity upon her face belying the fear that welled within her. Guy's life hung in the balance, to be decided by the perverse whim of a tyrant's lust.

There was silence. Time stretched out long and languorously, until Helena thought the mask would slip from her face.

But she need not have worried. Stephen wanted that which he could not have. 'Get him to his feet. Take him down to the bay.'

Helena watched Stephen's men manhandle Guy along the passageway and out of the front door. Her feet carried her step by step in Guy's wake, and at her side stalked the dark figure of Stephen. She could smell him and, even though he did not touch her, her skin crawled with his proximity. Not once did she let herself think of what she had promised Stephen. Not once did her mind stray to the horror of what lay ahead. She thought only that Guy was being set free. The waves rumbled upon the shore. Overhead gulls circled and swooped. The speckled gravel of sea-crushed shells crunched as the bottom of the boat was pushed over them to slide into the cold winter water. She watched as Guy began to unfurl the sails. Noted that he was no sailor, for he appeared to be having a problem with the inside of the boat.

Guy let the men march him outside. The light white sky was a contrast to the gloom within the castle. His eyes squinted instinctively against the brightness. He would have to act soon. Time was running out. He started to dig in his heels, to struggle against the arms that held him, but the men only dragged him harder and faster across the uneven grass and rocks, down towards the sand, down towards the water. Guy saw where it was they were taking him. Across the small distance, beached just out of reach of the water was a small sailing boat—Weir's sailing boat to be precise. It was all Guy could do not to smile.

He gave up resisting, save for a small token effort and let the men propel him over the sand and haul him into the wooden belly of the boat, before a knife blade snatched at his wrists to free their binding. He did not try to escape as four pairs of arms loosened the boat from its bed of sand and gravel. The boat bobbed upon the water and the men walked with sodden feet and legs back on to the beach. Guy was on his knees, but he was not praying. He pulled haphazardly at the furl of the sail, knowing it would partially shield him from Tayburn's view. Then his hands moved swift and sure to the stern of the boat and rested upon the long oilskin-wrapped object that he knew Weir always kept there. He remembered Weir's words: *Seagulls make for good target practice.* This time he did smile and the smile was harsh and resolute and determined.

Stephen's voice sounded beside her. 'So, Helena, Varington is free, just as you wanted.'

Her gaze clung to Guy's figure in the small boat for a moment longer, then she wrenched her eyes away. 'Yes.' The single word dropped between them. The bright clear light dulled to grey as the clouds moved to hide the sun. Helena turned away. She did not look back. She did not notice that Stephen's own large sailing boat was not beached upon the shore where he had left it. Stephen took her arm. She did not pull away, just let him lead her back towards Dunleish and everything that awaited her there.

As Stephen turned to look back at Guy, an almighty bang sounded. And when he looked round at Helena again, there was an expression of shock upon his face. Her gaze tore round to where Guy had been. Wisps of smoke billowed around the half-furled sail. She saw Guy draw back the rifle in his hand. Stephen's arm tightened around hers, and she watched as he clasped his chest as if he was suffering an attack of conscience. And when he took his hand away his skin was dripping with the deep crimson of blood. The red stain spilled out from his shirt so that even against the black of his coat Helena could see the soaking spread of blood. More shots ripped through the air. Helena gave a yelp and tried to withdraw her hand, but Stephen had trapped it tight under his right arm. He gave a grunt and slumped to his knees, pulling her down with him.

'No!'

But even weakened as he was, Stephen refused to release her. He did not speak, but his black embittered gaze held hers and she felt the resurgence of all of her fear.

Men shouted and she looked up to see Stephen's sailing boat bearing down upon Guy.

Stephen could not have seen it. The boats were to his back. But he knew all the same. For all the pistol shot that had lodged in his chest, Stephen's strength did not seem to have diminished. He pulled Helena closer, until her face was near to his. 'My love,' he whispered.

Helena's eyes opened wide in shock and fear.

'You would have given yourself to me?' he said.

A nod and the wind whipped her hair across Stephen's face.

He sighed and smelled its sweetness before Helena moved it away. He beckoned her closer, and despite all that he had done, she could not deny a dying man, so she lowered her head that she might hear the weak whisper that was his voice. 'And then, afterwards, I would have given you…' He coughed and the breath laboured upon his lips. 'I would have given you…' he said again, 'Varington's head on a platter. He would not have made it halfway across the water before my men had him.'

Helena did not hear the crack of rifle shots on the shore. Silence echoed Stephen's words.

Stephen smiled and the black eyes shuttered, and she was left staring in disbelief and horror.

'Helena!' Guy's voice pulled her from the nightmare. She looked up, saw him down on the sand, running towards her. There seemed to be none of Stephen's men left to follow him. 'Helena!' Guy shouted again.

She was shaking as she pulled herself clear of Stephen, and her breath came in ragged gasps. 'Guy!'

And then he was there, pulling her into his arms, stroking her hair, her cheek, holding her against him as if he would never let her go.

'Guy,' she said again, and she thought her heart would break for love of him.

His arm stayed around her waist as they walked back to the castle to free Weir and Senga and Caroline. She did not speak, just let herself feel safe in his presence. Behind them the bodies of Stephen's men lay still and lifeless upon the shore, like the master they had served.

She felt suddenly so tired that it was an effort to raise
each foot, to keep on taking one step after another. *It's
over,* she whispered to herself again and again, barely
able to believe it. She glanced behind her as if to make
sure that it really was. Stephen lay where he had fallen.
A great dark patch staining his coat and shirt. Dead.

Guy held Helena as they sailed the boat down the
island's coastline. Even when Emma, Agnes and Old
Tam were discovered and aboard, and Weir was steering
them back to the mainland, Guy kept his arm around her.
No one commented. Propriety was long forgotten. They
had survived, all of them. Tayburn was dead. They were
safe and they were going home. And nothing else
mattered. The boat skimmed over the water and,
although the hour was still early, barely three o'clock,
the day began to fade. Night and Seamill Hall beckoned,
and the nightmare that was Tayburn lay behind them.

Chapter Fifteen

The fire in the bedchamber was a warm golden flicker of flames. Helena stood alone, thawing the chill from her hands with its heat, staring into the magical array of flames. Stephen was dead. Dead. She was free at last. But no matter how much she knew the truth of it, she still felt an underlying unease. Every creak upon the stair, every howl of the wind, sent her eyes to the door and a shiver of apprehension straight to her core. A knock at the door sounded and she jumped, staring at it, heart beating wildly. The knock came again, this time accompanied by a maid's voice.

'I've brought warm water for you if you want to wash and Mrs Weir said to tell you that dinner will be served at half past five.'

Silence followed the maid's words.

'Do you wish me to come back later, ma'am?'

Helena roused herself from her stupor and, moving swiftly across the room, opened the door to where the maid stood. 'No, thank you, Martha,' said Helena and, rather than admit the maid to the room, she took the filled pitcher from her hands. 'It's kind of you to bring me the water. Thank you,' she said again, and forced a smile.

But the maid was not looking at Helena's face. Indeed, the maid did not meet her eyes at all. Martha's gaze remained fixed on Helena's shoulder.

No doubt the girl knew the truth of Helena McGregor. Kilbride was a small village. It was just a matter of time before they knew the rest.

So much had changed in the space of a single day, that it hardly seemed possible. A lifetime of changes in those few hours. Stephen was dead and, even had it not been so, what had happened in Dunleish meant that Helena would never be the same again. Emma was safe, and Agnes and Old Tam too. And Guy… She could not let herself think of him, not with the maid standing there so intently. The girl's face held an expression of horrified fascination and she was staring at Helena with distaste. 'Thank you, Martha,' Helena said a little more forcefully, and made to close the door.

The maid showed no sign of moving. Her gaze remained riveted upon the top of the green dress.

'Martha?'

At last the maid's eyes moved slowly to meet her own. 'Is that…?' She stopped and her hand came up hesitantly between them. 'Is that…?' She hesitated again. 'Blood, ma'am?' And her finger pointed at Helena's shoulder.

Helena twisted her head to follow where Martha's finger directed. The soft green material surrounding the shoulder and upper sleeve of her left arm was smeared with a dark stain. Stephen's blood! Helena felt her gorge rising. 'It's nothing,' Helena managed before shutting the door. She walked briskly across the room and sat the pitcher down upon the table beside the blue-and-white patterned china basin.

She tried not to think at all, just reached round to where the line of tiny bead buttons fastened at the back of her dress. Her arms contorted, her fingers prised. One button unfastened, then another two, but despite the stretch of Helena's arms she could not release any more. The lower line of buttons remained steadfastly resistant. Helena doubled her efforts. The buttons slid beneath her fumbling fingers, but would not be per-suaded through the buttonholes. Perspiration prickled and her arms began to ache. With every passing second she became increasingly aware of just what was soaked upon her dress. She knew she was being foolish, that she had been happy enough when she had been unaware of the markings on her clothes, but the thought of Stephen's blood repulsed her. She tried again, working her fingers harder, faster. It made no differ-ence. Her skin crawled beneath the darkness of the stain. Helena cursed and, as the beginnings of panic took hold, contemplated wrenching the material apart, regardless of what that would do to the buttons. She would never wear the dress again.

Knuckles rapped against the door.

She stilled.

'Martha?'

The door opened and closed again.

Helena glanced back.

It was not the maid that stood in her bedchamber, but Guy. His eyes burned with something she did not under-stand. 'The doctor has left. He said that Caroline is suf-fering from nervous exhaustion. Weir will write to her father to take her home to his country estate.'

She nodded, her hands dropping to her sides.

'Helena?' He moved towards her. 'What is—?'

She turned away. She did not look down at her dress. She did not want to see Stephen's blood. It was bad enough feeling the press of it against her skin, knowing it was there. 'I must change. It's his blood, you see,' she said, as if that explained everything.

Guy saw the colourless cheeks and the deliberate aversion of her face from the dark stain upon the material of her dress. 'Helena.' He reached out and took her limp hands within his.

'His blood is upon me,' she said, and swallowed hard, 'and I am having some difficulty with the buttons of this dress.' He could see her struggle to hold herself together. 'I…'

He looked down into her face and saw her need and felt her pain. Helena's emotions were raw and exposed. No mask, no pretence, not from him. His smile was small and gentle and understanding. 'I know,' he said, and released her hands.

She did not move, just stared up at him and waited, so trusting that it quite smote his heart.

His hands touched to her shoulders and he gently rotated her until her back faced him. Then slowly his fingers moved to the line of small emerald buttons and, one by one, he began to unfasten them. There was silence in the room save for the quiet flutter of the flames. He could feel her warmth through the layers of material that separated their skin. His fingers worked with a steady rhythm until at last the soft green wool gaped to reveal the white of her undergarments beneath. With all the buttons unfastened, he peeled the dress from her body, letting it pool upon the floor. Guy moved round until he faced her, took her hand and helped her step free. He paused, holding her gaze with his. 'The blood has soaked through.'

'Yes,' she said, and the single word resonated between them.

The red stains were bright against the pale petticoats and shift. He said nothing more until he had removed the layers of material and she stood naked before him. He did not look at the rich creamy velvet of her skin or the curve of her breast or hip. Instead he took her hand in his and guided her across to the table. He poured the water from the pitcher into the basin, took out his handkerchief and immersed it. 'The water is warm.'

'Martha brought it just before you arrived.'

He could hear the slight breathlessness, the tremor beneath her words. He longed to pull her into his arms, to envelop her, to kiss her and make love to her, but he could not, not when she had been through so much, not when she was so vulnerable. He squeezed most of the water from the square of white cotton, the drops splashing back down into the basin. And then gently, with the most infinite care, he pressed the wet material to her skin and began to wipe away Tayburn's blood.

He worked slowly, methodically, rinsing the handkerchief as required, until every last trace had been removed and her skin gleamed damp and pale and unblemished, and the water in the basin was a translucent red. He shrugged off his coat and wrapped it around the nakedness of her body. 'The blood is gone,' he said simply, although he wanted to say so much more, and dropped a kiss to the top of her head. He walked across the room and gathered up the abandoned and bloodied clothing, knowing how important this was to Helena, and moved to kneel by the fire.

Helena had felt Guy's patience and gentleness in every caress of the wet handkerchief against her skin. She gave herself up, letting each stroke wash away a little more of Stephen's marks, seeing in Guy's eyes a tenderness beyond anything she had ever known. His coat was warm and snug. They knelt side by side before the hearth, like a couple before an altar. There was no need for words. She knew what he was going to do. She wanted it. She needed it.

He placed the first item upon the fire. The flames embraced the dress, thrusting golden fingers around and through the green wool until it burst into a ball of golden light and then fell away to nothing. Piece by piece Guy burned each item of bloodstained clothing until, at last, there was nothing left, and they knelt together in silence and watched the remnants of what had been. Helena knew that the act had drawn them together like no other, for he had demonstrated that he understood. He had removed every last trace of the blood and Stephen was no more. He had saved her and cleansed her and freed her. He was looking at her now, and the ice blue of his eyes reached in and touched her soul, sending splintering sensations to shimmer deep in her belly.

'It is done.' He smiled and kissed the tip of her nose. 'Now you need to put on some clothes before you catch a chill.' He rose to his feet, but not before she had scrambled to hers.

'No.'

The word seemed to echo between them. He stopped and stared down at her.

She felt a wave of warmth heat her cheeks. 'That is…there is so much for us to speak of.'

'Yes, there is…' his smile was gentle '…but you have been through a lot today, Helena, and you need to rest. I shall send a maid up to you.' He allowed himself to stroke her cheek but only once, and then he moved away before temptation got the better of him.

She watched him walk across the room, watched his hand reach towards the door, his fingers wrap around the doorknob. 'Don't leave.'

He stilled and, even though he was not facing her, she saw the sudden tightening of the shirt across his shoulders. He turned. 'You want me to stay?' he said slowly, as if he could not quite believe her words.

'Yes.' The blood was rushing loudly in Helena's ears.

The distance across the room seemed to shrink so that she could hear the slight catch of his breath and see the surprise and hope dart across his features.

'Why?'

His question was so unexpected that she just stared at him for a moment. The answer was so simple that she wondered that he needed to ask the question. She loved him and she would love him for ever. She would be his mistress, she would bear the knowing looks of other men. She would suffer the exclusion from the decent world, and gladly so if it meant she would be with Guy. She loved him and she wanted him. She wanted to feel his body move over hers, to shiver beneath the gentle touch of his hands. She wanted to kiss him, and taste him and touch him. She wanted to give what he had refused to take. She wanted Guy, all of him and every last bit.

'Helena,' he prompted, 'you have not answered me.'

'Does it matter?' she said softly.

'Yes.' His answer was stark and uncompromising. 'It matters very much.'

'I thought I had lost you,' she said. 'When I saw Stephen's sword at your breast…' A sob sounded from her throat.

'Helena.' Her name was a sigh in the silence of the bed-chamber. He moved quickly, closing the space between them, taking her into his arms. 'Hush,' he said, and pressed his lips to her forehead. 'The nightmare is over.'

'Oh, Guy!' She stood against him, resting her palms flat against the breadth of his chest, feeling the hard planes of muscle through the soft cotton of his shirt. Her face tilted up to his and she looked directly into his eyes. They were standing so close she could see every minute detail, from the variations in the arctic blue of his iris to the stark black ring that surrounded it and each and every dark eyelash. 'He would have killed you.'

His gaze dropped to her lips before rising again to her eyes. 'Yes,' he said, 'but, thanks to you, he did not.'

She felt the stroke of his hand against her hair, swayed instinctively towards him as his mouth closed gently upon hers. It was a kiss of gentleness and reassurance. His lips were soft and undemanding, giving, never taking. And in the intimacy of their touch was a message of love and of longing. It was a kiss to last a lifetime. Even when he drew away and just held her against him, she could still taste him, his essence like a honeyed balm soothing her soul. 'Guy?'

'Yes?' He tilted her chin up so that he could look into her eyes.

And she knew that she would tell him the truth. 'I will answer your question.'

He waited. His chest rose and fell against hers. His breath was soft and light. Flames whispered in the background. Outside a robin whistled.

'I want you to stay, Guy, because I love you.' She drew back, opening up a small gap between them. 'I love you,' she said again, 'and I want to be your mistress.' There, she had said it. Silence rang after her words.

A smile curled at his mouth, and there was something warm and possessive and teasing in his gaze. 'Foolish love,' he whispered, and, wrapping an arm around her back, he pulled her close until the full length of their bodies were pressed together. 'You cannot be my mistress.'

She stilled, unsure of his meaning, his words and actions in blatant contradiction of each other. 'I do not understand.' A sudden fear tugged at her. 'Are you saying that you do not want me?'

'Helena…' his smile deepened with sensuality and suggestion '…surely you know better than that. I have wanted you since I first saw you, and for every minute of every day since.'

A blush flooded her face. 'Then why—?'

'Sweetheart, you cannot be my mistress…' he paused and rested his thumb upon the soft cushion of her lips '…if you are to be my wife.'

The world tilted on its axis. Helena stared at him and thought she must have misheard.

'If you will have me for your husband, that is,' he added with a grin.

'You want to marry me?' She felt her mouth gape open.

'I admit it is not the most romantic of proposals.' One dark eyebrow arched. 'So *will* you have me?' he asked.

'You are in earnest!' she gasped, and the room spun around her.

'Entirely,' he replied.

And it seemed that she had floated to a dream world of perfection and happy endings. 'Yes,' the word slipped quietly from between her lips.

The curve of his mouth deepened, showing the white of his teeth. 'You do not sound too certain, beloved,' he said.

'Yes!' she shouted, and a fountain of happiness welled up within her, and she thought that, in all the years that she had lived, she had never experienced such joy. 'Of course I will have you!' she said as he lifted her up and whirled her about the room. Their laughter entwined as their bodies pressed closer and their eyes sparkled with joy and excitement and happiness.

Guy's coat slipped from Helena's shoulders to lie abandoned on the floor. 'My love,' he breathed, and delivered her still laughing on to the mattress.

She lay naked beneath him, her eyes warm with love and desire, her skin soft and begging for his touch. He reached down and began to pluck the pins from her hair, uncoiling the long shimmering tendrils until it spiralled a deep spangled red over her breasts, reaching down to brush against her hips. He tangled his fingers through its length, immersing his hands in its silken texture, touching it to his lips, inhaling its scent. 'You don't know how much I've longed to do this,' he whispered. His eyes met with hers before he moved his gaze to wander down the contours of her body. 'You're so beautiful.' And then his fingers trailed lightly, seductively, along the path his eyes had taken.

He heard her gasp, felt the shiver beneath his fingers.

'You are cold, my love,' he said, and made to tug the bedcovers aside to cover her.

'No.' Her hand stayed his, then progressed up his arm with a slide until she reached his neckcloth. 'I am not cold.' And her fingers fumbled with the knot until at last he felt the linen strip loosen and unwind, and saw it flutter down to land beside them on the bed. She rubbed her hands across his chest, feeling the smattering of dark hair beneath his shirt. 'In fact, I believe it is you who are overdressed, sir.'

'Minx!' He growled a laugh. 'That is something that can soon be remedied.' Guy ripped the shirt from his body with uncommon haste, revealing his broad naked shoulders and the hard musculature of his chest. Her eyes widened at the sight of him. He smiled as he followed her gaze, then left the bed only long enough to divest himself of his boots, his pantaloons and underclothing.

Her eyes feasted upon his nakedness. Never had a man looked so glorious. He was strong and lean and hard with muscle. The dark hair covered lightly across his chest, narrowing to a line that led down across his abdomen to lower regions. His skin was pale, but of a different tone from her own. She had never seen a man like him, and the sight of him stirred anticipation deep in her belly.

When he came to her again, she opened her arms, pulled him down upon her so that flesh touched full against flesh and their bodies quivered with need.

'Helena,' he said with deep and guttural longing, and claimed her mouth with his own. Lips slid together, hard and urgent, hot and moist. The tip of his tongue brushed a tantalising tease, licking her lips, entwining with her own in motions set down at the start of time. Sucking. Gasping. Needful.

Helena's body was aflame. Desire burned her thighs; need clouded her mind; love overwhelmed her heart. Time ceased to be. Nothing existed outside this one single moment with the man that she loved. They feasted upon the intimacies of each other's mouth, sharing their breaths.

He stroked her hair, slid his hands down to capture the fullness of her breasts, feeling the hard budding of her nipples beneath.

'Oh, Guy,' she moaned, and arched her back to press herself all the harder into the exploration of his hands.

His fingers outlined magical patterns around the soft ripe globes, carefully avoiding their delicate pink centres, even though she wriggled in an effort to force them to his touch.

'Such impatience,' he said, but Helena could hear that his breath was short and uneven and his voice somewhat unsteady.

'Guy!' she pleaded, and drew her fingers down the length of his back to clasp the strong firmness of his buttocks.

A jolt of desperate need shuddered through him, but he reined himself back in, determined to take things slowly, intent on pleasuring Helena, not himself. His fingers moved at last to her nipples, rolling the firm buds between the thumb and forefinger of each hand.

She quivered and arched all the harder, thrusting her pelvis up towards his.

The groan escaped from Guy's throat before he could catch it back.

The erect nipples tightened and pushed against his fingers.

Where his manhood throbbed against her leg little shivers of pleasure and desperation vied for release.

His mouth left hers, his breath searing a pathway down her neck, down further still to replace his fingers over the rosy bead of one breast. He suckled, relishing the taste of her, hearing her small gasps of pleasure. He felt her need as strong and purposeful as his own, and his fingers crept between her thighs as his mouth moved to service her other breast.

'Guy!' She melted against his hand. 'I need you!' Helena could feel the tight urgency escalating within her. Something was happening that she did not recognise. She was reaching for something she did not understand, striving with all her being for that one thing. And all she knew was that she loved the man stretched over the length of her, and that she needed him inside her, to fill her completely and utterly with his love. He moved down her, rubbing the taut tip of his arousal against her. Her hands pulled his hips down on to her, but he resisted, manoeuvring her out to the side so that she lay almost at a right angle to him.

'Guy?'

But he just smiled and pulled her closer so that her legs wound round and through his, and she opened to him. And then, just when she thought she could bear it no more, he drove into her, filling her with himself, as his fingers touched her pearl of pleasure. Long sliding movements, in and out, and all the while his hand unlocked a world of hidden pleasure for Helena, until the tightening escalation exploded in an overwhelming flood of sparkling bliss that made her cry out his name and pull him to her, and kiss him and stroke him and bask in the heat of his love, until it cooled to a delectable throb. Only then, when he knew her own need sated, when he had stroked her cheek and kissed her

lips, did he move again, thrusting faster, harder, and all
the while holding her eyes with the blue fire of his gaze,
until she felt him shudder, spilling his seed within her,
and he collapsed down on the mattress by her side.

'My love,' he said, and touched his lips to her
forehead, her eyelids, her cheeks, in a myriad of whispered kisses. His hand moved slowly to stroke her hair,
to slide down against her neck. 'My brave love.'

The last traces of Stephen's influence had been oblit-
erated by Guy's loving. All the hurt of the previous
years rolled away. Helena's spirit soared. There was no
need for words. She nestled in closer to the warm curve
of Guy's body as he pulled the bedcovers over them. A
union of bodies; a union of souls. She would be his wife.
And on that last delightful heady thought, Helena
drifted to sleep.

The week had passed quickly since that dreadful day
upon St Vey, so quickly that Helena could scarcely
believe that tomorrow would be her wedding day.
Outside the sky was grey and an incessant patter of rain
drizzled against the window. She stole a glance at the
tall dark-haired man sitting by her side on the small sofa
in his room in Seamill Hall. He was so devastatingly
handsome, so wonderful and…he loved her. Her heart
swelled at that, so that it seemed to expand to fill her
whole chest. He loved her just as she was, knowing all
that he did of her. He loved her and he meant to marry
her. It was a dream come true. Love, happiness, a
husband, a family. Yet there was a shadow of unease that
lurked at the edge of Helena's mind, and she could not
sleep for the worry of it.

'You're very quiet, sweetheart. Is something wrong?'

Guy looked down into her face. 'Indeed, you've been growing quieter with each passing day. Not changed your mind about marrying me, have you?' He smiled a cheeky smile and her heart turned over.

She tried to hide the anxiety, tried to say the words of denial, but with Guy there could no longer be any pretence. With him she could only ever be herself. And she knew that she was going to have to ask him about the one last thing that lay between them.

There was a small pause before she asked, 'Have you told your brother that we are to be married?'

'You know that I have.' A line of puzzlement creased between his brows and he laughed.

'But he is not coming to the wedding, is he?'

A glimmer of understanding showed on Guy's face. 'The baby really is about to be born any day, otherwise both Lucien and Madeline would be here.' He stroked a finger against her cheek. 'It isn't some excuse he's concocted, my little worrypot.'

Another pause.

'Did you also tell him…' She hesitated and did not meet his gaze. 'Did you also tell him of my background?'

Guy reached over and took her hand in his. 'I told him all he needs to know, Helena, nothing more, and nothing less.'

Helena closed her eyes as her composure threatened to slip.

'Helena,' said Guy softly, 'you need not worry. Lucien will welcome you to the family. Ironic though it sounds, he has been trying to get me to reform my ways and take a wife.'

'I'll warrant that I'm not what he had in mind…well, not for your wife anyway.'

His hand tightened over hers. 'What manner of talk is this?'

'People will say that our marriage is a *mésalliance*. You are a viscount. Your brother is an earl. You know what I am,' she whispered.

'Yes, I know what you are,' he said, and there was strange expression upon his face. 'You are my life, my love, and tomorrow you will be my wife.'

Her eyes clung to his. 'Oh, Guy.' His hand was warm and strong over hers.

'Then what does it matter what others might think?'

'It matters what your brother thinks, does it not?'

Guy shrugged his shoulders in a dismissive gesture.

'What if he turns against you?'

'Why should he do such a thing?'

'You know very well why.' She chewed at her lip and looked at him. 'You cannot deny there will be a scandal over our marriage.'

'My family is not exactly scandal-free.'

'Will…will you be safe?'

'Safe?' Guy was looking at her as if she had run mad.

'From your brother?'

'From Lucien? Of course.'

'He will not seek to harm you over this?'

'Helena, why should Lucian seek to injure me over anything? He's my brother.' He quirked an eyebrow, and smiled a bemused smile.

'He is Earl Tregellas, is he not?'

'Yes.'

She hesitated before adding, 'The one that they call the Wicked Earl?'

There was a silence.

Guy sat very still. 'Where did you hear such a thing?'

'Stephen spoke of him…with admiration. He said Tregellas was a man after his own heart.'

The words hung in the air between them.

'Tayburn was mistaken,' said Guy. 'My brother is nothing like that fiend.'

'But they do call him the Wicked Earl,' she said softly.

He stared at her. 'I would not have thought you to judge a man by gossip and hearsay, Helena.'

She felt the warmth staining her cheeks. Too late she recalled Annabel Weir's words from what seemed a lifetime ago: *Promise me you will not heed any rumours that you may come to hear concerning Lord Varington or his brother…* And her own reply, *I do not let gossip influence my opinion of people.* 'Forgive me,' she uttered. 'You are right. I should not have spoken so.'

Guy gave a sigh and pressed her fingers once before releasing her hand. 'And I should have told you the truth of it all before now.'

'Guy—'

But he cut her off. 'You have a right to know, Helena. Maybe then you will see that there is nothing to fear from Lucien. He just wants me to be happy. Besides, there shouldn't be any secrets between us.' His stomach clenched just at the thought of talking about it. All that pain belonged in the past, not here, not now. He did not want her to see how much it affected him, to show this woman who needed him to be strong how weak he really was. And then he felt her hand slip around his fingers, felt the small squeeze of support.

'You don't have to tell me anything, Guy.'

'I want to,' he said. 'I need to.' And knew it was true.

She gave a small nod.

'It all started such a long time ago—more than six years. The woman to whom my brother was betrothed was murdered in the most horrific way imaginable. The shock of it killed my mother, and, as if that were not enough, the *Ton* believed my brother guilty of the crime. They called Lucien the Wicked Earl while the real villain, Farquharson, walked free.'

He saw the shock and compassion on her face.

'It was just a matter of time before Farquharson struck again, and this time his intended victim was Madeline. Lucien married her to save her from that devil.'

Helena's teeth bit into her lip. 'This Farquharson was the man you spoke of when you said that you had known a man like Stephen?'

'He was more like Tayburn than you can know,' he said.

'What happened to him?' He could hear the slight tremor of fear in her voice and was sorry that he had put it there, but, for all of its horror, Helena needed to know the truth, all of it.

'He's dead.'

'And your brother's wife is safe?'

He nodded and let the silence grow between them, unable to look round, unwilling to meet her eye.

'What is it that you're not telling me, Guy?'

Silence had never seemed so loud.

'I…' The words seemed to dry from his mouth. 'Farquharson captured my valet and me. He made me watch while he tortured my man. And there was not a damned thing I could do to stop him. Stupid, really.' He threw her a grim ragged smile. 'Spent years in the Peninsula surrounded by bloodshed and death, yet nothing prepared me for that. Collins, my man, survived. He's happily married and living in Dublin. But I can never forget…no matter what I do.'

'He tortured you too, didn't he?'

Guy felt her fingers stroke against his. He had never spoken of the details of that terrible night, not even to his brother. He nodded.

'Oh, Guy.'

He felt her arms wrapping around him, pulling him against her.

'My love, my sweet love,' she murmured again and again, and only when she wiped away the tears from his cheeks did he realise that he was crying. And even that did not seem to matter because he had told Helena the worst of it, and there was no more to tell.

She kissed him and took her hand in his and led him over to the bed. And she loved him with such tenderness, until there was nothing left of that terrible nightmare, until there was only Helena and her love.

They were married the next day in a quiet ceremony in the drawing room of Seamill Hall. Old Tam gave the bride away. Annabel, Emma and Agnes cried the whole way through. The last of the shadows in both their lives had gone, and as if to reflect that, the day was bright and clear and lit by sunshine. After the wedding breakfast they left their guests to their merriment and escaped down to the shoreline.

The sand was firm and golden beneath their feet as they stood on Kilbride's beach, looking out at the water beyond. The sea breeze caught at Helena's neatly pinned hair, freeing the curls to whip and dance free, and moulding her wedding skirts to her legs. She drew the fresh air into her lungs, smelling the tang of the sea in it, and knew that her happiness was complete. The sun warmed the chill from the air, and Guy's arm was warm and strong beneath her fingers.

Guy reached down and plucked a kiss from her lips.

'Guy!' she protested and with a rosy blush pushed his hand away. 'We are in a public place.'

He smiled a sensual smile and raised one wicked eyebrow. 'But there is no one about to see,' he teased.

He was right—there was not a soul to be seen. She smiled, tracing her fingers against the fine roughness of his cheek, remembering the dream from what seemed like so long ago, in which she had looked up into Guy's face and thought him an angel sent to save her. And Guy *had* saved her. He really was her dark angel of salvation. Their eyes locked and she revelled in the intensity of his love. For Helena there was, and had only ever been, Guy. It was as if they had been made to be together, as if each brought life to the other. In that moment was a lifetime of love. It flowed between them. Both knew it would flow for ever. No need for words. No need to say what the soul already knew.

His mouth moved to briefly nuzzle her fingers, never breaking the look that they shared. 'We could live here in Scotland. We would not have to uproot your sister and I know that you love the countryside.'

'And I know that you do not!' She laughed. 'You hate its wildness as much as I love it. My home is with you, even if that does happen to be in the pell-mell of London. And as for Emma, I fancy she will prefer London as much as you do.'

'I find I have developed a liking for this particular Scottish coastline. All the bracing sea air and plethora of precipitation.'

'You mean all the wind and rain!'

He smiled a teasing smile and dropped a small kiss first to one cheek and then the other. 'But what I like most of all is beachcombing. It's amazing what a man may find here upon the shore.'

'Lord Varington!' she huffed.

'Seaweed.'

She swiped at his arm in mock indignation.

'Shells.'

She placed her hands on her hips and raised her brows.

'And…' the teasing light vanished from his eyes '…his one true love.'

'Oh, Guy!'

She closed the space between them. Their lips met, and moved in passionate affirmation of their love.

Then he swung her up into his arms and began to tread the path back to Seamill Hall. And out beyond the sand, beneath the weak winter sun, the sea was a peaceful polished glass of pale ice blue.

* * * * *

Here is a sneak preview of
A STONE CREEK CHRISTMAS,
the latest in Linda Lael Miller's acclaimed
MCKETTRICK *series.*

A lonely horse brought vet Olivia O'Ballivan to
Tanner Quinn's farm, but it's the rancher's love
that might cause her to stay.

A STONE CREEK CHRISTMAS
Available December 2008
from Silhouette Special Edition

Tanner heard the rig roll in around sunset. Smiling, he wandered to the window. Watched as Olivia O'Ballivan climbed out of her Suburban, flung one defiant glance toward the house and started for the barn, the golden retriever trotting along behind her.

Taking his coat and hat down from the peg next to the back door, he put them on and went outside. He was used to being alone, even liked it, but keeping company with Doc O'Ballivan, bristly though she sometimes was, would provide a welcome diversion.

He gave her time to reach the horse Butterpie's stall, then walked into the barn.

The golden retriever came to greet him, all wagging tail and melting brown eyes, and he bent to stroke her soft, sturdy back. "Hey, there, dog," he said.

Sure enough, Olivia was in the stall, brushing Butterpie down and talking to her in a soft, soothing voice that touched something private inside Tanner and made him want to turn on one heel and beat it back to the house.

He'd be damned if he'd do it, though.

This was *his* ranch, *his* barn. Well-intentioned as she was, *Olivia* was the trespasser here, not him.

"She's still very upset," Olivia told him, without turning to look at him or slowing down with the brush.

Shiloh, always an easy horse to get along with, stood contentedly in his own stall, munching away on the feed Tanner had given him earlier. Butterpie, he noted, hadn't touched her supper as far as he could tell.

"Do you know anything at all about horses, Mr. Quinn?" Olivia asked.

He leaned against the stall door, the way he had the day before, and grinned. He'd practically been raised on horseback; he and Tessa had grown up on their grandmother's farm in the Texas hill country, after their folks divorced and went their separate ways, both of them too busy to bother with a couple of kids. "A few things," he said. "And I mean to call you Olivia, so you might as well return the favor and address me by my first name."

He watched as she took that in, dealt with it, decided on an approach. He'd have to wait and see what that turned out to be, but he didn't mind. It was a pleasure just watching Olivia O'Ballivan grooming a horse.

"All right, *Tanner*," she said. "This barn is a disgrace. When are you going to have the roof fixed? If it snows again, the hay will get wet and probably mold…"

He chuckled, shifted a little. He'd have a crew out there the following Monday morning to replace the roof and shore up the walls—he'd made the arrangements over a week before—but he felt no particular compunction to explain that. He was enjoying her ire too much; it made her color rise and her hair fly when she turned her head, and the faster breathing made her perfect breasts go up and down in an enticing rhythm. "What makes you so sure I'm a greenhorn?" he asked mildly, still leaning on the gate.

At last she looked straight at him, but she didn't move from Butterpie's side. "Your hat, your boots—that fancy red truck you drive. I'll bet it's customized."

Tanner grinned. Adjusted his hat. "Are you telling me real cowboys don't drive red trucks?"

"There are lots of trucks around here," she said. "Some of them are red, and some of them are new. And *all* of them are splattered with mud or manure or both."

"Maybe I ought to put in a car wash, then," he teased. "Sounds like there's a market for one. Might be a good investment."

She softened, though not significantly, and spared him a cautious half smile, full of questions she probably wouldn't ask. "There's a good car wash in Indian Rock," she informed him. "People go there. It's only forty miles."

"Oh," he said with just a hint of mockery. "*Only* forty miles. Well, then. Guess I'd better dirty up my truck if I want to be taken seriously in these here parts. Scuff up my boots a bit, too, and maybe stomp on my hat a couple of times."

Her cheeks went a fetching shade of pink. "You are twisting what I said," she told him, brushing Butterpie again, her touch gentle but sure. "I meant…"

Tanner envied that little horse. Wished he had a furry hide, so he'd need brushing, too.

"You *meant* that I'm not a real cowboy," he said. "And you could be right. I've spent a lot of time on construction sites over the last few years, or in meetings where a hat and boots wouldn't be appropriate. Instead of digging out my old gear, once I decided to take this job, I just bought new."

"I bet you don't even *have* any old gear," she challenged, but she was smiling, albeit cautiously, as though she might withdraw into a disapproving frown at any second.

He took off his hat, extended it to her. "Here," he teased. "Rub that around in the muck until it suits you."

She laughed, and the sound—well, it caused a powerful and wholly unexpected shift inside him. Scared the hell out of him and, paradoxically, made him yearn to hear it again.

* * * * *

Discover how this rugged rancher's wanderlust is
tamed in time for a merry Christmas, in
A STONE CREEK CHRISTMAS.
In stores December 2008.

Silhouette®

SPECIAL EDITION™

FROM *NEW YORK TIMES* BESTSELLING AUTHOR

LINDA LAEL MILLER

A STONE CREEK CHRISTMAS

Veterinarian Olivia O'Ballivan finds the animals in Stone Creek playing Cupid between her and Tanner Quinn. Even Tanner's daughter, Sophie, is eager to play matchmaker. With everyone conspiring against them and the holiday season fast approaching, Tanner and Olivia may just get everything they want for Christmas after all!

*Available December 2008
wherever books are sold.*

SPECIAL EDITION™

MISTLETOE AND MIRACLES

by *USA TODAY* bestselling author

MARIE FERRARELLA

Child psychologist Trent Marlowe couldn't
believe his eyes when Laurel Greer, the
woman he'd loved and lost, came to him for
help. Now a widow, with a troubled boy who
wouldn't speak, Laurel needed a miracle from
Trent...and a brief detour under the mistletoe
wouldn't hurt, either.

Available in December wherever books are sold.

REQUEST YOUR FREE BOOKS!

 Harlequin® Historical
Historical Romantic Adventure!

2 FREE NOVELS PLUS 2 FREE GIFTS!

YES! Please send me 2 FREE Harlequin® Historical novels and my 2 FREE gifts (gifts are worth about $10). After receiving them, if I don't wish to receive any more books, I can return the shipping statement marked "cancel". If I don't cancel, I will receive 6 brand-new novels every month and be billed just $4.94 per book in the U.S. or $5.49 per book in Canada, plus 25¢ shipping and handling per book and applicable taxes, if any*. That's a savings of 20% off the cover price! I understand that accepting the 2 free books and gifts places me under no obligation to buy anything. I can always return a shipment and cancel at any time. Even if I never buy another book, the two free books and gifts are mine to keep forever.

246 HDN ERUM   349 HDN ERUA

Name _____ (PLEASE PRINT) _____

Address _____ Apt. # _____

City _____ State/Prov. _____ Zip/Postal Code _____

Signature (if under 18, a parent or guardian must sign) _____

Mail to the **Harlequin Reader Service:**
IN U.S.A.: P.O. Box 1867, Buffalo, NY 14240-1867
IN CANADA: P.O. Box 609, Fort Erie, Ontario L2A 5X3

Not valid to current subscribers of Harlequin Historical books.

Want to try two free books from another line?
Call 1-800-873-8635 or visit www.morefreebooks.com.

* Terms and prices subject to change without notice. N.Y. residents add applicable sales tax. Canadian residents will be charged applicable provincial taxes and GST. Offer not valid in Quebec. This offer is limited to one order per household. All orders subject to approval. Credit or debit balances in a customer's account(s) may be offset by any other outstanding balance owed by or to the customer. Please allow 4 to 6 weeks for delivery. Offer available while quantities last.

Your Privacy: Harlequin Books is committed to protecting your privacy. Our Privacy Policy is available online at www.eHarlequin.com or upon request from the Reader Service. From time to time we make our lists of customers available to reputable third parties who may have a product or service of interest to you. If you would prefer we not share your name and address, please check here. ☐

HH08R

Harlequin® Historical
Historical Romantic Adventure!

THE MISTLETOE WAGER
Christine Merrill

Harry Pennyngton, Earl of Anneslea,
is surprised when his estranged wife,
Helena, arrives home for Christmas.
Especially when she's intent on
divorce! A festive house party
is in full swing when the guests
are snowed in, and Harry and
Helena find they are together
under the mistletoe....

*Available December 2008
wherever books are sold.*

HH29525

COMING NEXT MONTH FROM

HARLEQUIN®
HISTORICAL

- **HER MONTANA MAN**
  by **Cheryl St.John**
  (Western)
  Protecting people runs through Jonas Black's blood, and
  Eliza Jane Sutherland is one woman who needs his strong arms
  about her. Despite blackmail and dangerous threats on their lives, the
  attraction between Jonas and Eliza is undeniable—but Eliza bears
  secrets that could change everything....

- **AN IMPROPER ARISTOCRAT**
  by **Deb Marlowe**
  (Regency)
  The Earl of Treyford, scandalous son of a disgraced mother, has no time
  for the pretty niceties of the Ton. He has come back to England to aid
  a spinster facing an undefined danger. But Miss Latimer's thick lashes,
  long ebony hair and her mix of knowledge and innocence arouse far
  more than his protective instincts....

- **THE MISTLETOE WAGER**
  by **Christine Merrill**
  (Regency)
  Christmas is the perfect season for Elise Pennyngton to put the sparkle
  back into her marriage! Tired of what on the surface appears to be
  the most amiable but boring husband in England, she attempts to stir
  Harry Pennyngton's jealousy—little knowing that Harry is seething
  at her games! His concealed passion will guarantee that Elise will fall
  back into his arms—and the marriage bed—by the end of the festive
  season....

- **VIKING WARRIOR, UNWILLING WIFE**
  by **Michelle Styles**
  (Medieval)
  With the war drums echoing in her ears, Sela stands with trepidation on
  the shoreline. The dragon ships full of warriors have come, ready for
  battle and glory. But it isn't the threat of conquest that shakes
  Sela to the core. It is the way her heart responds to the proud face of
  Vikar Hrutson, leader of the invading force—and her ex-husband!